ON HER SIX

SIX

an *UNDER COVERS* novel

CHRISTINA ELLE

Entangled Publishing, LLC
2614 South Timberline Road
Suite 109
Fort Collins, CO 80525
Visit our website at www.entangledpublishing.com.

Select Suspense is an imprint of Entangled Publishing, LLC.

Edited by Alycia Tornetta
Cover design by LJ Anderson
Cover art from Dollar Photo Club

Manufactured in the United States of America

First Edition May 2016

To Keith for encouraging me to chase my dreams.
And to Jameson and Bennett for giving me the reason to.

Chapter One

This was *so* not the way Samantha Harper wanted to start her day. Running late to work *again*, she had just gotten her car door open when someone came up behind her.

"Gi-give me your ma-money," a gravelly male voice stuttered. Something cold and hard dug into her lower back. "*Now.*"

A gun. Inhaling a long gush of hot July air, she worked to slow her racing pulse and allow her training to kick in.

Keep him talking. Distract him. Buy some time to get out of the situation.

When she didn't move, he spoke again, "Di-did you h-hear me?"

"Yes, I heard you," she said.

"Then hand it over." She attempted to peer over her shoulder at the assailant, but the man pressed the gun harder into her spine, causing a slice of pain to the bone.

Wincing, she said, "I don't think that's a good idea."

"Wha-what?" the man said, surprised.

"There are less criminal ways of making a living. You don't

have to do this." She'd met plenty of people at the station who had forgone crime and now lived respectable lives. "I can help you."

"Shut your m-mouth and gi-give me your goddamn m-money!"

Something in the way the guy spoke told her this wasn't a regular mugging and he wasn't a regular criminal. No, he didn't seem like the usual drug-addicted men she'd helped book at the precinct. This one was more desperate. Frantic. Confused even.

"Are you okay?" she asked, once again trying to look over her shoulder.

There was a blip of silence where she didn't think he was going to answer. The pressure against her back lessened, before he came to. "I…I d-don't know what's wrong wi-with me." A slight tremor thrummed from where he held the gun. She caught sight of him rubbing his forehead as if suffering from a severe migraine.

She glanced up and down the vacant city street. No one outside due to the early morning hour. Only a handful of other cars parked along the curb. It was normally a quiet street. Neighbors took care of their houses, kept their hedges trimmed, and waved to one another when passing on the street. Things like muggings hardly happened in this part of the city.

The aggressive neighborhood watch group didn't hurt either.

The sun beat down. Her skin felt clammy. Her pastel yellow blouse suctioned to her skin like plastic wrap. The stifling air mixed with the adrenalin coursing through her veins made it difficult to breathe. And to think.

How was she going to get out of this? She didn't stand a chance against this guy without her weapons, which were currently locked in her Honda's trunk.

"Way to go, stupid." *Next time try listening to Grandma Rose when she tells you to carry some items in your purse.*

"Did you just call me st-stupid?" He growled and pressed the gun harder against her, causing her to take a small step forward. Then the gun full-out shook against her body, making it feel as if a mild earthquake was happening. "Two seconds," he grunted. "Or I'm gonna b-blow y-your brains out!"

"My back," she said without thinking.

"What?"

"The gun's pointed at my back. So technically you'd blow my back out." She immediately snapped her mouth closed and gritted her teeth. *Stupid, big mouth.*

The gun left her lower spine and landed along the base of her head with perfect precision. No shaking this time. "Better?" the man asked.

She glanced up to the heavens and exhaled through her nose. "Not really."

"C'mon, lady, d-don't make me do this. Just give m-me your purse." He grabbed hold of the strap on her shoulder and started to pull.

She gripped her purse and hugged it against herself. Not that it was expensive or contained anything besides her license and credit cards. Lord knew she didn't have much money in it. It was the fact that one day she would put away dirtbags like him. And what kind of future cop would that make her if she gave in to him now? If he got away, he would just be a statistic. One of the many addicts who died on the streets without proper help.

Just like Dad…

He pressed the gun firmly against her skull, cutting off that unpleasant memory. The dull ache increased into a slice of blinding pain, making her close her eyes.

Gritting her teeth, she prayed for Grandma Rose or one of the other members of the watch to look out their neighboring row house windows. Someone. Anyone.

Not that she'd want Grandma running out guns-a-blazin'. But she could call Martinez or Sinclair at the station. Webb was doing his rounds about this time. He could pop by.

No one came. No screaming, no sirens, nothing. Just the sounds of the city in the distance as people went about their day.

Oh God. She had to handle this thug by herself. This was really happening. And she didn't have anything at her disposal aside from her two hands.

She bit her bottom lip. If she flung her purse into the middle of the street, enticing him to chase it, it might give her enough time to distract him. She could jump on his back, maybe knock him unconscious, and try to disarm him. Or make a run for her car and get the trunk open.

The plan wasn't promising, but it was better than nothing.

Click. The gun's hammer pulled back.

This was it. It was now or never.

She prayed for courage and strength from her father and grandfather—two of the bravest cops she'd ever known.

Heart thundering in her chest, blood pounding in her ears, she fingered the smooth leather hanging near her waist. As she started to turn, a second voice spoke.

"Put your hands up and back away slowly." Deep. Ominous. No-nonsense. One did not want to mess with the man who belonged to that voice.

Her eyes widened, body stilled. The ground seemed to shift beneath her sandals, but she didn't dare move.

Where did he come from?

She didn't stand a chance against two thugs—knowing at least one was armed—so she shot her arms toward the sky.

"Not you, Blondie," the no-nonsense voice said. "Him."

Him? So the two men weren't working together? Relieved, she released the breath she'd been holding and dropped her arms.

"Do it now," the voice spoke again, even more fierce, almost a snarl.

The gun lifted from the back of her head.

She spun. As she'd been trained, she took in each man's identifying characteristics.

Not much taller than her, her attacker was nondescript at about five-seven. He had dark hair from what Sam could tell by his eyebrows and wore a gray sweatshirt with the hood covering his head.

A sweatshirt in this heat?

Shaking her head, she continued her perusal. Eye color was hard to make out given his face was angled toward the street. He appeared around twenty years old. Gangly and pasty white, his body hunched over still shaking. Stark white hands were hoisted in the air, gripping a 9mm. What could make someone his age so desperate for money?

Then she zeroed in on the mountain of a man behind him.

Quite *descript* indeed. Well over six-feet, piercing blue eyes, military-cut dark brown hair, and strong jawline. The black tattoo on his neck was something. It dipped below the neckline of a white T-shirt that stretched across his broad chest. She took in the full view of his pecs, which appeared to be double the size of hers. Ignoring that fact, since really, a toddler had bigger boobs than she did, Sam focused closer on the tattoo. It was tough to decipher what it was. It looked like feathers. Maybe from a bird. She'd need to see him without his shirt to determine—

Wait a minute. What the hell was she doing? She blinked to clear her thoughts away from the man's chest and dragged her gaze up to his.

Dark. Sinister. Like he thought he was the only person in the universe who mattered.

"You okay?" her rescuer asked. One eyebrow quirked,

and he wore an expression that said saving her had been a huge inconvenience.

Plus, the looker of a man held a 9mm of his own, pressed against her assailant's head.

"Who are you?" she asked.

Chapter Two

The woman wasn't wearing the pale, frightened expression Ash Cooper had expected. In fact, her eyes were strikingly clear and her skin flushed.

Her light-colored eyes glanced at the kid between them and a myriad of emotions crossed her face. Surprise. Curiosity. Interest. This chick was going to be trouble. She was perceptive. Too perceptive.

Her gaze locked on Ash, staring in a way that made him feel exposed. Naked, even. Her eyes widened, and she inhaled a quick breath of surprise. The pink on her cheeks deepened as her gaze traveled down his neck and chest. It had been too long since a woman looked at him that way.

He almost choked on a laugh. Yeah, like that was gonna happen.

Ignoring her question, he growled in a low voice and held out an impatient hand. "Give me the gun."

The thug's shoulders dropped as he released a ragged exhale.

"Nice and slow," Ash said. "That's it." He snatched the

weapon and stored it in the back waistband of his cargo shorts. "Who are you? What do you want? And where'd you get the gun?"

"N-no one, man," the thug spoke, gripping the hood covering his head. "M-money. I just need m-money."

"Money, huh?" Ash laughed, thrusting his handgun against the back of the kid's skull. See how he liked it with the roles reversed. He pushed a little harder, satisfied after the kid grunted in pain. "Hell of a way to go about getting it. Ever heard of getting a job?"

Christ, it was hot. Sweat dripped from Ash's forehead and down his cheeks. The idiot in front of him shivered and clutched his midsection as if a few feet of snow lay on the ground.

Dealing with this shit was the last thing he needed right now. He'd been given strict instructions to stay hands-off on this assignment. Ash's DEA teammates were assigned to discover, track down, and take out the Vamp drug supplier by any means necessary. No clue as to who the dealer was yet, so the team was spending most of its time collecting intel on the big dealers around the area. Ash's bullshit job was to observe any unusual activity in the city and report it to his new acting team leader, Bryan Tyke. No action. One more wrong move and Ash would be demoted from field agent to trash collector. He'd already been demoted from team leader, for shit's sake.

"Just give me m-money, m-man." Tremors shook the kid's body. "Then I'll le-leave. I-I swear. I just need money. Just m-money. Plea-please, man."

"Oh my God," the woman gasped, her hand covering her mouth.

Now what? Ash tightened his grip on the gun.

She cocked her blond head, and her nose wrinkled as she leaned toward the kid. "What's wrong with you?"

Keeping the gun pointed at the attacker, Ash circled to

stand next to her.

Blood red eyes with black pupils. Shit. "A vamp." A user of the drugs Ash's team was trying to stop.

Ash quickly glanced around the street. They usually didn't travel in packs, but he needed to be careful. Especially if the kid was as desperate as he appeared.

"Vamp?" Blondie asked, her eyes growing wider than the rusted hubcaps on her Honda. "As in *vampire*? But—but—"

Ash shook his head. "Drug user."

Vamp—more potent than heroin and a hell of a lot more addictive. The official name of the drug was a lot longer and more scientific sounding; Ash could never remember it. Vamp was the street name, because that's what addicts looked like: vampires. He cursed himself for not picking up on the kid's cues earlier. After extended use, the drug took over the body to the point that the user appeared more monster than human. Shaking. Desperate. Confused. Pasty skin with a dry, chalky texture. The whites of the eyes a deep red color as if filled with blood, pupils so dilated there wasn't any color around them. No blue, brown, or green. Just black.

"Drugs? What kind of drugs do *that*?" He didn't think it was possible, but her eyes grew even wider. "I don't understand. I've never heard of Vamp." If he wasn't mistaken, she sounded kinda pissed about it.

And I'm going to make damn sure no one around here ever does. He shifted his weight on his feet. "You complaining?"

She stiffened at his comment. "Well, no. I just—" He didn't like the way her eyes suddenly narrowed in his direction.

The addict's trembling spasms increased. His gaze darted around as if he couldn't control it, and he licked his chapped lips repeatedly.

Blondie leaned even closer to the guy.

Did she have no common sense? He was dangerous.

"Why do his eyes look like that?" she asked.

The Vamper's attention went everywhere—the cloudless sky, the unevenly paved street, the line of brick row houses behind Ash. He was in need of a fix soon, or it would be a short withdrawal period.

The drug was constructed so users lasted a matter of hours between fixes. Without another taste of the drug, their organs started to fail. Talk about dependency. At this stage, vamps were uncontrollable and unstable, willing to do anything— even kill—to get their next hit. Ash couldn't think about what would have happened to the woman if he hadn't shown up when he did.

Whatever made the drug so addictive—the DEA was still trying to figure it out—made the body crave it so bad that, after one direct taste, it couldn't live without it. Like air in the lungs and food in the stomach, the body physically couldn't function without Vamp in its system. There had yet to be any medicinal assistance to wean users off the drug.

Once a Vamp addict, always a Vamp addict. Until death.

Blondie took a step back and inched toward her car.

He leaned into the addict's face, using his height as intimidation, and bared his teeth. "Where'd you get it?"

When the kid hesitated, Ash hardened his stare and all but shouted. "*Where?*"

"Clu-club Hell. 27th St-street!" he barely got out as a wave of violent spasms took over his body. "C'mon, m-ma-man!"

The addict didn't seem to know what he was begging for—money, another hit, or to be put out of his misery.

Now the dilemma: try to apprehend and get more information out of him in front of the woman? He wanted to laugh. Right. That would go over well. She'd be all up in his business while he interrogated the addict. It wasn't worth risking it just to torment the fool. And if the kid remained silent, he'd be dead in a matter of an hour or two anyway.

"Damn it," Ash said under his breath. He lowered his weapon and reached in his back pocket, pulling out two fifties. He tossed them into the street. "Get the hell out of here. And don't come back."

"Wait, what?" Blondie surprised him by saying. She took two commanding steps forward. "You're letting him go?"

The vamp leaped forward to retrieve the cash.

"Yeah," he said. Blondie was saved. The addict was retreating. Mission accomplished. Ash could get back to his boring-ass surveillance assignment in peace.

Ash started to turn toward his row house—

"Oh, no, you don't." Blondie leaped forward and caught the kid by his hood. She yanked his head free of the cover, making him scream in more pain.

Squeezing his eyes shut, he clawed at the air around him. "What are you doing? Get the fuck off me!" The addict yanked at his dark, shaggy hair as if he would take pleasure in pulling every strand out by the root.

Ash found it pretty damn interesting the kid didn't stutter when the sun's sharp rays stabbed his eyes.

Since the addict was only a hint bigger than Blondie—he was scrawny, really, and incapacitated by the sun; plus she had the element of surprise—she easily snapped his arms behind him.

She shoved the kid toward the back of her car and popped open her trunk.

What the fuc

Ash's mouth actually dropped open when she pulled out a pair of handcuffs. What the hell was she doing with *those* in her car? Who was this chick?

Probably out of mercy for her ears, she flipped the man's hood over his head. "Oh, hush." She latched one of the thug's wrists and then the other. "I'm taking you in. It just so happens I'm on my way to the police station right now."

Ash continued to gape, a ridiculous thing for someone with his skill and training. This woman was beyond anything he'd ever seen. Anyone else would have run in the other direction. Not her. She faced danger head-on. Seemed to welcome it. Panic and exhilaration overcame him as he watched her. His pulse quickened, but all he could do was stand there and blink like an ass.

"I'll need you to make a statement." Her long slender neck turned to face him as she shoved the kid into the passenger side of her gold POS car. "Once I get Dracula here settled into the backseat, the front's all yours." When he didn't respond, her eyebrows rose in question with a look of, *Yo, dumbshit. Anybody home?*

"What?" His mind recapped. *Handcuffs. Police station. Statement.*

No way. He grabbed the woman around her upper arm, causing her to jump. "No cops." That's the last thing he needed. If he went to the precinct or any cops came around here, his cover would be screwed for sure. Not only his cover, but the entire investigation. The DEA had discovered enough dirty BPD cops that they had to be on guard. No telling who was clean or who could be trusted within BPD. This was strictly DEA territory now. All it would take was one leak to alert the dealer that the team was onto him and he'd go underground. They couldn't allow that. They were too close to nailing the son of a bitch.

Her forehead creased, and a beet red color seeped into her face, despite his hand clutching her arm like a baseball bat. She inched onto her tiptoes and shoved her scrunched-up face into his personal space. "Why? You got something to hide? You know an awful lot about this Vamp stuff. Maybe I should grab an extra pair of cuffs and force your butt down to the station, too. As a proud employee of the Baltimore City Police Department—"

She's a fucking cop? That explained the handcuffs.

"—I am well within my rights to—hey!"

He let go of her to snatch the addict. Never without a key—old habits and all that—Ash snapped the cuffs open, releasing the thug from the metal hold. "Go." He pointed in the direction of 27th Street. Maybe the kid would make it the eight blocks to Club Hell. "Now."

Blondie's head swept from the direction of the handcuffs to Ash and back again. "How did you—?"

The young thug stumbled away, clutching his stomach, not bothering to glance back.

"Get back here!" she shouted. Then she turned her fury on Ash. She actually stomped her foot. "Oh! You—you... imbecile!" She stretched up on her tiptoes again, even farther than before, barely putting her at his chin level, and shoved her bony finger in his face. "What's wrong with you? He should be arrested!"

Ash shrugged and turned toward his house. He was done dealing with this. The issue wasn't the kid being addicted. It was the source of the drugs. And he'd just gotten a strong lead on the latter.

She followed him. "Oh, great. That's just great. Ignore me, why don't you?" She practically stepped on his heels. "Do you have any idea what you just did? You said that guy's a drug addict!"

And the perp had had a gun to her head, but that didn't seem to matter to the insane woman. "Your point?" He kept his back to her. If she was a cop, then she'd ask all sorts of questions. Questions he sure as hell wasn't going to answer.

"Right, it's not your problem," she continued, trailing him like a fucking shadow. "You obviously don't give a crap about other people. If you did, you wouldn't have let that guy go. You know what I should do? I should lock you up for obstruction of justice!" Her footsteps stopped, and he peered over his shoulder. She seemed lost in her own little world. Her eyes clouded, and she stared down the vacant street, chewing on the inside of her cheek. "Yeah, that's what I should do. I mean, I couldn't officially lock him up. But I could get Martinez to do it. He owes me from last week's poker game." Her gaze raked from Ash's buzzed-cut head to his scuffed sneakers as if sizing him up.

His lips curled at the corners. *I'd like to see you try.* That would be a sight. She thought she was such a badass with her handcuffs, but she'd never faced anyone with his kind of training. The Special Forces and later the DEA had seen to it that he could tackle any situation. No way would a tiny, annoying thing like her get the drop on him.

The smile broadened into a grin. That is, unless he wanted her to.

He could imagine it now: she'd get a few touches in as she tried to maneuver him into submission. He'd let her get one arm behind his back. Make her think she had the upper hand. That's how pushy broads like her operated—always dominating everything. But after a few moments of playtime, as she reached for his other arm, he'd reverse her hold, and get her under him so fast she wouldn't know what hit her.

Keeping his thoughts and smiles to himself, he proceeded toward his front door in silence. That would aggravate her more than if he spoke. He liked knowing that.

"Wait, you live here? Next to me?" She sounded devastated. "*You're* the new neighbor? Ugh. Of course you are. Just my luck." He could almost hear her eyes rolling.

Ash couldn't suppress a smirk.

"Aren't you going to say anything?" Approaching his porch, her footsteps grew heavier, the soles of her shoes pounding into the earth. "I want answers!" When he didn't provide any, she switched tactics. "What if that druggie comes back? What if he finds Carrie London and her baby a few houses down? Huh? How will you feel when you hear about a single mother and her child getting hurt knowing you're the one who let it happen? And gave the addict money for his next hit!"

Fuck. Ash halted with one foot on the first step. In his book, women and children were always off-limits.

Jesus, what did he do?

No, he'd taken the addict's gun and given him money. He was long gone by now.

As if hearing his thoughts, she placed her hand on his arm. "So you do care."

He shot a sharp glance at the physical contact but didn't turn around. Such a contrast—her tiny hand to his large, powerful arm. His fists clenched and unclenched. "Remove your hand."

She pulled back as if she'd been stung. Smart girl. "Who are you? Why do you have a gun? And how do you know so much about Vamp?"

Screw twenty questions. He took the final steps to his house two at a time and then rested his hand on the screen door latch.

Surprise, surprise—she was right behind him.

"And why don't you want cops involved?" She peered around his body to catch a glimpse inside his house. He didn't care. All she'd see was that he was scarce on furniture and needed to dust the place. "What are you hiding?"

He pulled on the screen door, giving her only a second to move out of the way, before he stepped inside and pulled it closed. Turning, he debated whether to speak.

Nah.

Grasping the oak door, he shut it in her face. *Take that.* He grinned as he pictured her stunned expression—wide eyes, red cheeks, pouty lips pinched together.

The woman was the complete opposite of his usual taste—

buxom brunettes with more than two handfuls up top—but damn if she didn't have something that attracted him. Despite her barely-there curves, she had a spark.

Confirming his thought, she yelled from the other side of the door. "You are the rudest man I've ever met! I hope you don't plan on being in the neighborhood long, buddy, because I'll be keeping a very close eye on you! I can be extremely annoying when I want to be!"

Yeah, he'd already figured that out.

A thud sounded as if something hit his door. Then a loud groan.

Stealing a glance through his peephole, he watched her grab her foot and jump around on one leg.

He chuckled. Scratch that. This chick had more than a spark. More like a bolt of lightning.

"You're welcome, by the way," he said, knowing she wouldn't hear him through the door.

Shaking his head, he turned. This was going to be a long fucking assignment.

• • •

Ugh! What an ass!

Sam hobbled down her neighbor's unstable cement stairs and crossed the street.

A drip of sweat at the back of her neck trailed under her shirt and ran the path of her spine. She pulled the damp blouse from her body, giving her a bit of relief, before pounding on her grandmother's front door. "Grandma!" Grumbling, she pounded harder. Stupid man with his stupid door. "Grandma!"

The door opened. "What? What?" Her grandmother held a cup of coffee in one hand and pushed her bifocals higher on the bridge of her nose with the other. "I'm watching— Samantha? What are you doing here? Shouldn't you be at work? If you're late one more time, Major—"

Sam held up her hand, silencing Rose. "I met the new neighbor."

Rose's eyebrows lifted above the metal of her petite frames. She peered across the street at the jerk's house and squinted through the daylight now peeking over the horizon. "The hunk next door? Really?" She leaned against the doorjamb and crossed her arms. "And?"

"Let me see." Sam began counting on her fingers. "He's rude, arrogant, psychotic, and an enabler."

"That bad?" Grandma Rose frowned before taking a sip from her mug.

"Did I mention he keeps a 9mm in his waistband?"

Her hand froze midair, and her green eyes bulged out of her head.

"Oh, and he gives money to drug addicts."

Grandma's jaw looked like it had come unhinged. Thank you, Fixodent, for keeping those chompers in her mouth.

"You better call Maybel and find out what she knows."

Rose's shoulders sagged as she exhaled. "She's been watching him since last night. I didn't want to say anything until we were sure, but he made a few calls to some guy named Tyke. Maybel said it sounded suspicious. Now based on what you're saying…"

You sneaky, sneaky man… The wheels in Sam's brain spun out of control. The gun, the information about Vamp, the big muscles—she didn't feel at all at ease with her new neighbor living on their street. They needed to find out what he was up to fast. And force the jerk out of town ASAP.

"We need to get to the bottom of this," Sam said. "Gather up the girls. When I get back from work tonight, we're hosting a stakeout."

Chapter Three

The drive to work was all of seven minutes, nowhere near enough time to rest Sam's throbbing foot. Her plan was to get to her desk, elevate her bruised tootsies, and try to find out as much as she could about her neighbor.

"Harper!" the Major's unmistakable roar shot through the halls of the southeastern precinct.

The building looked like any other station. Old and dusty. Desks littered with stacks of papers, bright halogen lights gleamed from the drop-tile ceiling, and clamor from the dispatch radio echoed all around. It had a distinct musty smell that always gave her a sense of calm when she entered.

This particular precinct was responsible for the dealings in the southeastern part of Baltimore City. More blue collar than the rest of the city, so none of the craziness and debauchery she would prefer, but beggars couldn't be choosers. No one else would hire her, and since Major Fowler was a family friend, Sam was happy to simply gain the experience until she passed the police exam and became a real cop.

"You're in big trouble now," Officer Daniel Martinez

said as Sam passed him on the way to her desk. "He's been shouting your name for thirty minutes. We're all taking bets on whether he's going to can you for real this time."

"How much is it up to?" Sam asked, amused. She dropped her purse into the bottom desk drawer and turned on her computer.

"Fifty bucks."

"That's it?" She stuck out her bottom lip. "Come on, Martinez, you know I'm worth more than that."

His brown eyes crinkled at the corners when he laughed.

Martinez had been at the precinct for a few months, his first assignment after graduating from the academy. He helped process bails and book criminals once they were brought to the station.

A bit younger than Sam, but a whole head taller, he was a good-looking man. Lean and fit with tanned skin and a smile that could light a room. No matter what kind of day Sam was having, Martinez could always make her laugh. He was one of the only friendly faces at the precinct. Most of her other coworkers, those who'd been around since the days of her father, tended to steer clear of her. Or bad-mouthed her family behind her back.

She glanced at her computer, then down the short hallway toward the Major's office. Eh, what's another minute or two? He'd be in a bad mood no matter when she showed up.

"How's your grandma doing?" She frowned at the abundant stack of reports next to her monitor. Secretary to the Major had its perks, but the monotonous workload definitely wasn't one of them.

Relief sparkled in Martinez's eyes. "Better, thanks. The hip replacement went well. Doc says she can move back home tomorrow."

"That's great news." She sat and drummed her fingers on the mouse. The computer always took forever to boot up when she was in a rush.

"Yeah, I told her no more stairs. My heart can't take it. I'm moving her into the first floor bedroom."

"Think she'll let you boss her around?" Sam smiled, knowing Grandma Martinez was a firecracker, despite her age.

He laughed. "Probably not."

She'd just opened the first search program, when another bellow sounded from the Major's office. It ricocheted off the white walls. "Harper! Is that you?"

"You better get in there before he has a coronary."

Fearing Martinez might be right—the Major *really* loved his triple-decker sandwiches with bacon—she left the computer program open and limped down the hallway toward the rear of the precinct.

She looked through the glass front of her boss's office to assess his mood.

Major Louis Fowler was a stout man, his navy uniform shirt not quite fitting, the buttons straining against the pull across his chest and bulging belly. He'd lost most of his hair, leaving nothing but a shiny dome on top that could double as a mirror. His bushy eyebrows and thick mustache were sprinkled with shades of brown, gold, and platinum.

His desk was always in disarray, and today was no different. When she stood in the doorway, he didn't lift his gaze from the stack of papers on his desk. Based on the deep crease in his forehead and the way he slouched, he seemed to be reading a disturbing report. "You're late. What's your excuse this time?"

"Hi-ya, Lou." Maybe her chipper tone would reverse his mood and get her out of his office pronto. Her leather sandals itched to get back to her desk. "You're never going to believe why I'm late."

"Take a seat." He rubbed his temples, still not looking at

her. "This better be good, Harper."

She settled into the dark leather chair opposite his desk but sat on the very edge of the cushion. "It is, I swear." The shock had worn off considerably. Her voice was calm, like she was reading an article from the newspaper. "I got mugged."

He dropped the report and abruptly looked up. Alarmed brown eyes raked over her. "My God. Are you okay?"

Well, at least that diverted the attention away from her lateness. She leaned back and stretched her arms across the leather. "I'm fine. It was an almost-mugging. Perp on drugs put a gun to my head and demanded money, but I didn't give it to him."

"A gun? Drugs?" Fowler swiped his broad forehead with the back of his hand. "Samantha!"

Her eyes slanted to the doorway. "I'm fine. Look at me." She stood, turning in a carousel move and inched for the exit. "See, not even a scratch."

"How?" A vein pulsed on his forehead as if ready to burst.

"Well, I had this whole plan worked out where I was going to chuck my purse into the middle of the street and wrestle the guy when he wasn't looking—"

"*Wrestle him?* Jesus, Samantha!"

"—but I didn't have to because my next-door neighbor came out with a gun of his own and demanded the guy surrender."

Fowler's eyes were huge, and the vein on his forehead throbbed double time. "The eighty-year-old man next door?"

"No, no." She waved her hand in the air back and forth and rolled her eyes. "This is a new neighbor. Just moved in on the other side. Big, really annoying guy." The emotions swam across the Major's face—worry, confusion, relief. "Who's handling the report?"

"No one," she said before she thought better of it.

The Major waited.

Oops. "My neighbor didn't… I mean, I didn't want…we bickered…he shut the door…I kicked it…"

"Sam," he said through a sigh, "we've been through this. You're not a cop. You can't go around taking the law into your own hands. You should have called Young or Webb."

She fought to belie the disappointment washing over her. "Come on, Lou, I've got more training under my belt than both of them combined, and you know it. The only thing they have over me is a badge."

He shot her a look that said, *My point exactly.*

She picked at her fingernails. "You know neither one of them would've jumped to help me anyway. Even if I'd called. They still think—they think I'm…"

His gaze shifted from hers, taking keen interest in the dead plant hanging from a hook on the ceiling behind her. His chest expanded a few times before he brought his attention back to her. "No one holds what your father did against you."

A sharp current of heat zapped down her spine, making her jerk upright. "What my father did?" she hissed. "He didn't *do* anything! My father wouldn't, he *couldn't*, be a dirty cop. You were his partner. You knew him better than anyone."

"I know, I know," he said. "Calm down, kid. I wasn't implying he was. It's just…it's hard for some of the guys on the force to get over the rumors. I'm not saying it's right. It's just the way it is."

It was rumored that after a year of working undercover for a local drug dealer, Viktor Heinrich, Sam's dad had stopped reporting back to his handler. Weeks passed with no word, so a team from BPD Narcotics assembled to go after him and bring him in. But they never found him. After awhile, people on the force started suggesting he'd either become a dirty cop or he was dead. Sam didn't believe either theory. Who knew the truth? Only her father and Heinrich.

She'd tried to use her limited resources as Major Fowler's

secretary to find one of Heinrich's locations and go looking for her dad. But those files were locked up tight. Only the officers on the case were given access. And since no one trusted her because of what they thought her father had done, they refused to offer up any information on the case or Heinrich's suspected whereabouts.

Eventually everyone moved on with their lives. Except Sam, who had a missing piece of her heart that would never be filled. Her father would forever be disgraced in the eyes of Baltimore City Police. And there wasn't anything she could do to clear his name.

"I'm sorry I brought it up, Sam," he said. "I didn't mean anything by it. But promise me if something like this morning happens again, you'll call the precinct, okay?"

Her lips flattened into a thin line, and she resisted the urge to bark at Lou. To tell him he should stick up for his old partner. *Make* people believe her father would never turn against the badge. But the piercing pain in her stomach stopped her. There wasn't anything out there to prove his innocence. "No one was hurt, Lou. If it makes you feel better, I'll give a description of the perp to Henderson so she can do a sketch to post around town." She took two more side-steps toward the door.

Fowler stared at her for a moment longer, seeming to weigh her words, and then nodded. "You know your old man would have your hide if he was here and heard you'd tried to wrestle a man with a gun."

She tried to offer a smile to mask the pang of anger and sadness. "I know. But he's not. So I'm your problem to worry about, remember?"

"Yes," he said, through a wry smile. "I do." His eyes misted as he shook his head. "Sometimes you're more trouble than you're worth, kid."

"It's a good thing I'm so lovable then, huh?" This time the

smile did come, spreading across her face with ease.

"Get out of here before I fire you." He grinned before dropping his head and massaging his temples once again.

"Yes, sir." She gave him a mock salute and turned on her heels content in the fact that the Major must have completely forgotten why he'd called her into his office in the first place.

Standing at her desk, she glanced at the piles of reports. Later, she promised. Right now, she needed to do some investigative work.

Dropping into her office chair, she moved her mouse to wake up her computer. She flexed her fingers as the Baltimore City Police's database homepage appeared. The program was invaluable in finding perpetrators with prior records.

Her eyes shifted from her screen in a wide arc around the precinct. She and Martinez were the only two in the front room. Webb, Hirsch, and the rest of the gang were out patrolling the streets. Martinez sat behind his desk, phone resting on his shoulder, typing on his keyboard. He must have been taking a complaint from a citizen. As a probationary officer, Martinez gathered the facts and then sent an officer to the scene to handle it. Most of the calls that came into the precinct were non-emergency, *my cat is stuck in a tree* or *my neighbor parked in my spot* kinds of things. If it was a real emergency, people called 911, and the central dispatch center handled the calls and correspondence with officers on the road. Sam listened idly to the consistent chatter on the dispatch radio. Mostly domestics and B and Es; nothing she needed to respond to. At least for now.

She maneuvered the pointer to the search box. If her neighbor was as dangerous as she thought he was, then his butt would definitely be in the database. She was counting on it.

"Bird tattoo on neck." She typed and clicked SEARCH. She waited, tapping her fingers on the keys of the keyboard.

4,367 RESULTS.

Yikes. That would take forever to sift through.

"Hmm, okay, how about *black* bird tattoo on neck."

1,287 RESULTS.

Impatience rose from her stomach and lodged in her throat.

"Let's try black bird tattoo on *male* neck." Her fingers pounded each letter on the keyboard. The program took its sweet time processing the search.

"Hey, Sam," Martinez said across the room. "You busy?"

She held off a groan, pulling her gaze from the computer screen. "Kinda, why?"

"Sinclair just called and said he's got a 10-95 coming in. Guy's hopped up on PCP. He's gonna need extra hands. Can you cover the phones while I help?"

She looked sideways at the phone on her desk, praying it wouldn't ring until he got back, and nodded.

Then she glanced back at her computer screen. *435 RESULTS.*

Holy momma! A rush of excitement blasted through her from head to toe.

Sam scanned the first three pages of results, growing more impatient with each passing minute. Her dinosaur computer kept locking up, and the server was busy, so it took forever to get to the next page. At this rate, she'd get through all four hundred entries by quitting time.

There had to be another way.

Rocking back in her chair, she looked up at the drop-tiled ceiling. A hum from the bright halogen lights invaded her ears. "What else? What else? Come on, Sam. Think." She closed her eyes and white orbs flashed behind her eyelids.

Opening her eyes, she leaned forward. "Hey, Martinez."

The young, dark-haired officer lifted his head from his computer screen, smiling. It was different than his usual smile. One that held an excited hint. The amber in his eyes was brighter, too. He must have been thinking about the impending arrival of the PCP user.

That look made her want to chuckle. She'd seen officers on probation come and go. They all had that nervous anticipation whenever they had a chance to get their hands dirty. Hell, she felt it, too. "If I want to get information on a guy, but I don't know a lot about him, what can I do?" The stakeout and Maybel's contact would tell them more about Mr. Grumpy next door. But she was too impatient to wait until tonight. She wanted info now.

A grin erupted on Martinez's face. "Someone catch a case of the Salt Water Pinchers?"

"The *what*?"

"Crabs. You sleep with some guy and he gave you something nasty down below?" He swirled his hand around his lap.

"Eww, no!" Her face contorted. "Why would you even go there? You know I'm not like those floozies you hang around with after work." Martinez was a man-whore, and he flaunted it proudly. "It's my neighbor—"

His grin widened to the point of almost touching his ears.

"—whom I have *not* slept with. *Ever.*" Just to clarify. "I want to find out more about him. Since he's new and living near my grandma and all. I just want to make sure he's legit." Mentioning her grandmother would surely pull Martinez's mind far away from STDs.

He shot from his chair and stomped across the room in his black military-grade boots. He stood beside her with his feet spread and shoulders squared. "What do you know about him? Name? Hair and eye color? Type of car? License plate number? Any identifying marks on his body? Tattoos? Piercings?"

"He's tall. Well over six foot. Six-four, maybe? Dark hair.

Blue eyes. Huge body."

Martinez tilted his head to the side and raised his eyebrows. "Come again?"

"You heard me. Huge body. Real fit. Like, muscles everywhere."

Martinez seemed to be fighting another grin. "Okay. Keep going."

"He's got a tattoo on his neck. I could only see the top of it poking out of his collar. Looks like feathers. Maybe it's a bird or…or one of those Vegas showgirls. You know, the ones in bikinis with feathers strategically placed on their head and body." Yeah, Big and Brawny looked like the type to have a scantily clad woman tattooed across his bulging biceps.

When his eyebrows touched his hairline, she clarified. "I'm not saying that's what it is, I'm just saying that all I saw was feathers. Could be anything. I'll have to get a closer look next time I see him."

"Sounds like it'll be soon," he said, crossing his arms over his chest.

She turned to meet his gaze. "What do you mean by that?"

He shrugged. "Just sounds like you wouldn't mind seeing this guy again is all."

"He's my neighbor, Dan. Of course I'm going to see him again. With my luck, it'll be all the damn time."

She got the sense she and Martinez were having completely different conversations.

"Anyway," she said, "He didn't have piercings or any other identifying marks that I could see."

No need to mention her neighbor's handgun and her almost mugging. Martinez didn't need a reason to worry.

"You check Book 'Em yet?"

She nodded. "Checked that first."

"Hmm." He rubbed his clean-shaven jaw. "What about NCIC?" he asked, referring to the National Criminal

Information Center.

Bending over her shoulder, he peered at the screen. He was so close she smelled the woodsy scent of his soap.

Shaking her head, she said, "Can't. I don't have his name, social, or DOB."

Martinez nodded once. "Oh, right."

She scooted her chair forward a bit, creating a few inches of space between them.

He leaned in farther, resting his palm on top of her desk. "That cancels out Dashboard, too, then."

She slid her chair forward again and turned her head, ready to tell him to back up. Before she could get the words out, his eyes widened. "You know what'll work though?"

She slid to the edge of her seat, her pulse revving in anticipation.

"Let's try—"

The front doors swung open, slamming against the interior wall with a crash. "What the fuck, Martinez!"

Sam fell against the back of the chair, slouching into the leather. She was so close.

Officer Sinclair entered, holding on to a man in handcuffs. "I thought I told you to meet me outside in ten? Quit flirting with Harper and get your ass over here!"

Martinez straightened and hustled toward the front of the station.

The man in Sinclair's grasp wasn't large. He was around Sam's height and probably only weighed about twenty pounds more than she did. But he had a crazed look in his eye, like he thought he was as big as a sumo wrestler. He swung his head toward Sinclair with teeth bared. If someone pulled out a red cloth, the guy was going to charge it like a bull. He was doing his damnedest to free himself, thrashing and pulling away from Sinclair. Which was a feat since Sinclair was more than six feet and almost as wide as a tractor trailer. When Martinez reached for the guy's other arm, the man kicked a nearby chair, sending it skidding into Sam's desk.

"Hey!" she said. "Watch it!"

The man yelled obscenities at her, involving something about a woman and a spoon.

Sinclair gripped the man's nape and shoved him forward. "Watch your mouth in front of the lady."

The perp cussed again and then jerked his head to spit in Sinclair's face.

Sam didn't blink, but her mouth dropped open. *Oh boy.*

Momentarily stunned, Sinclair's grasp on the guy loosened, freeing one arm. The perp used the opportunity to swing his shoulder toward Martinez, landing a hit square in Martinez's chest. Dan stumbled two steps and landed on his butt.

"Damn it." Martinez scrambled to get up.

The perp dashed toward Sam with a broad, crooked grin. *Oh, no you don't.*

She reached for a half-empty bottle of water from her desk and clunked it on the guy's forehead. It obviously wasn't enough to injure him, but it stunned him enough to stop his progress.

His heels dug into the tiled floor and he shook his head as if to clear it. He shouted another profanity and came around the side of her desk. His face was red, and he was panting like a wild beast. Sweat poured down his temples and spit trailed out of his mouth.

Probably due to the raucous screaming, two plain-clothes officers from the back of the precinct came rushing in. With alarmed expressions, they swung their attention from Sinclair and Martinez approaching the perp to the perp himself who had caged Sam in behind her desk.

Her back was to the wall, and the psycho stood in front of her wearing the grin of a serial killer. Before she made a move,

Sinclair slammed the guy's face into the computer monitor on her desk, and the other two officers, including Dan, contained the man from all sides.

Once upright, blood dripping from his nose, the guy flailed his legs wildly and wailed like a caged animal causing one of his ankles to tangle with the cords under her desk. When the officers yanked him back, her keyboard went first. It dropped onto the floor and skidded a few feet. Her mouse clanked onto the tile next. Then she watched almost in slow motion as the computer monitor slid across the top of her desk and dropped. Right onto her already throbbing foot.

"*YOW!*" she shouted, as the thing rolled off her foot and onto the floor in a steaming heap of plastic. It *zapped*, then *sizzled*, before the screen went black.

"Holy freakin' mother of a biscuit on toast with jelly!" She held her foot and jumped around as Martinez, Sinclair, and the other officers pushed the PCP user toward Booking.

"Mother Mary in Heaven and Wilbert, too," she whimpered.

"Sam?" Major Fowler said from behind. "What the hell is going on in here?"

She turned to see his furrowed bushy eyebrows and wrinkled forehead.

Squeezing her eyes shut and wincing, she pointed to her foot, which was still cradled in her other hand. "*Ow,*" she squeaked.

Chapter Four

As Ash parked his '98 Dodge pickup along the curb, his stomach grumbled. After getting settled in last night, and then the incident with the Vamper this morning, he hadn't eaten. He couldn't wait to get inside and devour his lo mein.

He lifted the manual lock on his driver's side door and glanced up and down the street. Always vigilant.

The street was quiet; it was midday so most neighbors were probably at work or staying inside to beat the heat. Based on what he'd seen so far, the community was made up of blue-collar workers. Some wore a shirt and tie, but the majority wore uniforms and drove company vans. The other half he'd seen walking the streets during the day were much older than him, probably retired, their hair gray and posture slumped from years of backbreaking work.

Perfect place to blend in and learn what he could about the local drug scene. First, because this area was near the port, which was where the DEA suspected the Vamp supplier was bringing drugs into the city. Second, he knew from personal experience on the job that the quietest streets and people were the best sources of information.

The DEA knew about Vamp and what it could do to a person once hooked, but they didn't know how and where patrons were getting addicted in the first place. The incident with the addict this morning was a great start. Club Hell on 27th Street. Ash's portion of this assignment was to learn information like that and then pass it on to his team leader, who would decide what to do with the intel. Which pissed Ash off because that used to be his job. Before his major fuckup on their last assignment, that is. Out of habit, he rubbed the left side of his chest, his fingers gliding over the notch of round, raised skin just above his heart. A constant reminder.

If he wanted to get his team back, if he wanted to be team leader again, he had to play by Director Landry's rules. Observe the city, see what he could learn about where addicts were getting hooked, and pass the info on. Do not under any circumstances take matters into his own hands.

That last order was going to be his greatest struggle. Ash was a hands-on kind of guy. It wasn't in his nature to sit back and watch.

But he wanted to stop the drug pandemic that seemed to be taking over. It was why he joined the DEA in the first place. That shit didn't belong on the streets. And users most definitely didn't deserve to die because of it.

Still gazing out the driver's side window, he glanced at Blondie's house and thought about their unorthodox introduction this morning. *Boyish and athletic* had been his first thought when he'd spotted her. But it was something in the way she moved that had caught his attention. Fluid and confident. Shoulders back and spine straight gave the illusion she always got her way.

A bitter laugh escaped. And now he knew she was demanding and overbearing, too.

Snatching the take-out bag from the seat, he slid out.

He made it five steps.

"Excuse me!" a female voice called out behind him.

He glanced down at the bag in his hand and sighed. So much for chowing down on his lo mein. Stopping on the first step leading to his house, he turned.

"You there—are you the new neighbor?" A woman hurried after him, making great strides despite her age and size, her full hips swaying with a purpose. Behind her she dragged a scraggly-haired mutt that looked about a hundred years old. Even the dog's four legs couldn't keep up with her two. The pair reminded him of Paula Dean and Old Yeller.

The woman stopped in front of him, the top of her poofy white hair coming up to his chest. Her plump head tilted back, revealing narrowed eyes. Ash sensed it wasn't because of the bright sun.

She wrapped the leash around her wrist, ensuring her dog couldn't escape. Not that he would. The damn thing dropped to the ground the second she stopped walking. His tongue hung out of his mouth, and his broad chest expanded in exaggerated motion.

"I'm Maybel Ray," she said, sticking out her free hand. "And you are?" Her eyes narrowed farther in challenge, as if she knew he wouldn't answer.

Ash thought long and hard about doing just that, but that wouldn't help his cause to blend in and gather information. So he forced a pleasant smile and lied. "John."

"John, huh? You have a last name, John?" She popped her hip out and placed her hand on it. The movement tightened the slack on her dog's leash, causing him to yelp when it restricted around his neck.

"Oh! Oh my. Sorry, Rufus." She patted the dog's head, and he fell back onto the pavement, snoring.

Maybel turned to Ash. "How about that last name, John?"

He wanted to give her a narrow-eyed expression of his

own but chose to keep the smile in place instead. Intel. *It's all about collecting intel*, he reminded himself. "Black."

"John Black," she echoed. "All right, Mr. Black. Are you from Baltimore? When did you move here? What do you do for a living?"

A car engine revved somewhere from the right. Ash glanced in that direction, spotting a dated Buick moseying toward them, but Paula Dean didn't take her eyes off him. A lesser man would have crumbled under her direct gaze. Not Ash. He'd faced down drug lords, hard-core criminals, and some of the world's worst terrorists. One old broad and her decrepit dog weren't going to break him. Just the thought made him want to laugh.

"Are you in a gang?"

Now that was a first. He laughed out of honest amusement. "Why do you say that?"

She glared at his neckline. "You have a tattoo. Gang members have tattoos."

So did a lot of other groups. Like Special Forces and SEALs. He glanced down as if he could see the ink on his neck and chest. "From my Army days."

"Hmm." Her eyes opened a fraction more, and the creases on her face softened. "So you're a vet?"

He gave a nod.

A look of approval crossed her features. "What brings you to 19th Street, John?"

He hooked a thumb through his belt loop and crossed one foot over the other. "I grew up around here before I joined the Army. I'd been deployed a bunch of times and was getting tired of life in the desert. So when I was getting out, I wanted to grow roots where I had some ties."

Maybel tilted her head as if assessing if his story was legit. She must have deemed it was, because she dropped her full chin once.

His turn.

"What about you? You and old Rufus lived here long?"

She glanced down the street with a far-off expression as if she was looking into the past. "Moved here in the eighties with my husband. He worked in DC, and I got a job at the local school. It's a great area. Always has been." She inhaled a deep breath, then blinked a few times, coming to. She looked at him directly. "We're a tight-knit group here on 19th Street. We watch out for each other. We don't take kindly to new people disrupting the balance." She slanted her head to the other side. "You're not going to disrupt the balance, are you, John?"

He would've taken offense to her insinuation, but he couldn't ignore the blatant pride she had in her hometown. They had the same agenda: to *keep* the balance in Baltimore. Specifically for him, it was to stop men like Viktor Heinrich from causing devastation and misery.

He looked her square in the eye. "No, ma'am. I'm just looking for some R and R."

She loosened her hold on the leash, letting it drop onto the cement. The mutt rolled onto his side and began scratching his stomach with his back leg. The woman mirrored Ash's casual stance, crossing a foot over the other, but contradicted it with a Mafia stare-down. The DEA could use a broad like her. She almost intimidated him. Almost. "I'm glad to hear it. You stay out of trouble, you hear, John?"

"Yes, ma'am," he said again. "Is there trouble I need to be looking out for?" Might as well see if the old broad had heard of anything out of the ordinary. Based on the event this morning and the way she was drilling him, 19th Street was a lot more active than she was leading on.

She stepped toward him, her overabundant chest almost brushing his stomach, and jutted her chin out. "Just keep your nose clean, young man. If you cause trouble, you'll be sorry."

The woman reminded him of his genteel grandmother. She was soft and round in the midsection and probably baked cookies every day for fun. But his grandmother would never make threats she couldn't keep. And Ash could guarantee Maybel Ray didn't, either. From her firm stance and hard gaze, the woman meant business. He was also damn certain that she knew more than she was saying.

"Take care for now, John. I'll be seeing you around."

He gave her a final smile for good measure. "Looking forward to it, Ms. Ray."

She turned and reached down for the leash, which was no longer where she'd left it. Instead, it was about ten feet away, trailing behind the curved body of Old Yeller who was taking a dump on his front lawn.

Before he could pull the plastic bag off his take-out and make her pick up the dog's crap, his cell phone vibrated in his pocket. Sliding it out, he glanced at the screen. *Tyke.* The new team leader. Ash's replacement.

His movement caught Maybel's attention, and she leaned in to catch a glimpse at his cell phone. Ballsy, he'd give her that.

He kept the smile in place and signaled to his phone. "My baby sister. We're supposed to meet for dinner tonight."

Her perceptive eyes didn't waiver. "Best get going then."

His phone dinged, alerting him that he had a voicemail. "See you around."

She gave a little wave, then whistled to her dog. Old Yeller kicked his feet backward, uprooting chunks of grass to cover his pile, before trotting away like he'd just won the Eukanuba Nationals.

Ash would worry about that particular pile of shit later. First priority was getting on the horn to Tyke to report what he'd learned about the Vamper and Club Hell.

Dashing up the front cement stairs, he entered his house.

Dropping the food on the kitchen counter, he pushed a button on his cell phone to access his voicemail.

"Hey, asshole," Tyke's gruff voice said. "Avoidin' my call? Real fucking mature. Why don't you do yourself a favor and call me when you get this? I'd like to know you're doing some kind of work on this assignment. Or did you already find some woman to screw off with?"

"Fuck you, Tyke," Ash mumbled. It was one time. One. And it was going to haunt him for the rest of his career.

"Just call me back," the message continued. "I wanna know what else you've found out about Heinrich. Anything out of the ordinary going on in the city? Do your goddamn job so I can do mine."

Ash was marooned by himself in Baltimore because of his involvement with Lorena Serrano on their previous mission. She had been an informant offering information about Jose Serrano, an immensely powerful and wealthy drug creator. Of course, when Ash fell in love with her, neither he nor the Agency had any clue that Lorena was Jose's daughter. Ash might have figured it out if his head hadn't been up his ass with stars in his eyes. She was beautiful, with curves in all the right places. He fell for her, and he fell hard. Started ignoring direct orders from the director. Missed meetings with his team. Even thought about leaving the DEA for her. It wasn't until after they arrived at Jose Serrano's chateau in Buenos Aires that he discovered the truth. That was also the night Ash sacrificed an innocent boy's life and was then shot by the supposed love of his life and left for dead.

All of which put him on Director Landry's shit list. And for good reason.

Fun times.

Somehow Ash got to a hospital and survived. But his career didn't. Landry yanked Ash out of Argentina and placed him on desk duty for a few months to recoup and cool off. Good move since all Ash had wanted to do was head back to South America and track down Lorena and her father. Once the director felt like Ash was in his right mind and could handle something other than getting coffee and filing reports, he sent him here to Baltimore. Still punishment since he wasn't allowed to rejoin the team, but better than being a paper pusher. He'd take it.

Staring at his lo mein on the counter, he inhaled. *You did this to yourself. Suck it up and play along.*

Chapter Five

After spending six grueling hours waiting in the emergency room, Sam finally made it back home. The doc said her foot wasn't broken, thank God, but she should stay off of it for a day or so. That was fine with her, since the next two days were going to be filled with sitting on her bum and spying on her neighbor.

She knocked on the door at Grandma Rose's house and heard voices yelling from inside.

Grandma opened the door and peered down at Sam's foot with a worried expression.

"I'm good," she said. "Just have to keep it elevated and put ice on it. The pain's more in my rear-end than my foot." It still throbbed like an extra heartbeat, but the doctor wrapped it good and tight. Even if she walked into a wall, it wouldn't hurt it any further.

"That's good news. When Lou called and said he'd had to practically drag you to the ER, I didn't know what to think."

More shouts erupted from inside Rose's house. Sam looked over her grandmother's shoulder.

"They've been here since noon." Rose smiled and motioned with a swing of her arm for Sam to follow.

Sam ambled into the back of the house toward the kitchen, where the rest of the women from the 19th Street Patrol huddled around the table like a pack of lions devouring a fresh kill.

Grandma's house was identical in layout to Sam's. Living room with TV just inside the door, a short hallway with a powder room, then the corridor opened to a dining area with sliding glass door to the right and kitchen to the left.

Sam stopped in the doorway between the dining room and kitchen, gripping the inside of the doorjamb.

Evening had descended. The moon was full, sending its white rays through the window, acting as a spotlight to gadgets laying on the kitchen tabletop.

"No," Maybel snapped, yanking a video camera with infrared technology from Estelle's hands. "I told you, *I'm* going to use it. I have better vision than you do." Maybel, Vice President and oldest member of the neighborhood watch group, was what most people would consider a typical grandmother. Wearing a blue short-sleeve cotton shirt and khaki culottes, she appeared as the essence of simplicity. One would never guess that behind that easy-going facade lurked a woman with an unquenchable thirst for information.

During the Cold War, Maybel had worked as an operative for the CIA. She usually clammed up when Sam asked her about what happened, but Grandma Rose had said Maybel played a part in the peacekeeping efforts between the U.S. and the Soviets. Whatever that meant.

She must have had a pretty huge part, because she still had connections at the Agency and beyond. She never spoke about the who and the what, but if the 19th Street Patrol needed anything, Maybel could provide it.

"But my hands are steadier," Estelle barked, snatching

the piece back. "You can't hold the camera still long enough to see what's going on. Always looks like the suspect's being sucked into a damn hurricane." Estelle wore a spaghetti-strap top and a tight denim skirt, looking more like a barmaid than a grandma. She'd lived alone, five doors down from Grandma Rose for forty years. Never married, but never without a list of adoring suitors at her beck and call.

"What do I get to do?" Celia asked no one in particular. At sixty, she was the youngest and most proper of the group. Dressed in her usual Sunday best—cashmere top, pearls, kitten heels, and hair pulled into a perfect chignon—she reached cautiously across the table for a dart gun. She marveled at it and then pointed the barrel at her face.

"No!" Sam leaped forward, pulling the gun from Celia's hand before the woman figured out how to pull the trigger. Celia shooting herself in the face and passing out from the tranquilizers wouldn't be a great start to the evening.

Voices continued to holler over one another, arguing about who was going to handle which device. Excitement at the prospect of gathering information on their mysterious neighbor had taken over the room. Sam let their racket go on for another minute, before forcing order.

"Ladies! Ladies!" She bobbed her hands in the air like a teacher trying to calm an unruly class of first graders. "Ladies, please listen."

The arguing continued.

Grandma Rose stuck her fingers in her mouth and let out an ear-piercing whistle.

All eyes turned and gave Sam their undivided attention. "Thank you for coming. We have a very important mission tonight. We need all hands on deck for this one. As you know, we have a new neighbor. And he's a slick one. I had a run-in with him this morning. Big, bad, and carries a pistol."

A collective gasp erupted.

Sam nodded for effect. "The man is dangerous."

Maybel dropped her binoculars onto the table with a *thud*. "I bumped into him while I was out walking Rufus this afternoon—"

"More like spying on him," Estelle said out of the side of her mouth.

She shot the woman a stern sideways glance. "I questioned him is all." She straightened her spine and lifted her chin. "As VP of the watch I have a right to." She paused, seeming to wait for someone to challenge her logic.

"And?" Estelle said, drumming her fingers on the table. "What'd you find out? We're waitin' on baited breath here. Some of us might die soon."

"His name is John Black. He moved back to town after serving in the Army. He grew up around here."

"That's it?" Estelle asked. "That's all he said? What about the juicy details?"

Juicy details was right. He might have moved back to his hometown, but then why the gun? And how did he know so much about those drugs?

Maybel slumped in her chair. "There weren't any. I could tell there was more to his story though. Much more."

With an eager expression, Estelle rested an elbow on the table and leaned over it. "Like what? Firefighter by day, Magic Mike by night? That kind of thing?"

Maybel sent a deadpan look to her friend. "No, Estelle. I was thinking more that he was hiding something of importance."

The other woman leaned back and shrugged. "You don't think a man who can gyrate like Channing Tatum is important?"

Celia bent to whisper to Rose. "Who's Channing Tatum?"

Rose waved her off. "I'll show you tomorrow afternoon during tea."

Satisfied, Celia nodded and folded her hands in her lap.

"What I *meant*," Maybel said in a stern tone, "was that I don't believe his story about who he is and where he's from. He's definitely hiding something and I want to know why."

Sam's gaze shifted to the windows looking out to the back alley. She focused on the aged-wood fence outlining her grandmother's small yard.

A vision of her brawny neighbor came to her, and her heart suddenly beat double-time. "He's arrogant," Sam mused. "But I guess he can be, since he's all buff and what-not...he's wide like a tractor-trailer and just as tough...a bit roguish, but it's a front. He's not fooling me with that tough-guy exterior." She snorted. *But man, the way he'd saved me from that kid and took control of the situation. Capably. Securely. Forcefully.* She shuddered. It was meant to be in disgust, but it definitely wasn't. *His muscles are enormous. And he has this commanding way of—*

"Is he a bad guy or a hero in a romance novel?" Estelle said through a sly smile. "Sounds like Channing Tatum ain't got nothing on Beefy next door."

Sam jumped and glanced at the smirking faces staring back at her. She'd said all of that out loud. How embarrassing.

Estelle threw her shoulders back, showing off her low-cut neckline. "From that description, I'm thinkin' we should go over and welcome him to the neighborhood, if you know what I mean." She nudged Maybel in the ribs and winked. "Might not be such a bad thing havin' a little eye candy to stare at."

Sam's focus cleared and snapped to the women at the table. They had to understand the importance of tonight. "He's no piece of candy. And if he is, he's a...a...chocolate-covered maggot."

There was a shared, "Eww."

"Yuck," Celia whispered to herself, her face turning an

ill shade of green. She pulled a handkerchief from her pocket and placed it over her mouth. "Why would anyone want to eat a maggot covered in chocolate?"

"No one eats 'em, Celia," Estelle responded. "It was a figure of speech. A poor one, but one nonetheless."

Sam narrowed her eyes at Estelle but didn't comment.

Estelle shot her a mega-watt smile and batted her eyelashes.

"Oh." Little red patches appeared on Celia's cheeks.

"Chocolate maggot or not," Grandma Rose interjected, "I'm grateful to him. He did, after all, save you from that horrible drug addict."

Another collective gasp.

Sam's arms waved up and down to calm the group. "It was nothing. I could've handled it on my own." But she hadn't. Ash had saved her. Her voice didn't sound as confident as she would have liked, and the awkward silence and worried expressions on the other women's faces told her they had picked up on it.

Sam turned to Celia with the intention of getting them back on track. "You can handle the audio. It's important we hear what our new neighbor has to *say*." *Not what he looks like.* "Your job is the most important." She pointed to the corner of the room where the Long-Range Laser Listening Device sat propped against the wall. It was a tall, camera-looking thing on a tripod typically used by law enforcement or military. All Celia had to do was point the laser at their neighbor's house, into one of his windows, and they'd be able to hear him moving about. The device attached to an amplifier unit with audio recorder, so if he said anything really interesting, they'd have it on tape.

Celia sat up straighter in her seat and grinned.

"I'll be the lead on this investigation," Sam continued. "Grandma, I need you to install the GPS on his car."

Rose flashed a cocky grin. "Done. Installed it this afternoon."

All at once, the women reached and grabbed equipment from the table, eyeing each device carefully, acquainting themselves in preparation for their assignment.

"Are we sure he's really bad?" Celia placed a pair of headphones in front of her. "Maybe he carries a gun for hunting."

"You don't hunt with a handgun," Maybel responded.

"There must be a good reason," Celia said. "What if we go through all this to find out he's a good guy?"

"That's what we're hoping," Rose spoke up.

"Yeah, right," Sam muttered. *Good guy, my ass.*

"But then why—"

"Remember the Wilkensons?" Grandma Rose said.

"The family that died?"

"*Killed*, Celia," Maybel said. "By their neighbor. He seemed like a perfectly normal, nice young man and then one day he shot them both dead in their house. No one on the street had any clue he had mental issues." Her eyes closed as a shudder ran through her body. "Thank goodness the kids were at their grandparents' that night."

"That's why we're doing this," Rose added. "So hopefully children like them never have to wake up without their parents again."

Sam remembered the day clearly. Maybel and Rose had formed the group the day after the funeral, and they'd been adding members and keeping watch over their neighbors ever since.

A hush fell over the group as the women took an unofficial moment of silence for the Wilkenson family.

After a few moments, Sam's head snapped up and she grinned. "Let's get started."

• • •

Ash savored his last bite of Chinese food. Now all he wanted to do was relax. He'd set up a nineteen-inch TV in his living room to the right of the front door and directly under the bay window. All that hung over the window was a grimy pair of sheer ivory curtains that had probably been white at one time. They suited his purpose.

The room was bare apart from the curtains. No pictures, no rugs, nothing to add warmth to the house. A TV on a milk crate, a worn sofa, an end table, and lamp without a shade were all he'd set up. He wasn't planning on staying long.

He settled onto the soft sofa cushions and turned the channel to ESPN, catching up on baseball scores from around the country.

His eyes grew heavy and his blinks slowed. He laced his fingers over his stomach and dropped his head to the side, giving in to the tiredness.

When his cell phone rang, his eyes shot open. Leaping from his lounged position, he scrambled into the kitchen to retrieve his phone.

"Yeah," he answered, rubbing the sleep from his eyes.

DEA Northeast Regional Director Joseph Landry spoke, "Status report."

Fuck. He'd forgotten to call Tyke and report what he'd seen with Blondie and the Vamper.

Ash cleared his throat. "Had an incident this morning with a Vamp. Held a local woman at gunpoint demanding money. I handled the situation."

"Really?" he asked. A few silent beats passed, prompting Ash to elaborate.

"Just some punk in need of a fix. He came out during the daylight though. Must've been desperate."

"You're sure he was on Vamp?"

"Yes. Same red and black eyes, chalky skin, shaking like a leaf."

"I see."

"Said he buys his stash at Club Hell. Viktor Heinrich's joint."

"Anything else?"

Ash paused.

"Spit it out, Cooper."

"The incident with the Vamper. The woman involved… she was asking questions."

"Who is she?" The director's voice turned weary.

"Next-door neighbor. She noticed the eyes, sir."

Landry stayed silent for a moment, then said, "You're a capable agent. You'll figure something out." He paused a fraction of a second before saying, "But, Cooper, if you blow your cover, you can kiss reinstatement to team leader good-bye."

"Understood," he replied through tight lips.

"I shouldn't have to say this, Agent Cooper—"

Here it comes…

"—but I'm going to, so listen up. You're not leading this investigation. Got that? You're there to observe and collect intel on the area around the port. We're expecting a drop anytime now, so activity should be hopping. Pass anything else you see on to Tyke for the team's analysis and action. He'll take it from there."

Ash gritted his teeth. "Yes, sir."

Landry sighed. "Christ, Cooper. You think I want you off doing grunt work? Of course not. I want you with the rest of the team at Heinrich's compound. You're the best agent we've got. Well, you were, before you got involved with *that woman*."

His teeth clenched harder. Fucking Lorena.

"Tyke's leading your team fine," Landry continued. "But

he's not you. Know what I mean? If things were different…if you hadn't…" He sighed again. It was a rare reaction from the man who was usually so buttoned-up. "You know why I have to do this. Just follow orders. Keep a low profile and stay out of trouble. For your sake?"

"Yes, sir."

It should have been Ash's job to bring down Viktor Heinrich. Not sitting on the sidelines watching his second-in-command take over leadership of his team. He hadn't spoken directly to Calder or Reese since they'd left Argentina. Neither of them would talk to him. Hell, maybe Landry told them to back off. That Ash was a lost cause and would drag them down with him.

He dropped the phone from his ear and looked down at the offending item. Waiting for the wave of pissed-off to pass, he gathered his thoughts and dialed Tyke.

Get a grip, man. Do your job.

As usual, Bryan Tyke picked up on the first ring. "What've you got?"

"Not much. Yet," he said, knowing Tyke would question his ability to collect intel. "We're getting close. I had a run-in with a Vamp this morning. Went after a woman on the street."

"Shit," Tyke hissed. Tyke might be a big mean bastard, but when it came to protecting the innocent, there was no one more devoted.

"There's been no sign of Heinrich. But I just got here, so there's time."

"He's been active at his compound," Tyke said. "Adding extra security. It looks like the drop's gonna happen there. Sawyer said his team hasn't seen anything out of the ordinary at Heinrich's house. You got anything else?"

Ash ran down the events of the last twenty-four hours, making sure to call out that he'd be paying a visit to Club Hell. He figured he fell within the purview of observation. If the

Vamper said he got his stash at Club Hell, then Ash was going to check out the place and see what else he could learn about Heinrich's operations.

As for Heinrich himself, all of his activity had been at his compound in Upper Marlboro, a city about thirty minutes east of Washington, DC. Tyke and the boys had that covered. And Sawyer and his team were watching Heinrich's house in Alexandria, VA. The mission was to figure out Heinrich's plan for Vamp and who his supplier was. Heinrich was expecting a large amount of Vamp in the coming weeks, and they needed to be ready to nail the son of a bitch and his supplier. Or at least Tyke, Calder, and Reese needed to be ready. All Ash was good for was stopping annoying blondes from getting themselves shot.

Knowing him too well, Tyke said, "Remember, Coop, you're hands-off. Don't try to be the hero because you need to prove yourself. Let me know what you find. Reese, Calder, and I will move in if needed. This isn't your fight anymore."

But it should be! His fist tightened on the phone as he made an incoherent sound like a grunt. He glared out the kitchen window into his small yard. The fence between his property and Blondie's leaned, ready to fall if a stiff breeze pushed it. He'd have to remember to fix it before he left. He sure as hell didn't want to give her another reason to bitch at him.

"Look, man, I'm just following orders," Tyke said. "Remember those? That's what got you in this situation in the first place. Director Landry said you're stuck there doing bullshit work until you get your head on right. That's the way it is. You knew that when you signed on. You made a decision; you gotta live with the consequences."

Another grunt.

"You're pissed off, I get it. You think I'm happy with the way things went down? Hell, you know I'd turn the reins over to you today if I could. Do us both a favor and fly right. Then things can go back to normal. Got me?"

A huffed grumble was all Ash could produce in response.

Tyke took a deep breath and let it out in a quick rush. "Like talking to a goddamn brick wall. It's Buenos Aires all over again."

Ash sucked air into his lungs with a sharp hiss.

"That got your attention, didn't it, asshole? Remember that while you're out in the field *not* following orders." Before Ash could say anything back, Tyke snapped, "Call when you've got more." The phone went dead.

Tempted to throw the goddamn phone, he simply ended the call and shoved it into his pocket. Being excluded from the group was the worst sort of punishment, and Landry knew that. He was part of the team, but at the same time not part of the team. He was exiled. Left to gather information, then pass it on to Tyke.

And it was killing him. He wasn't the kind of guy to sit and watch others save the day. When he started something, he for damn sure finished it. And because of one stupid mistake with one beautiful woman, he was now on his own until he could prove to the director that he could listen to orders. That he could carry out his assignment without getting anyone killed.

He whirled from the window in search of something to take his mind off—

He took one step and froze. All thought about Tyke and his shitty comments evaporated as an eerie sensation crawled up his spine. The hair on his arms stood on end.

Someone was watching him.

He hated that feeling. Always had. As a Special Forces sniper, he'd been trained to blend in, go unnoticed for hours, even days. Now, standing out in the open, it made him seethe with anger. He loathed being spotted when he didn't choose to be.

Casually, as not to tip off his prowler, Ash proceeded up the stairs to the front bedroom overlooking the street. Standing at the edge of the window, out of plain sight, he scanned the area. The street was clear except for the usual neighborhood cars. Using the light from the street lamps, he searched trees and row house windows, paying special attention to the second story. A professional would be up high to make sure he had the tactical advantage.

Where are you, you son of a bitch?

Then he saw it.

A red blinking light. In the top left window of the house across the street. The same house Blondie had gone to after their incident with the Vamper this morning. An older woman around Maybel's age had opened the door. Ash had written the exchange off, given the older woman's surprised reaction when she'd opened the door. But now, he was starting to think there was more to the story than just Blondie telling her neighbor about a drug addict.

Locating his night-vision binoculars, he focused on the group of bodies standing behind the light. Five women— *women!*—two of whom he recognized. The first was the pushy one with the dog. And the second was Blondie.

He groaned. "You gotta be kidding me." Who the hell were these women?

Definitely not cops. They couldn't be, right? Apart from Blondie, the rest were as old as Maybel.

If he didn't get these women off his back, his cover wouldn't last another day. Landry would quarantine his ass behind a desk for the rest of his miserable career. Christ, Tyke would have a field day if he heard a bunch of grannies duped Ash. Obviously ignoring the women hadn't helped.

Maybe he needed to do the opposite.

Within seconds, he hatched a plan. If old women had nothing else, they at least had propriety. And he was going to exploit the hell out of it.

A harsh cackle tore from his chest as he thought about the ridiculous length he was about to go to save his career.

Chapter Six

Sam couldn't breathe. No scratch that, she was panting. No, she was suffocating.

Heinrich?

He'd mentioned Heinrich—the same dirtbag drug dealer who had been involved in her father's disappearance. Her pulse leapt, pounding against her skin. What did that have to do with her neighbor? Was he involved in a deal with Heinrich? Or worse, was he working for Heinrich? Did he know anything about her father?

Sam and the grannies heard everything he'd said. The red and black eyes. Chalky skin. Club Hell.

Then nothing.

The women huddled on folding chairs in Rose's narrow spare bedroom, situated at the front of the house. It was the room Sam used to stay in when her dad was on assignment. The same daybed with pink lace pillows and a small white nightstand still decorated the room.

Estelle and Celia wore headphones, tuned in to any sound John Black made. Sam perched in front of the television monitor hooked to the video camera Maybel operated. Rose held binoculars,

"What's he doing now?" Sam's words were clipped. She spun to the window. "Do you hear anything? Anything else?"

Celia and Estelle both shook their heads.

"He's doing a lot of grunting."

"Maybel, can you see anything?" Sam asked.

She, too, shook her head from behind the video camera.

"He's involved in something," Sam said. "Viktor Heinrich. The port. This isn't a coincidence. It has to have something to do with Dad's case. It just has to."

None of the women contradicted her theory.

"Keep eyes on him," Sam insisted. "Where is he now? I want to know every move he makes."

"We lost him," Estelle said. "He was near the couch, and now he's…gone."

"Gone? *Gone?* He can't be gone. Keep looking."

The ladies surveyed his house.

Silence.

Sam had never been very good with silence. "Anything?"

"Nothing."

She didn't feel anything but the pounding of her impatient heart. Not the soft carpet beneath her bare feet. Not the sweep of cool air from the overhead vent. "Where *is* he?"

"I think…" Celia began. Sam jerked her head to the woman. "Wait."

"Wait, what?" Sam bit off. "Celia, *what*?"

"I hear something. Music, I think."

"I have movement," Maybel said from behind the video camera. "Top right window. Lights just went on."

"Got it." Sam lifted high-powered binoculars to her eyes. "There you are, you—"

Wow.

Not expecting the view, Sam stopped breathing.

He stood in the middle of the empty room, with music blaring, completely nude.

As in *naked*.

His entire front bare for them to see.

He appeared to be doing a workout routine on the hardwood floor. Since the room was empty, there was nothing else to look at but him.

Tear your eyes away. Tear. Your. Eyes. Away.

She tried, God she tried, but she physically couldn't. She was transfixed by his body, corded with muscle. His movements fluid with every twist. Massively wide shoulders, strong arms, and a firm abdomen flowed into a tight waist and sculpted legs. She couldn't begin to describe what lay between his legs. That, too, deserved praise. Holy. Hell.

Sam's mouth went bone dry.

Ten hours. That was her first coherent thought. He must work out for ten hours a day to have a cut body like that. No real human man could achieve it otherwise. Or he's an alien. That was the only other explanation. He was an alien from Asgard or Krypton. Yeah, that had to be it. Chris Hemsworth had moved in next door.

The only sound emanating from the room were the breaths each woman heaved while watching him curl his hunky arms with weights and then do jumping jacks.

Up, down, up, down.

Inhale, exhale, inhale, exhale.

"Is everyone seein' what I'm seein'?" Estelle spoke in a breathy tone. "I'm not imaginin' his throbbin' banana bouncin' like that, right? It's really happenin'?"

"Uh-huh," Maybel said behind her, fixated on the room with binoculars. Sam thought the older woman might have even licked her lips. "He appears to…" Her throat rippled as she swallowed. "…*enjoy* working out."

"Well," Estelle spoke, barely audible, doing some

swallowing of her own, "he might be a drug dealer, but at least he's…*fit*."

"Uh-huh," Maybel said. "Fit."

Sweat streamed down his muscled chest, mingling with the light dusting of dark hair. Sam imagined running her tongue along the path, tasting the salty sweetness of his tan skin. It probably tasted like sunshine. She'd never wanted to taste someone's chest so badly in her life. A primal need to lick him all over grabbed hold of her and refused to let go.

God, the way his strong legs flexed and constricted.

Her own skin heated; small droplets of moisture collected over her body. What would his lips and tongue feel like on her? A shiver ran through her at the thought.

A burning ignited in her lower abdomen—a yearning that seemed to grow and take over. Her fingers and toes went numb, and she was sure her heart had dropped into her stomach. Something inside kept mounting, reaching; for what, she couldn't explain. Her breathing picked up and her chest heaved with each of his movements. A strangled gasp escaped so quickly she couldn't stop it.

This was a man who knew how to use his body. God didn't give people muscles like that and not show them how to put them to good use. She wanted to squeeze his butt and run her hands along his thick thighs, making them clench under her touch. She wanted his strength around her, grabbing her hard and leading her to a place she'd never been—teaching, guiding, stroking.

She felt wanton. Wild. Daring. *Hot*.

She shook her head. Where were these thoughts coming from? She'd never had such vivid images flash through her mind.

At twenty-eight years old, of course she'd dated. But no one had ever inspired the insane horny-as-hell feelings coursing through her.

"Oh my." Celia's gaze darted toward the mauve carpet. "I shouldn't…we shouldn't be…" She shot from her chair, the force of her movement making it wobble and snap closed. She turned from the window, walking as far as the doorjamb. Away from the show, but not completely out of the room.

"I'm not sure this is a good idea anymore," Maybel said next. "I feel like we're spying on the man in his element. Just doesn't seem right."

With the break in silence, Sam started to come back to earth. Her heartbeat slowed, and her body belonged to her again. She blinked twice to clear her head.

"I agree," Rose said, placing her binoculars on the folding table under the window. "We can leave the audio on, but maybe turn the video off." She glanced at Sam as if questioning her thoughts.

Her thoughts…what exactly *were* her thoughts? She couldn't seem to locate them at the moment.

Up, down, up, down.

Inhale, exhale, inhale, exhale.

Sam waited for Estelle to chime in.

She didn't. She remained at the window, binoculars glued to her eyes, not uttering a peep aside from her deep sighs.

Sam dared two more peeks before agreeing with her grandmother that it was indeed wrong to spy on her naked neighbor. She did have limits. And morals. Grandma had made sure of it. Staring at him with everything under the sun shining back at her—bobbing and weaving, glistening in the soft evening light, inviting her womanly desires to partake—wasn't right.

No matter how good he looked.

And man, he looked good.

So good.

With every sliver of willpower she possessed, she peeled the binoculars from her eyes and turned from the window. She checked to make sure the audio recorder was still on and then followed Rose, Maybel, and Celia downstairs to the kitchen.

Maybe they could try again in an hour or so. He'd have to be done with his workout by then, right?

Chapter Seven

"You're going to be a good boy and slide in nice and easy, right?" Sam eyed the box she'd brought up to her bedroom from her trunk. "Momma needs you *really* bad. Just do what she says, 'kay?"

As soon as she got this bad boy crankin', she was going to collapse spread eagle on her bed until every last drop of sweat evaporated from her body. It was going to be glorious.

Sam approached the box with a knife, taking a deep, strenuous breath. She made one clean slice, and the lid popped open. "See, that didn't hurt a bit, did it?" Reaching in, she lifted the portable air conditioner unit and aimed for the window frame.

She shifted her weight on each foot, unsuccessfully matching the perimeter of the machine into the open window frame. "Come on. Just. Go. In!"

Balancing the contraption on her shoulder, she teetered on her feet a few steps. She almost lost her balance but used her last remaining strength to hurl it forward.

"A-ha!" Sam brushed her palms together, admiring her

handiwork. "Like a glove. I knew you could do it."

Turning, she spied the box it came in. "I believe you came with instructions." She retrieved the lengthy pamphlet and began to read. "Make sure to take off the protective film before operating. Mmm-hmm… Make sure it's level. Ah huh, got that… Make sure plug is accessible…" She turned to the window. "Where's the plug?"

Dropping the instructions, she turned to the AC. It was nowhere in sight.

Shit. The cord had slipped outside the window.

As she neared the contraption, her back and shoulders screamed in protest from carrying the stupid thing up her steep, narrow stairs.

Sam leaned in and braced her body for the impending weight. She was about to pull the AC toward her when something caught her eye through the window.

A *big* something.

A *muscular* something.

A *next-door neighbor* something.

Sam froze in the awkward forward position, arms stretched, chest against the device. She narrowed her eyes at the figure in an attempt to get a better view.

Her mysterious, more-complicated-by-the-day neighbor stood about ten yards away in his backyard, mending the fence. It was about two-hundred and fifty degrees outside, and he was close enough that she could see the sweat gleaming on his bare chest and broad shoulders as he pulled and tugged on the main two-by-four holding the fence upright. His dark tattoo stretched from the base of his neck to his right pectoral. The wings of the animal seemed to flap each time the muscle flexed.

His cargo shorts were slung low across his trim hips, presenting a pack of defined abs like the showcase showdown on the *Price Is Right*. A path of thick, dark hair trailed from his midsection and dipped below his waistband. For as low as his shorts were, the top of his underwear should have poked out the top. It didn't. Which meant…

A hot zing ran up her spine, making her shiver. *Commando.* She tried to swallow, but just like the night before, her mouth dried up.

He swung a sledgehammer, drilling the post into the hard ground. His movements were precise and compact, not wasting any additional energy. It gave her the impression he always did everything with such finesse. Such care and attention.

She sighed. What a strong, capable man.

Yeah, strong and capable of killing you if he wanted to.

"But, boy oh boy, would it be nice to have your murderer look like that." She leaned closer to the windowpane for a better look. Her breasts flattened against the warm plastic of the AC unit, the buttons and knobs jabbing at her already sensitive skin. She yearned for the damn machine to be out of the way so she could stick her entire body out the window and properly gawk.

"Having that stand over me, staring down all brooding and conflicted…" Her tongue jutted out to moisten her lips. "I'd die with a big, goofy grin on my face if that's what I got to see right before the end."

Smashing her face against the top window, she took in his display of primal mechanics. A man that well-built would command all of her attention and energy. Her breathing picked up, and her nipples began to ache. Those nimble, skin-seeking fingers would run along her soft curves. Goose bumps spread across her skin as she imagined those powerful hands sliding over her breasts, stomach, hips, down her thighs, and traveling inward. He'd set a scorching path, hungry for her—

She blinked and shook her head. What was she thinking? He was the enemy. She shouldn't be thinking about his—

A long, scraping sound sliced through her thought.

"What the—" Sam jerked back. The air conditioner no longer rested against her body, but instead teetered on the border of the window ledge outside.

"Oh, shit." She clawed at the smooth exterior but couldn't latch on. "Shit." Her breaths came in ragged staccato pants as she hoisted her head, shoulder, and arms through the open window. "*Oh, shit!*"

She hung half out of the opening, her legs dangling inside behind her as she watched her only salvation to the scorching heat falling to its death—

—on a direct collision course with her neighbor.

Her arms waved wildly. "*OH! OH! EECH!*" was all she could get out before the useless plastic device landed within a foot of his side.

"What the fuck!" Her neighbor leaped back, landing in an attack pose. He crouched on one knee, arms open, seeming ready to disfigure an enemy at a moment's notice. He'd pulled a gun from God knows where and gripped it in his right hand. Facial expression hardened and eyes narrowed, he surveyed the area around him. Like a lion ready to fight for its survival. Determined and skilled. Quite impressive, actually. And a little unsettling. Where exactly had he learned to do that?

His focus snapped up to Sam. His scowl sent arctic shivers across her body. "What in the hell are you trying to do? Kill me?" He got to his feet and dusted himself off with short, jagged strokes.

"No," she shot back, immediately defensive—her normal reaction to overly embarrassing situations that were entirely her fault. "Didn't you hear me scream? If I wanted to kill you, I wouldn't have given you warning first."

"Scream? You mean that animal wail I heard right before this…this…*thing* almost splattered my brains everywhere? I'd hardly call that a warning, Tarzan. Next time try a 'hey, watch out!' or 'get out of the way!' *Jesus Christ*." He shook his head before doubling-over, hands on his knees, sucking in huge gulps of air.

"Look," she spoke. "I'm sorry. I didn't mean—"

His head jerked up, and he shot her a frightening stare.

Her lips cinched into a tight, thin line. He obviously needed a minute or two.

After a few excruciatingly silent seconds, she tried again. "It was hot. I—"

His hand went up, again halting her speech. Still bent at the waist, his breathing started to level out, his back rising and falling at a more normal pace.

"But I—"

"Are you physically incapable of keeping your mouth closed?"

Her lips parted and then snapped shut. She bit down on her tongue as long as she could. But her lungs filled to the max and threatened to explode if she didn't get it out. "You're a…a…a…"

"There you go again."

"I was trying to be nice and apologize," she cut in. "Isn't that what people do when they hurt someone? Or when they shut a door in their face?" She couldn't resist.

He let out a humorless laugh. "Nice," he echoed. "Yeah, I'm sure that's what you were being. Just do me favor—shut your window so you don't drop a bathtub or anything else on me while I'm out here."

As if he didn't seem intimidating enough, he stretched his body, lengthening every muscle so he appeared taller and more imposing. His shoulders rose. The darkness in his eyes cleared and the tenseness in his frame relaxed. He stored his weapon in the back of his waistband.

"But—" she tried again.

"Just go." He turned his back to her and bent to collect

the plastic rubbish littering his yard.

Slowly, so she didn't follow the same fate as the air conditioner—'cause God knew her neighbor wouldn't catch her—she snaked her way back into her bedroom, closed the window, and slumped onto her bed.

"Excellent work, Sam. If he is dangerous, he'll be coming after you first, just for making him mad. Perfect."

And to top it off, she'd be spending another night glued to her sheets by sweat.

Double perfect.

. . .

No one got the drop on Ash Cooper.

No one.

Which was why the incident with the damn air conditioner made him more than unnerved. He'd been spacing out too much over the last twelve hours, and it had to fucking stop. What was it about this woman that put his head into such a goddamn scramble?

All he'd been thinking about was her reaction last night, those light-colored eyes opened wide, and how he'd like to see that sweet expression as he drove into her. Hard. Her perfectly arched eyebrows had risen so high they'd almost disappeared into her hairline, and her soft lips formed an ideal round shape. Yeah, she'd be beautiful lying under him sated and exhausted.

No, goddamn it. The point of last night had *not* been to arouse her. Or himself.

Flashing a group of women—older women at that—wasn't something he did on a regular basis. But he'd needed to do something to get the lot of busybodies flustered. His bared male form had certainly done the trick. The wrinkled biddies quickly left their perch by the window not long after he started his unorthodox workout. Thank Christ it had been eighty degrees last night. If it had been a frigid winter night, he wouldn't have dared it. He'd wanted to shock the old biddies, not freak the shit out of them with a case of shriveled dick.

He picked up the demolished heap of plastic and carried it to the front yard.

Crushing the plastic in his arms, he dropped it on the edge of the curb for trash collection the next morning. He spun and headed for the backyard.

At the fence, his hand rested on the latch. He stole a glance next door.

No movement near the windows.

No prying eyes peering out.

He opened the gate and entered his yard.

Odd. For a woman so determined to learn more about him, she wasn't doing a very good job. He'd expected more from—what did she call herself?—*A proud employee of the Baltimore City Police Department?* Not much of a cop if she didn't know how to carry out a discrete investigation.

A branch cracked beneath his foot as he took a step and then froze. *An investigation…* Was that what today was? Something to test his reaction? Learn his weaknesses?

No. Now he was being paranoid. If Heinrich hired someone to run surveillance on him, it wouldn't be a handful of elderly females led by a pain-in-the-ass woman. No matter how tempting the ringleader may be to him.

Her apology and embarrassment was real. Her face lit up into thirty shades of red, and her eyes were wide like a cartoon character's. She hadn't intended to drop the air conditioner on him.

Even so. He grinned wryly. *Pretty good aim if she had.* Another inch or two to the left and he'd be pleading his case for entry into the pearly gates.

He glanced back up to the window he assumed was her

bedroom.

The image of her hanging out of it wearing just a thin, low-cut tank top sent him reeling. That kind of distraction was the last thing he needed. He reminded himself again that he wasn't in Baltimore for vacation, though he needed one. Bad. It was so easy to think about the sweet-looking blond next door rather than the mission at hand.

Damn it, he was doing it again. Letting a woman get in the way of his work. Just like he had with Lorena.

Beautiful, exotic, and tempting. The first three words that came to mind when Lorena walked into that bar in Buenos Aires. He'd literally lost his breath when she locked onto his gaze and smiled.

"Damn idiot." Ash kicked the fence post hard enough to make it rattle. A searing pain shot up his calf, but it only fueled him. He deserved the punishment.

He needed to find out as much as he could about this group of women. Between Blondie with her handcuffs in the trunk and the state-of-the-art equipment the group had been using last night, he suspected there was a hell of a lot more to the story. He reached into his pocket for his cell phone and dialed the agency. Giles, the computer guy who could hack into any computer anywhere, answered.

"Ash, this is a surprise. How goes it?"

"Not bad. How've you been, Giles?" He cradled the phone on his shoulder as he bent to retrieve the hammer and a nail.

"Ah, can't complain. Director Landry locked me in this hole they call the IT department, but I manage. What can I do for you?"

Ash took a deep breath. "I need a favor."

There was a pause.

Shit. Giles knew about his history with Lorena and the botched assignment in South America. Ash was a pariah.

No one at the agency wanted to help him for fear of being dragged into the sewers with him.

"What do you need?" Giles asked hesitantly.

Ash held the nail in place with his left hand and swung the hammer with one quick stroke. "Information on a group of women." Good. He sounded casual. Not pathetically pleading. It didn't matter at this point if Blondie and the grannies heard him or not. Hell, maybe it would help if they knew he was onto them. Maybe they'd back off.

"Hmm," Giles murmured into the receiver. "Women, you say? What information are we talking about exactly?"

Yep, Giles was definitely thinking about Lorena. "Names, backgrounds, anything you can find. The sooner, the better."

There was another silence on the other end.

"Giles?" Ash asked, sickened by the desperation in his voice.

"I don't know, Ash. I mean, I really want to help you out, but Director Landry—"

"I think it may be life or death," he added. To his career, at least.

Another moment passed, and then, "No promises. I'll see what I can do."

Chapter Eight

Sharp afternoon rays pierced the windows in Rose's house, rivaling the cool air circulating from her perfectly working air conditioner.

In the spare bedroom, the women sat in their folding chairs as they'd been the day before.

"Interpol's got nothing on him," Maybel said to the group. "Neither does the FBI or CIA. Jackson couldn't find a lick of information anywhere."

Jackson was Maybel's contact. She wouldn't tell the group his last name or which agency he worked for. All they knew was Jackson could find anyone, anywhere, at any time.

Except now.

"That's impossible." Sam's teeth clenched and her eyes turned to the TV screen. No movement or sound had occurred since last night's stakeout. "There has to be something. A birth date, place of employment, anything."

Maybel shook her head. "It's like he doesn't exist. Someone went to an awful lot of trouble to cover his tracks. I asked Jackson to look up this Tyke person he keeps talking to.

Still nothing. I'm concerned."

Why would someone need to go to that kind of trouble to hide his identity?

John Black was collecting a lot of strikes.

Each watch member turned and gave the woman next to her a worried glance. Anxiety blanketed the room.

"We've still got eyes and ears on him," Estelle said from behind the binoculars. Sam didn't think the woman had moved from her post the day before.

"Yes, we do," Rose said, squaring her shoulders, bringing confident order back to the group, "and if he does anything, we'll be ready."

The other women nodded in agreement.

"The important thing right now is to collect as much information as we can." Maybel spoke in a dark tone, a contradiction to her attire for the day—a simple light pink shift dress and flats. "Intel is the most important weapon one can possess. We have to learn his routine, his habits, his *weaknesses*." She stared each woman down as if she was a platoon leader readying her troops for battle.

"I agree." Estelle fanned herself as she peered across the street. Since she had been gulping massive amounts of ice-cold lemonade and Rose's AC worked just fine, Sam didn't think it was because of the summer weather. "Let's keep watchin' him. He needs to be watched. Closely."

The women raised their eyebrows and turned to Estelle.

Sensing the silence, Estelle unglued her gaze from the window. "What? I'm just sayin' if we need to videotape him more, I'd be willing to do it. Hold the camera and what not."

Maybel smirked. "You know, we have a tripod."

"We'll keep that in mind, Estelle," Rose said through a crooked smile.

"Ladies." Sam stomped her foot. "Did we get anything on GPS yet?"

Rose sobered and shook her head. "He hasn't gone anywhere."

"I haven't gotten anything on audio, either," Celia added, holding the headphones firmly in place over her ears. "He hasn't made a sound since last night."

"He's in there." Sam tapped the TV screen. "I saw him go inside after doing yard work. We just have to wait. He'll make a move, and we'll get him."

Thirty silent minutes passed, and no one caught sight or sound of the target.

Having left her post for a brief bathroom and pastry break, Maybel sat behind the video camera and asked, "How'd everything go with the exam, Sam? You never said."

Kudos to Maybel for asking with a bright face and positive tone, but the cautious looks the women exchanged told Sam they had already figured out the answer. Hell, if Sam had passed the police entrance exam, she would have jumped up and down and screamed for the entire world to hear. Everyone would have known immediately. Not days later.

Sam's lips tightened into a thin line, and she shifted her eyes in Maybel's direction. She shook her head once.

"Aww, honey, I'm sorry."

"The same part givin' you trouble?" Estelle asked.

Sam's lips remained thinned and she nodded.

"Don't give up." Estelle placed a hand on Sam's shoulder and squeezed. "Until they tell you otherwise, you drag your butt back there and try again. And again, if that's what it takes."

"That's right," Maybel chimed in. "Make them turn you away."

Celia nodded, her head bouncing, causing a hair pin to drop out of her bun.

Rose approached with open arms. Hugging, she whispered in Sam's ear, "I'm sorry, sweets. I know how important it is to you to follow in your dad and pop pop's footsteps." She smoothed a hand down Sam's shoulder-length blond hair. "I hate seeing you hurt."

"So do the rest of us," Maybel added, rubbing Sam's back.

Sam attempted a smile but released a choked sound instead. It's all she wanted. To carry out the Harper family legacy. To serve and protect as an officer with Baltimore City Police. To do her father honor by being loyal to the badge, just as he was, proving to her coworkers that the Harpers were trustworthy.

"That's how I feel about all of you. I need to keep you safe. Now that Dad's"—she swallowed hard—"now that he's gone, it's my responsibility to protect you. I have to find a way to pass that test." She took a ragged breath. "If something happened to any of you—"

"Nothing's going to happen to us," Rose replied. "We may be old, but we're not helpless. We can take care of ourselves."

Estelle crossed her arms over her full chest, causing her cleavage to poke farther out of the top of her low-cut shirt. "Damn right."

"I didn't mean to imply—"

"Yes, you did," Rose said through a grin, "but at least your motives were noble. You worry. It's understandable. There are bad people who do bad things that you can't control. What you can do is love those around you and spend as much time together before the end. It's anybody's guess when that will be. You can't stop it, but there are things you can do to lessen the pain."

Sam hugged her grandmother again, squeezing hard. "God, if anything happened—if I lost you too—" Her heart constricted to the point of being painful. First Dad. If she lost Grandma Rose, too… Suddenly the small bedroom seemed even smaller. The air in the room thickened, making it hard to pull a breath.

"I'm not going anywhere, sweets. Not when I have you and this bunch of crackpots to look after."

"Hey!"

"Who you callin' crackpot?"

"I take offense to that!"

The tension evaporated, and the room filled with its usual laughter.

Rose peered through her bifocals at the clock on a nearby table. Estelle, Celia, and Maybel followed suit. "Sweets," Grandma Rose said, "it's getting late. We have the fund-raiser at church. Father Stephen is counting on us to be there."

"Go, go," Sam said, not taking her attention from the TV screen, even though she was going cross-eyed. "Don't let me keep you."

Maybel stood and smoothed the wrinkles from the front of her dress.

Estelle remained by the window. She dropped the binoculars from her eyes for a second, then lifted them, then dropped them again. When Grandma cleared her throat, Estelle grunted and rested the binoculars on the table.

"Go home." Rose put her arm around Sam's shoulders and kissed her cheek. "Get some rest. We'll leave the recorder on."

"Take the GPS tracker," Maybel offered.

Grandma approached the doorway and craned her neck back. "Let's go, Estelle."

"Yeah, yeah," she said and stood. "I'm comin'."

Keeping her eyes on the monitor, Sam said, "Thanks for your help, ladies. Have fun."

• • •

Sam sat in her grandmother's spare bedroom until the sun set. She allowed herself a ten-minute break to go to the bathroom and get food. She threw chips and a turkey sandwich on a plate and ran back upstairs, stuffing her mouth as she went.

John Black or whatever his name was hadn't made one damn peep.

A little after nine in the evening, she gave up and went to her house. Her back ached, and her eyes screamed from the strain. She left the lights off and dropped onto the couch in her front room, closing her eyes.

Her stubborn nature refused to give up. She heightened the focus of her ears, listening through the open window. But her eyes grew heavy. She fought to stay awake. Then a door clicked open and closed, and footsteps tread down her next-door neighbor's front steps.

Vaulting from the sofa, she peeked out the front window, making sure to stay hidden in the shadows behind the curtain. He looked in her direction and then lowered his head, before jumping behind the wheel of his pickup truck.

With the GPS tracker gripped in her palm, Sam watched the path he took. He drove around the city for a bit, before stopping in a crummy part of town, just shy of 27th Street.

Sam's heart pounded and giant sparks ignited throughout her body. That was where Viktor Heinrich's club was located. *This is it!* The break she'd been waiting for.

She had to go. She needed to find out what John Black had to do with Heinrich's drugs and see if she could gather clues about her father.

Dashing into her bedroom, she rooted through the closet for anything appropriate to wear to a lowlife's club. Blending in was key in surveillance. She tossed on a simple white tank top and black miniskirt, found a pair of strappy black heels hidden in the corner of her closet, and sailed out the door.

Before getting behind the wheel, she searched her trunk for defense items. She shoved earplugs, a few cans of pepper spray, and two air horns into her purse, and then hopped in the car.

A hum of excitement radiated inside the cabin of her Honda as she sped through the city toward 27th Street.

Chapter Nine

"Christ, *this* is it?"

Ash stood on the street in front of the rundown warehouse known as Club Hell. He patted for his gun, making sure it was still in his waistband. After assessing the neighborhood, and now the club's patrons, he should've also brought his .38.

Trash littered the sidewalks, and a foul stench hit his nostrils like a jackhammer. The surrounding buildings were dilapidated, with shattered windows and graffiti-covered walls. Not exactly the type of neighborhood one ventured into unless necessary.

Between Tyke and the spying grannies, he'd already been on edge before leaving the house. His current surroundings diminished his mood even further. Had he lost his mind? Maybe he deserved a desk job. Had he really gotten so careless that a group of grannies could watch him and he didn't know it?

He'd made team leader in a matter of months. An unheard-of achievement. And now look at him. Demoted just as fast. A disgrace. A laughing stock. A geeky IT guy wouldn't even help him.

His jaw clenched. How could his entire life be in shambles because of one goddamn woman? If he'd never met Lorena, none of this—

He shook his head. No, that wasn't true. He'd *had* to meet Lorena. It was part of the job. What he didn't have to do was get involved with her.

Fucking moron.

Lately, whenever he thought about Lorena, he immediately thought of Blondie. Why, he had no idea, because the two women couldn't be more different. And yet both had unnerved him to the point he didn't know which way was up. Lorena with her effortless sex appeal and Blondie with her bumbling innocence.

Thinking about one or the other made his blood boil, but now that both were in his brain at the same time, he wanted to rip someone's head off. Fucking women.

His phone vibrated, reminding him he'd told Tyke they were on communication lockdown. Another joy he didn't want to explain to the new *team leader*. But it was necessary. If Blondie was spying on him, then he'd make damn sure she wouldn't get any useful information.

He'd been texting and emailing Tyke and the director like a fool for the last twelve hours. His big fingers punching the wrong keys, cursing and deleting, trying again before taking a break to cool off. It would have been so much easier to pick up the damn phone and just call someone.

At Club Hell yet? Let me know what you find. Tyke's message said. *No recent sign of Heinrich here at compound.*

He sent a quick reply, then tucked his phone back in his pocket.

Club Hell. The name of the joint fit. Without ventilation or airflow, a putrid smell of sweaty bodies and something damn close to death filled the air. Ash gagged a number of times from the initial shock. It was impossible to imagine none of his deployments in the military had prepared him for anything close to the disgusting hole he found himself in.

Cement floors. Lights dim and scarce. The only illumination came from a few scattered, faintly powered light bulbs hanging on strings from the ceiling. As expected, the music was loud and pumping. He didn't recognize the song. It didn't have words, just some squealing synthesizer shit. The bass thumped through his body like an extra heartbeat. No Guns 'N Roses or Metallica in this place. Shame.

Ash could make out a line of bars framing the length of the exterior walls, with bartenders standing shoulder to shoulder, ready to take patrons' orders at a moment's notice. Employees of Club Hell were easy to spot, as all of them resembled Hulk Hogan on steroids. Ash hated being outsized. It wasn't often accomplished. He wasn't threatened; it just meant he wouldn't walk away as easily if a brawl broke out. And he certainly wasn't planning on starting anything.

Observe and report back to Tyke.

It was alarming to see so many people working in a club of such low quality. Still early in the evening by club standards, the room wasn't packed, but he couldn't imagine the place drawing large enough crowds to warrant the excessive coverage. It made him wonder why the large staff was needed—in quantity and body size.

He surveyed the area, taking in anything and everything. There were only two exits—one he entered through in the front of the building and one behind the bar in the back right corner. Judging from the layout outside, the bar exit led to the side alley, its path dumping onto 26th Street, which fed onto the highway. Convenient for a quick getaway.

Thirty minutes had passed, and the club had filled with people. Dark shadows of bodies crowded the room from entrance to exit and every space in between. Apparently, eleven o'clock was the magic hour for people to come out of their caves and party.

College-age kids poured in, reeling in eagerness of what the night had in store. They moved to the middle of the room, transforming the space into a dance floor. They grabbed each other, grinding and sucking face as if they'd never seen the opposite sex before that moment. Hormones raced and libidos soared. The air was thick with it. They hadn't ingested Vamp yet. Their skin hadn't taken on the dry, chalky texture others acquired after long-term Vamp use. Their eyes hadn't changed color, either. But they exhibited the horny side effect quickly. *Residuals*, the agency called them. The drug was highly potent and easily transferrable from one person to another through bodily fluids.

Small groups of experienced vamps were easy to spot. Their sinister eyes appearing even darker in the dimly lit room, their bodies beginning to shake in slight convulsions. To the innocent onlooker—the college kids, for example—the addicts appeared to be moving in disorganized dance steps, shaking and jiving as an uncoordinated cohesive unit, but Ash knew better. Right now the vamps were high as a kite, reveling in the ecstasy the initial hit of the drug offered. They shook in pleasure, not pain. He glanced again at his watch. Give it two hours when the high wore off, and those slight convulsions would turn into epileptic seizures. They'd be ready to kill everyone in this room for another hit. He needed to be far away from Club Hell by then.

He perched on a stool in the back corner of the room. It was more than packed, making it almost impossible not to bump into someone. And the more crowded the room became, the harder it was for him to tell the regular patrons from the vamps. The club crawled with trembling bodies.

"Can I get you *some-sing*?" an accented voice said behind him. "A *bee-ah*?" Ash turned to the bar. One of the goliath-size bartenders smiled as he pushed a glass of amber liquid toward him. The guy looked like a thug from Ash's favorite movie *Die Hard*. White-blond hair and German accent included. "It's on za house."

"No thanks, man." He offered a casual smile. "How about just a bottle of water?"

The corners of the man's mouth wavered. "But alcohol is on za house."

"Nah, I'm good. Water would be great though."

A vein pulsed in Die Hard's neck, the beat growing more rapid by the second. "It's on za house," he said without a smile.

What the fuck. "Just a bottle of water."

The bartender's jaw ticked and he paused for a second before finally reaching under the bar to, Ash assumed, retrieve his water. Then the guy made a motion like he was going to twist the top, but Ash stopped him.

"Hey, man," Ash said, pushing the sleeve of his shirt up to flex his biceps. "I can open my own water. Thanks for the offer though."

Die Hard grinded his molars for a few more seconds, then slid the bottle across the bar and turned to the other patrons.

Ash returned the favor and pushed back, spinning on the stool. He wasn't here to provoke anyone for Christ's sake. He just wanted to gather information and get the hell out of this shithole.

Making his way across the room, he spotted another bartender, identical in looks to the first, holding a glass of clear liquid below the bar. The guy looked around, then focused on the lowered glass.

Keeping his head in one direction and his peripheral vision in another, he watched the man drop a shard of something white into the glass. A tiny square, barely visible to the naked eye dissolved into the liquid within seconds.

The bartender then handed the glass to a young woman

on the other side of the bar, who laughed with her girlfriends, unaware her drink had been tampered with.

"Not on my watch," Ash growled, kicking the bar stool out from under him. With a forced smile intact, he was at their side within seconds. "Ladies, how are we this evening?" His eyes lowered to the glass of clear liquid, seeing nothing out of the ordinary.

The brunette and her two friends smiled back.

"Hey there," the brunette spoke for the group. "What's your name?" Batting her eyelashes, she slid a finger across his chest. Her girlfriends' eyes sparkled as they looked him up and down like he was this season's latest handbag.

All three were dressed similarly in heels and short dresses with low-cut necklines. The brunette was in black; her friends in blue and purple.

"John," Ash lied. "The name's John."

"Hi, John," the ladies spoke in unison like a choir of muses.

"You're a cutie, you know that?" the brunette in black said, running her tongue along her upper lip. "And *big*." She squeezed his biceps. "I'm River. This is Sonya and Kendra."

He nodded and smiled to each woman. The bright whites of their eyes shined back, and he released the breath he'd been holding.

"What did you order?" He directed the question at River.

She'd had the glass almost to her mouth, suspended in midair when she responded, "Vodka and Sprite with lime juice." She smiled at him, baring all her teeth, and pushed her breasts higher into his view. Running her index finger along the swell of one breast, she dipped it between her cleavage.

He grimaced, which made her pause. "That's too bad."

She frowned and her eyebrows furrowed in confusion.

"I overheard the bartender say the lime juice turned." It's the best he could come up with. "Some guy ran to the bathroom after having some of it. I was just in there. Wasn't pretty." In case the women didn't catch his drift, he covered his mouth with his hand and puffed out his cheeks to imitate pre-puking.

The women turned green. "Um, like, yuck."

"Here," he said, taking the glass from her hand, "let me get you something else." He smiled and glanced deep into River's brown eyes for effect. Her hand willingly opened. "In fact, let me buy all of you a round."

They grinned and giggled.

Ash held up his finger. "Be right back. I promise."

He dropped the glass into the first trashcan he came across and nestled his way between two people at the bar. "Three vodka Sprites," he said when the first available bartender glanced his way. He didn't take his eyes off the bartender's hands. Never once did Die Hard III lower the glasses or drop anything into them.

Ash had cash ready when the bartender came back.

"It's on za house," he said.

Arm suspended in the air with cash in-hand, Ash asked, "You sure?"

The man nodded. "It's on the za house."

Odd, but he didn't question it. Instead, he carried the three glasses to River, Sonya, and Kendra as promised, a surge of chivalry surging through him for having saved the women from what could have been a terrible evening—and beyond.

Movement caught his attention. After years as a sniper, Ash could spot a fly in the middle of a dark room.

But this was no fly. This was an annoying, blond cockroach who didn't know when to mind her own goddamn business. The woman was going to kill him. If he didn't kill her first.

Grinding his teeth, he handed the drinks to River and her friends. He kept his gaze on Blondie, who made her way toward the back of the club with a purpose.

"What a gentleman!" Kendra purred as she ran her free hand up his arm to his shoulder.

"Our hero!" River followed, repeating the motion on his other arm.

The touches reluctantly turned his attention to the muses. "My pleasure, ladies."

When the three women took a sip from their respective glasses, he turned back to Blondie. She had stopped in front of a door in the back left corner of the room, her back to him.

His eyes narrowed, and his blood pressure rose to dangerous levels. *What the fuck is she doing?*

Pissed his surveillance would have to be cut short in lieu of dragging his neighbor back to her house and throwing her over his knee, Ash spun on his heels to fetch her.

He didn't make it two steps before all hell broke loose.

• • •

There was no one at the door to pat Sam down or search her bag. Not a good sign. Especially given the broken-down look of the place. Didn't these kinds of places have metal detectors or those magic wand things looking for weapons?

People crowded in front of the door, pushing and shoving one another to get in. Their bodies were strung tight, their muscles taut with excitement.

She took her place in the back of the group, wondering what all the hype was about. This Vamp stuff her neighbor referred to must be why these people were at the club. The joint didn't look very special. If anything, it looked the exact opposite of special.

Shuffling along with the crowd, she didn't bother looking down at whatever her heels sloshed through on the pavement. Based on the foul stench around her, she didn't want to know.

Most of the club's eager patrons looked pretty normal.

Guys wore blue jeans and button-down shirts; girls wore short skirts and belly-baring tops.

Within minutes, she was inside the most disgusting place she'd ever seen. "No wonder there's no bouncer," she mumbled as she made her way into the dim room. "They probably let all sorts of people into this junk hole."

The walls were plain aside from the grime and mold climbing to the ceiling. The air was stale and hot, making her the tiniest bit thankful for her situation at home. She might not have working AC, but at least the air was clean. She'd have to breathe through her mouth for the remainder of the night. The floor grabbed the soles of her heels like bubblegum as she brushed past groups of people, who didn't seem to notice or care about the filth surrounding them. The place reminded her of Chuck E. Cheese during summer break—lots of soiled kids and germs lurking everywhere.

The party was in full swing, crowds bunched together, jumping and shaking to the music. Couples lined the dance floor, groping each other and kissing as if it was their last dying wish.

She had to fight her way to an open seat at the bar. She peered over the crowd in search of her neighbor but came up empty. When she turned to the bar, she met eyes with a hunky fair-eyed bartender.

He nodded his greeting, sliding a martini glass with blue liquid toward her.

"Oh," she said, surprised, "I haven't ordered yet."

The bartender offered a sweet smile. "It's on za house."

"Well, that's nice." She allowed him to push the glass in front of her. The free drinks were probably a way to make up for the lacking decor. She fingered the stem of the glass as she scanned the room again.

Lovers at the bar.

Lovers in the shadows.

Lovers on the dance floor.

The man next to her had his hand so far up his lady's leg it was hard to tell if she was a woman or a puppet.

Is everyone making out? What kind of club is this? And where is John Black?

She turned to the bartender who had given her the complimentary drink. "Must be something in the drinks, huh?" She nodded her head toward the man and his puppet.

The bartender chuckled with a wicked hint. "Ya." He bobbed his head toward the full glass in front of her. "You drink."

She lifted the glass to her mouth, smelling the inviting aroma of fruit and liquor, before remembering her reason for being at Club Hell.

"Hey, Sven—can I call you Sven?" she asked through a convincing smile, setting the drink on the bar.

He shook his head. "Hans."

"Okay, Hans. Is Viktor Heinrich around?"

His smile dropped and his spine snapped to attention. *A soldier preparing for battle.*

Interesting. His reaction gave her the answer she wanted. If Heinrich wasn't here tonight, he was definitely involved in the club.

She leaned forward and rested her forearm on top of the bar. "I'm an old friend. We go way back. I just want to pop in and say hi. See how he's doing."

Hans didn't blink once while she spoke, his stare so intense it was as if he peered down into her soul and pulled out the lie she'd just fed him.

Then after a moment, his eyes cleared and he blinked. "Don't know Viktor."

Her fist rested under her chin. "Hmm, you sure? I could have sworn he told me he owned this place."

Hans's eyes betrayed him for a brief second, flitting to the back left corner of the club, before he recovered and gave her a slight shake of his head. Then he turned to the bartender standing next to him—a bit too close, in Sam's opinion—and whispered something. The second bartender, who could have been Hans's twin brother based on looks and size, turned and gave her the same evaluating gaze. Both men's lips curled into snarls.

Sam may not be a cop, but she had instincts, and at that moment, they were on full alert.

She shot from her chair, a nervous chill running through her. Leaving the free drink behind, she pushed her way past the people making out and crossed the dance floor.

"Hey!" one person shouted, spraying saliva. "Watch it!"

"What the—" came another.

Sweat-drenched appendages slid across her skin as she moved farther through the crowd to the back of the club. Gross. She swiped her slick arms on her tank top to be rid of the nasty sweat.

In the back corner, she spotted a door covered in shadow. That must have been where Hans glanced. Was it Viktor Heinrich's office? Was he in there? Was he alone?

Only one way to find out.

She looked behind her. Her legs wobbled and threatened to give out. This was the moment she'd been waiting for. She unzipped the top of her handbag and reached for the can of homemade pepper spray. It contained Maybel's extra-special recipe. The woman had learned a hell of a lot more than just peacekeeping tactics during her time with the CIA.

"C'mon, Viktor," Sam said, her lip curling. "Just show me your miserable face." She hoped the pepper spray would disable him enough for her to interrogate him. She hadn't had enough time to come up with a rock-solid plan. She'd had to seize the moment. But no matter what, she'd find out once and for all what happened to her father. She had to. By any means necessary.

Two more steps and she was there.

With her free hand, she reached for the door handle.

Her heart hammered against her ribcage. *Finally!* She was finally going to meet Viktor Heinrich face to face. She couldn't suppress the giddy anticipation bubbling inside of her.

Commotion exploded to her right. Screams erupted.

She turned.

The overgrown bartenders huddled around a body almost matching in size to theirs, manhandling him, five against one.

Three women stood to the side, in short dresses of black, blue, and purple. They turned their heads long enough for Sam to notice their eyes.

Red and black.

Vamps.

The man flailed his arms, screaming at the bartenders, "How did you do it? Tell me, damn it! How did you fucking do it?"

Sam searched the room in a frenzy. No one around her seemed to notice or care about the fight. Everyone went about their business, groping one another.

Then her heart caught in her throat. She lost her ability to breathe when she realized every eye in the club looking her way was *red* and *black*.

Oh God.

No. No. No. This couldn't be happening. Not when she was so close to busting Viktor Heinrich.

One bartender held the large man's arms behind his back, but he still managed to kick two of Hans' twin brothers in the face. The captive man fought to free himself of the tight muscle-bound hold, twisting and writhing, when Sam caught a glimpse of his face.

John Black.

No! Her knees were definitely going to give out. Blood rushed to her head. She blinked rapidly to keep herself from fainting.

Another bartender pushed his comrades out of the way and punched John in the face. Sam gasped as blood spewed from his mouth, trailing down his chin and neck. He spit a red patch back at the men in front of him and smirked.

The man John kicked in the face recovered, eyes glowing in fury, shouting something Sam didn't catch. It sounded foreign. *German?*

The bartenders surrounding John snapped to attention as Hans had done when she asked him about Heinrich, and they hauled him toward a back door in the opposite corner of the club.

No. No. No!

Her gaze darted from the office door to John. John to the office door.

Do the right thing and try to save John, who apparently couldn't save himself? Or stay and get her long-awaited revenge?

As she contemplated, the seconds ticked by in her brain like resounding gongs. She'd waited for this moment and now it was within her grasp. Could she let it slip away with the probability it may never present itself again?

Her knuckles screamed in protest as her grip tightened on the door handle, the other on the can of pepper spray.

Who was John Black to her anyway? Only her neighbor. No one special to her. She didn't have an obligation to him like she did to Rose, Estelle, Maybel, or Celia. Had one of them been in trouble, Sam would have flown over the crowd and pummeled each and every one of those German brutes.

She turned toward her neighbor, nibbling on her bottom lip.

If he was being beat to a pulp and forcibly removed from

the club, she could bet he wasn't partners with Heinrich. He couldn't be. Plus, he'd saved her when she'd been attacked by that vamp. She owed him.

Another quick glance at the office door and then at John. Her grip relaxed on the door handle. "You better be worth it!"

Pepper spray still in hand, Sam ran as fast as her legs would carry her, ignoring the looks and shouts of the other patrons as she knocked them out of her way.

Within range of the scuffle, and running on pure adrenaline, Sam shot two of the burly men in the back of the neck with the spray.

They squealed and twisted in agony, hunching over. The skin on their necks began to peel away, leaving deep, irritated welts. Blood oozed onto their shirt collars. What had once been crisp, white cotton was now drenched with dark, scarlet stains.

Noticing their brothers wounded, two more broke away from the pack, headed in her direction.

John screamed, "No! What are you doing? Get out of here!"

Yeah right.

Once the two men were close enough, she sprayed their faces as if she held a can of Aqua-Net and was determined to destroy the Ozone layer in one shot. They fell to their knees screaming, gouging at their closed eyes, which started dripping with blood.

With eyes wide and mouth open, John glanced at the bleeding bartenders and then at Sam.

Surrounding vamps convulsed and their eyes darkened.

Out of nowhere, three more Germans came after her. John was still being forced toward the exit.

"Get back here!" she screamed.

"Go!" John shouted back, still flailing and shifting. "Run,

goddamn it! Run!'"

Vamps closed in on her, their teeth gleaming like feral beasts, a frantic thirst on their face. Even if they weren't *actual* vampires, if they couldn't get a drink from the bar, she was sure they'd be fine with a drink from her neck. They appeared that desperate.

Withdrawal. They must be going through withdrawal. Just like the perp who held her at gunpoint. She'd escaped that scenario. But a group of them? There was no way she'd survive.

Step by step, at an agonizingly slow pace, the giant men and dark-eyed monsters drew closer, ready to swallow her whole in the dark heart of the circle.

She had to do something or she wouldn't live to see Viktor Heinrich brought to justice. She'd never know what her neighbor's involvement was. Her father would forever be considered a traitor. And, she'd never hug Grandma Rose or laugh with the 19th Street Patrol gals again.

Thoughts of her grandmother whirled through her mind as the darkness closed in around her.

Chapter Ten

Sam squeezed her eyes shut and scattered the remaining pepper spray in the direction of anything that moved. Screams pierced her eardrums, but she kept her finger locked on the trigger.

When the can sputtered, she chucked it at one of the incoming bartenders. It bounced off his forehead as he advanced.

"Run!" John screamed again. "*Now!* Get out of here!" He was almost to the door.

Did he really think screaming the same thing over and over would make her listen? She was committed to the situation now. There was no backing down.

If they made it outside, who knew what would happen. She had to save him.

Another circle of Hanses and vamps closed in around her. Sweltering body heat stifled the air, smothering her, robbing not only her breath, but her courage, too.

"Leave her alone!" John strained against the powerful hold. He sounded like a wild man about to draw his last breath. "Over here! Come get *me* you sons a bitches!"

John wiggled one arm free, managing to elbow a Hans in the face; blood spurted from the man's mouth before his comrade restrained John's arm. Bloody-nosed Hans gave John a four-knuckle shot of his own. Sam winced and cried out as John doubled over.

Sweaty hands clawed at her body, pawing along her skin as she tried to squirm away.

Like possessed zombies vying for a taste of her, the monsters huddled into the circle, reaching, angry, and hungry.

Keep moving. Come on, Sam! Keep moving!

Sinking to her hands and knees, she opened her purse in search of her next homemade weapon. An iron-clad grip yanked at her hair, pulling the follicles from the roots. A wail tore from her lungs, but she continued to rummage inside her purse, pushing away the piercing pain in her head and neck.

Where are *they?*

A strong arm reached around her neck and tightened like a rattlesnake strangling its prey.

"No!" As she'd been taught in self-defense class, she dipped her chin and bit down hard on the forearm. A howl cut through the room as the arm yanked back. She tasted salt, but not metal. Thank God. She wanted to hurt the person, not draw blood into her mouth.

Another grabbed her, forcing her to her feet. She wasn't giving in. Blindly throwing a right hook, she connected with the bartender in front of her. His head snapped to the side and he stumbled backward, finally allowing her to locate what she was looking for in her purse.

Earplugs.

She shoved one in and then the other as she watched John being propelled through the back door. The look of desperation and fury on his face was almost enough to crush her will.

The door slammed closed behind him.

While arms reached and voices screamed at her, she yanked the air horn out of her purse and let it howl.

Everyone but Sam doubled over, grabbing their ears and screaming at the slicing sound.

She inhaled a deep breath, starving for the oxygen left in the wake of the dissipating bodies. One by one they fell like dominoes.

It was as if she was the only person in the room — a statue standing among an ocean of bodies lying flat and lifeless on the ground.

The man who had received her right fist removed his hands from his ears to see his palms covered in his own blood. Dark red clumps dripped onto the floor. Other vamps ceased moving all together, stretched out on their backs, barely breathing as their bodies convulsed and blood ran from their ears onto the filthy cement.

She kicked off her strappy heels and ran toward the back door. Lightheaded, she leaped over bodies. Adrenaline on high alert, her heart pumped blood to her brain in rapid amounts. She was sure her heart was going to burst out of her ribcage at any moment. She was like a ticking time bomb.

Thump, thump. Thump, thump.

She threw open the door and spotted John on the pavement. His arms braced as if he'd just finished doing push-ups, except he was covered in smears of dirt and blood. He swiped his forearm across his mouth, blood streaking across his cheek.

His head turned, and he locked eyes with her, relief clear in his expression.

The Hans quintuplets turned as well, scowling at the interruption. Three remained with John and two headed toward her.

John's eyes expanded. He tried to leap to his feet, but a

foot stomped onto his back.

"Wait!" she yelled.

The Germans paused.

Pleading with each eastern European staring back, she said, "Please don't kill him yet."

John's eyebrows rose. "*Yet?*"

The beefy Germans raised their eyebrows too, but in amused curiosity. The one with his foot on John's back smirked as if to say, *Go ahead, humor me.*

"Uh, yeah…please don't kill him just yet." She coughed and cleared her throat. "Please?" She batted her eyelashes, desperately trying to recall the year of German she'd taken in the tenth grade. "I mean, *bitte?*"

A few of the Germans offered appreciative smiles.

"*Ja, deutsche* talk." She nodded after noticing their pleased reaction. "Me and *meine* man-*freund…*" She spoke slowly, deliberately, winking at the Germans as her hand gestured to herself and then her neighbor.

She was pretty sure John rolled his eyes and groaned, but she didn't care. At the moment, he was alive and not being beat to a pulp.

Smirking, the Germans looked at her and then to John, seeming to forget that moments ago she'd made their brothers suffer in agony. "Ahh," they said. "*Liebespyrchen.*" They nodded to one another. "*Dein Mann!*"

"*Ja! Ja!*" she said, boisterously happy her plan to delay their torture was working. "My man. *Ich* like to, uh…say *guten*-bye…" She waved her hand in the universal gesture of farewell. "…before you…*killen* him." The last part was spoken in question since she had never learned the German word for "kill." Not much use for it in the tenth grade.

It seemed to get her point across. Their smiles grew wider, so she took a step toward her neighbor. They grabbed him by the shoulders and yanked him up.

Frau Weber would be so proud! Sam squared her shoulders and took another step and then another, silently scolding her racing heart.

She stood within inches of John by the time his feet hit the ground. She was so close the heat from his body mixed with hers, and his musky male scent enveloped her. She took in two deep breaths, calming herself.

"What the hell are you doing?" he muttered, looking into her eyes with a mixture of both disapproval and awe.

"Just go with it," she murmured without moving her lips. "My man," she said, turning to smile at her new German friends. "*Liebe* man." Sam caressed a hand across his cheek, slight stubble tickling her fingertips. "Oh, *meine liebe* man."

"Is that your extent of the language?" he whispered. "Because if so—"

Sam pinched his cheek and twisted.

"YOW!" he shouted.

"*Liebe, liebe* man!"

Grunts and groans echoed from the Germans. Apparently they liked her dominance.

So she did it again.

"ARGH!" His face contorted into a scowl, and his eyes darkened. "Stop that, damn it!"

The Germans now moved in syndication, closing in on the pair, circling in attentive voyeurism. They nodded in encouragement and nudged one another in the ribs.

"Oh, *meine liebe.*" Sam tried to mimic the raspy voices she'd heard on TV for those 900-numbers. "*Ich* going to, uh… *essen du.*"

"*Eat me*?" John blanched, and Sam pulled his head toward hers with a swift and effective tug on his ear.

The Germans continued to smile and grow red in the face, their sharp white teeth shimmering in the dim night.

On her tiptoes, she placed a soft kiss on his neck. Though

meaning to, she didn't stop there. Her mouth worked its way across his cheek, slowly depositing soft kisses. His face dipped in response, and her mouth searched for his. Body heat rising, she forgot herself as their lips touched.

Both exhaling loudly through their noses, it was as if they had been holding their breaths until that moment. The Germans must have let go of him, because a pair of strong arms wrapped around her, steeling her in place against him.

He tangled his fingers in her shoulder-length hair and tugged back for better access. When his mouth took hers, she forgot about their audience and location. It was simply the two of them.

He kissed her good and thoroughly, his tongue demanding an improper introduction with hers. He wasn't gentle, and he wasn't slow as he parted her lips with haste.

She gave in and opened for him, enjoying the pleasure of his warm, wet tongue dueling with hers. Never one to be dominated, Sam met him stroke for stroke, grasping his head tight as she sliced her tongue along his.

His hands dropped to her backside. They lingered, as if deciding, then his fingers dug into the fabric of her skirt and rammed her forward, cradling her against his erection.

How can he be turned on at a time like this?

As if hearing her thought, he pulled back and looked into her eyes with a clouded expression. He looked to be in pain.

Before he blew the con, and the Germans realized what she was doing, she dipped into her purse and grabbed the remaining pair of earplugs.

She reached her arms around his neck and grazed her lips along his jaw line. Her fingers climbed toward his ears, and she pressed the buds into his canals.

When his eyebrows dropped and his forehead creased, she whispered, "Trust me."

The Germans closed in. They now wore expressions of

wary concern rather than horny curiosity.

John must have thought she lost her mind. "What are you—?"

Sam yanked his face to hers and planted a sloppy resemblance of a kiss that would have been fitting if she'd been about twenty years younger and eating an ice cream cone instead of kissing her hot neighbor.

Lips still locked, she lowered her purse between their touching bodies, blocking it from view as she searched inside.

The bartenders, now snarling, stood shoulder to shoulder, trapping Sam and her neighbor in the center with their massive bodies.

John's body went rigid, every muscle locking into place. He was going to try to take on these thugs.

Before he could, Sam raised her arm to the heavens and pulled the trigger of the second air horn. With her other arm, she bear-hugged John as if they were on a ship in the middle of a monsoon. He tightened his arms around her waist.

Like in the club, the Germans dropped to the ground and began to bleed from their ears.

John's head whipped around, watching the massive bodies fall.

Darkness invaded her vision as she looked up at him, smiling proudly. She'd saved him! She'd actually done something right, and she'd saved him! Without a badge. Without backup. Without anything but her brain and some homemade weapons.

And now it was time to get the hell out of Dodge.

Throwing his arm around her shoulder, she held him close as they hobbled toward the street.

He paused, bending to retrieve a gun from the ground, and tucked it into his waistband, before leaning on her again. His taut muscles pressed against her, and she realized it must be difficult for him to rely on anyone for help. He didn't seem to have friends or comrades. No one ever visited. And aside from the Tyke guy he talked to, John seemed to be a loner. The thought pulled at her heart. Everyone deserved someone they could rely on for comfort and love.

Once they approached her car, he spoke. "What in the hell did you think you were doing?"

"Saving your ass, obviously." She dug in her purse for her keys. She staggered a step as they approached the curb where her car was parked. "You're welcome, by the way."

"Saving *me*?" He laughed without humor. "I had it under control."

"Looked like it."

"I told you to run."

She leaned him against the passenger-side door. Taking in his battered appearance, she ignored the urge to shake her head at his ridiculous statement.

Black spots invaded her vision as she ran to the driver's side and struggled to get the key into the lock. Success after three tries, she sat behind the wheel. "Can you get in okay?" Noticing his drooping frame, still covered in mud and dried blood, she opened the passenger door from the inside.

He fell into the seat, expelling a few sharp breaths. He buckled himself as she started the car and raced down 26th Street.

"Again," he said, wincing as he turned to her. "What did you think you were doing?"

"Can we worry about that later? Right now I'm concentrating on getting us out of here." She stole a few glances in the rearview mirror. The view tilted, so she narrowed her eyes, concentrating.

He looked in the side mirror and then craned his neck to look behind. "You can slow down. No one's following us."

She breathed a sigh of relief and slowed the car's pace to the speed limit.

"What was that?" he asked.

"Are you okay? You look pretty banged up."

No verbal response, but she sensed his eyebrow raise.

She sighed. "An air horn."

"That wasn't a regular air horn. Where'd you get something like that?"

She shrugged like it was no big deal she had a contraption that made people's ears bleed. Thanks to the CIA for their research in the sixties on unorthodox methods of warfare.

He pulled the earplugs from his ears and held one up to examine it as if it was a rare gemstone found only in the most remote and dangerous cave.

"Where's your gun?"

"My gun?" She removed her earplugs and placed them in the cup holder. "What makes you think I have a gun?"

"You're a cop."

She snapped her head to look at him. "No, I'm not."

"You work for Baltimore City Police."

Her jaw clenched and pain sliced down her neck. "There are other jobs in the department besides being a cop."

She turned off 23rd Street, heading toward 22nd. They'd be home in a matter of minutes. If only her eyes would focus on the road. The glow from the streetlamps was doing funny things to her vision, creating large yellow orbs in front of her windshield. She blinked to clear her sight.

"What were you doing at Club Hell?" he asked again. More like demanded.

Why was her heart still racing? They'd escaped trouble, her body should have slowed by now. But it hadn't. The blood in her ears drummed against her skull and she felt—actually *felt*—her veins stretching from the excess liquid pumping at accelerated rates through the canals. She was sure her stomach had just dropped out of her midsection. And her head. Good Lord, her head was like a balloon, growing lighter by the second. Any time now, it was going to detach and float away.

"Uh, I think I'm..." she said in a breathy voice.

She must have swerved because the steering wheel jerked and John shouted, "Hey. You okay?"

Glancing in his direction, she tried to focus on his features. But her eyelids grew heavy and her body went limp.

Then everything went black.

· · ·

Shit! Ash grabbed the wheel, steering the car away from the light post they headed straight for. Blondie's head had dropped back, and her eyes were closed.

"Damn it," he muttered, turning his attention to the road ahead. They were still one block from their street.

He threw the car into neutral and guided it to the curb. Without stability or traction control, it was difficult to force the car anywhere. He used his remaining strength to yank the wheel, cussing and wincing as he pulled. The car hit the raised cement curb with more force than he'd wanted. There was a loud scrape and then white smoke drifted to the sky, and an acrid stench of burnt metal filled his nostrils.

Oh well. He'd worry about that later. It's not like the POS couldn't benefit from a visit to the auto shop.

First priority was to get Blondie to his house and assess her condition.

He pulled her from the car and hoisted her onto his shoulder, ignoring the gut-searing pain. Die Hard and his buddies had done a bang-up job on his ribs and stomach. He'd be more than black and blue tomorrow. But for now, just like he'd been trained, he pushed forward. He'd get first aid once he was back at camp.

Sprinting up the block, he reached his front steps within minutes.

He laid her on the worn sofa in his front room, taking care not to bump her head on the arm. He pried her eyes open, bracing himself for the telltale sign of Vamp use. He hadn't seen her enter the club, so he had no way of knowing if she'd ingested any of the free drinks being shoved down everyone's throats. The drinks were obviously laced if River and her girlfriends had been affected.

Blondie's blue eyes stared back, and he said a silent prayer of thanks. There was no red. Or black. Just light blue. Like the color of the sky on a crisp fall day.

His finger brushed a damp strand of hair from her forehead, before checking her pulse, which was racing. Her skin was clammy and on fire.

She must have gotten a residual high from direct contact with a vamp. Much like a cold or flu, the effects of the drug could be passed from person to person by bodily fluids. Not as potent or deadly as ingesting the actual substance, but she'd be horny as hell tonight and might have a blinding hangover tomorrow. He wasn't sure if she'd have a mild addiction afterward or not. All residuals were different. She was already reacting differently than other residuals—he'd never seen anyone pass out from contact as she had.

He'd need to keep watch over her tonight and make sure her temperature didn't spike to dangerous levels. Also, he'd need to keep her close so she didn't go out looking for someone on the street to ease her raging hormones.

There was no doubt about it. She was staying with him tonight—whether she hated him in the morning for it or not.

First step was to bring her temperature down.

Ash checked her pulse and breathing once more. No change. So he picked her up and hurried up the stairs to the bathroom.

He turned the knob and practically dropped her into the porcelain tub, clothes and all.

She sucked in a sharp breath as ice-cold water hit her bare skin.

"I'm sorry," he said, pushing away a strand of errant hair. He stroked his hand along her shoulder and down her arms. She shivered.

Movement. That was a good sign.

"Can you open your eyes?"

No reaction.

"I wish I knew your name, Blondie." Ash continued to caress her skin. Smooth, he noted. His neighbor was really something up close. Not that she wasn't when she hung out her bedroom window or bounced down her front steps smiling, but it was her simplicity—natural makeup, arched eyebrows, daintily sloped nose, and high cheekbones. She was breathtaking. Why was he suddenly stunned to realize it?

He went to the closet and grabbed a towel. Dipping it into the water, he placed it over her forehead.

This woman was the first one he noticed as just that—a *woman*. Not a pain in the ass—though in the short time he'd known her, she was definitely that. No, this one wanted to walk alongside him in danger. Not get him into it.

She'd never let herself be the victim. She had proven herself less cowardly than most of the troops he'd served with in the Middle East. Blondie had a confidence that was ninety parts arrogant and ten parts naive. A disastrous formula concocted to blow up in his face any moment.

It only made him like her more.

She'd ventured out tonight in search of something so important she'd risked her own safety to obtain it. He was going to find out what that something was.

Just as soon as he made sure she lived through the night.

He placed his hand on her forehead again. The cold towel had helped. Perspiration was less evident. Her temperature seemed to be lowering.

Her eyes fluttered once. "Grandma?" she asked in a strangled voice.

His hand stilled. "No."

She turned to him, the blue in her eyes empty and dull. "I'm so cold."

"I know. I'm sorry. I have to bring your body temperature down." Hopefully the cold water would help minimize the next symptom as well, he thought grimly.

He took the towel from her forehead, soaked it in the cold water, and squeezed it over her shoulders.

She shivered again, and her teeth chattered. Her lips turned the same color as her eyes.

He went to the closet to get more dry towels. "Just a few more minutes. I promise."

She nodded once, the movement choppy in conjunction with her shudders.

Jesus, it killed him to see her in this condition. She'd been so strong. So capable. And now she was so damn vulnerable.

Once he thought she'd had enough, he yanked her from the tub and wrapped her in a towel. When she curled into his chest, he softened even more as he carried her into his bedroom.

"You'll warm up soon," he said, rubbing her back. Sooner than she realized since his AC was broken.

He pulled back the sheets and laid her on his bed. Taking a deep breath, he laughed. "You're definitely not going to like this when you wake up."

His hands worked her skirt down over her narrow hips, doing his best not to look at the small bit of fabric remaining. Then he sat her up to remove the flimsy top, not daring to look at her bra.

He covered her up to her neck with the sheet and then reached under to slide her drenched panties down, shaking his head in disbelief as the thin material slid over her ankles.

"This is definitely a first."

Making sure the sheet stayed in place over her, he unhooked her bra. His breath hitched at the feel of her soft skin against his callused hands. It was impossible not to wonder what she looked like under that sheet.

Needing distance, he hung her clothes on a nearby chair by the open window.

Filling his lungs with the warm night air, he turned to see the body of his neighbor lying so still.

Soon, very soon she'd be awake. And in need. Though he'd have to wait to find out which of her needs would outweigh the other. The drugs. Or her libido.

Chapter Eleven

Removing everything from his body except his boxer briefs and a pair of gym shorts, Ash crawled into bed next to his neighbor, too damn tired to worry about administering first aid on himself. He'd splashed water on his face and wiped away most of the blood and grime. It had been a trying night. Rest was what he needed. He normally slept naked, but he definitely wasn't putting himself in that situation tonight. Not with Blondie's condition, the fact that they barely knew each other, and the awkward explanation it would cause tomorrow morning. Tonight had been weird enough.

Reaching for her forehead again, he breathed a sigh of relief that Blondie's temperature had leveled out. She rolled, whimpering as she huddled into him. He hated himself for noticing how well her head fit onto his shoulder and her hips curved into his.

When she shifted onto her side, her hair lifted, fanning out on the pillow behind her. It gave him full view of her slender neck.

Best place to start kissing a woman…

He grinned at the thought. Lips were fine, but that soft patch of skin at the back of the neck really warmed the blood. Scandalous and sweet, all at the same time. She was just the right height for it, too. Perfect for his six-three frame to caress the sensitive spot with his tongue. His groin tightened as he imagined other things he could do to her with his tongue.

Giving in to the heat, he closed his eyes and thought about wrapping himself around a woman, holding her close, catching a trace of her sweet scent. It had been so long; he'd almost forgotten how amazing women smelled. Jasmine, lilac, vanilla, lemon. Even the simple scent of shampoo wafting into his nostrils got his blood started. Each woman's scent was different, but in a way the same, too. They all smelled like their own piece of heaven.

A violent shiver shook her body, yanking him away from his thoughts.

The woman's injured. Pull yourself together!

"Shhh," he whispered, wrapping his arms around her. "You're going to be okay, Blondie. The drugs just have to work their way out of your system."

He caressed her back and shoulders, trying to create as much friction as possible to warm her up. The long-ignored stir low in his belly rekindled, and he fought to keep his thoughts in check.

No. He told his subconscious.

Why not? It asked back.

I can't.

How long's it been? Months?

Not going to happen.

Why? the voice persisted, almost in a whine.

He continued to stroke her back, sliding his fingers along the plane of her spine, down and up again, imagining how it would feel to give in to his needs.

Ash hadn't been tempted after Lorena. Hadn't allowed

himself to. Women had always been a means to an end. He'd accepted that.

But this one—he didn't know what to make of her.

Bringing him back to the present, Blondie pulled her arms from under the covers and threw the sheet down past her stomach.

He stopped breathing. There was just enough light from the street to filter streams along her bare skin. Oh Christ. The shape of her petite round breasts were visible. They were already pert and aroused. His groin tightened further, and his subconscious laughed at him.

This was going to be a long night.

Eyes now open wide, she ran her fingernails up his exposed chest, over his shoulders, and gripped his biceps.

He closed his eyes and imagined the situation differently— that she wasn't under the influence and she had come to him willingly.

Huge mistake.

She rolled off the pillow, positioning herself over him, and laid sweet wet kisses on his neck, jawline, and cheek. He hissed in a breath at the feel of her tight nipples running along his chest. His hands lifted to her back but halted before contact was made. "Not like this," he reminded himself. He balled his hands into fists at his sides, trying with all his might to regain composure. His body reacted to every movement she made, humming to life, hardening beyond comprehension.

It's just been awhile. This was a normal reaction after the drought he'd been through.

What a crock of shit. He wanted this woman. Bad. And it pissed him off that she'd snuck under his radar.

Blondie was doing things to him. Making him feel things…things he had vowed to never feel again.

She trailed her hot mouth along his chest, abdomen, and then reached the line of his waistband. With its own agenda, his cock jumped, straining against his shorts.

Like a bolt of lightning, his fingers gripped her shoulders and yanked her toward the headboard. Fuck. There was no way he'd stop her if she started touching him down there.

As if reading his thoughts, her lips formed into a wicked curve. Jesus, he'd give his entire pension to read what was going through her head.

He held her still, suspended above him, his blood coursing through his veins in protest for not allowing this beautiful creature to have her way with him.

His subconscious said a few choice words he chose to ignore.

"What's your name?" he asked, hoping to distract everyone involved.

The corners of her mouth curled higher in knowing anticipation. Like a black widow, luring her lover close before she snapped his head off. "Anything you want it to be."

He groaned. Yep, long night. Tipping his head to the side, he raised an insistent eyebrow.

She let out a loud sigh and rolled her eyes. "Samantha. Happy? Now can I continue?"

"Wouldn't you like to know my name?"

"Not really." She jolted forward, catching him off guard, and planted her lips on his.

Soft and perfect, that's all he could think. She was eager and she was here, making it extremely hard to remember he was a gentleman.

Hard. Yeah, definitely hard. Dangerously hard.

It brought back images of their kiss outside Club Hell. When she saved him. When she took control. Damn, he loved when a woman took control during sex.

She opened her mouth and ran her tongue along his lips, then dipped inside and moaned.

His body shot to attention, ready to engage. If he didn't

stop her now, he wasn't going to.

And he *had* to.

She somehow managed to crawl on top of him—when or how, he had no idea—and straddled him.

Now. Definitely now. Stop her now.

With every ounce of restraint he had left, he planted his hands on her shoulders and pushed her away. He flipped her onto her back and used his weight to pin her onto the mattress.

She gave him a grin that almost stopped his heart.

He held her wrists above her head. The hold didn't help his control as it lifted the swell of her breasts. They were there for the taking. All he had to do was lean down…

No. Remaining still, he willed both of their bodies to come down from the high that wouldn't find release tonight. He pulled the sheet up and tucked it around her chest, burying his hands beneath her to make sure she couldn't wiggle free. If he could have wrapped her like a fucking burrito, he would have.

She frowned and squirmed beneath his hold, but her small frame was no match for his strength. "Please?" She gave him a convincing pout. His resolve started to crumble. If he stared any longer at that face—those sad blue eyes and full inviting lips—he'd be a goner for sure.

"Samantha." He closed his eyes and exhaled. "We can't."

"Why?"

He wondered the same damn thing. "Well, for starters, you're under the influence." He was fairly certain she wouldn't be as outgoing without the residual Vamp in her system. But then again, how the hell would he know? She'd been hell on wheels the second she'd walked into his life. "And you'll regret it in the morning."

Her eyes sparkled with erotic promise. "No, I won't."

He groaned. Images of her naked body on top of him—sliding and stroking to completion—blinded him.

"Please." As if her plea wasn't difficult enough to fight, she slipped one arm between them and grazed her palm against his rock-hard erection.

He groaned again as his eyes slammed shut.

Goddamn torture.

"Oh," her voice was pleasantly surprised. His eyes fluttered open to see her gaze lower to her errant hand, as if she just now noticed his attraction to her.

Ash smiled wryly.

She closed her fingers around the shaft, acquainting herself with his shape. She moved a little slow for his taste, but that could be fixed. Her hand squeezed tighter, and the pace picked up.

Terrible idea. This is a terrible idea.

"You're *really* big," she marveled. "And hard."

He grew even harder.

His body started to give in, lowering itself toward her. The thin cotton sheet brushed against the hair on his chest. He moved closer, breathing in her sweet scent as he sought out the sensitive spot on her neck.

Letting instincts be his guide, he placed his lips on her pulse. It leaped in response to the soft caress. By its own desire, his tongue slid out, tasting her satin skin.

Salty. Sweet. Delicious.

Perfect.

His left hand, feeling grossly neglected, sought out her breast. Beneath the sheet, he filled his palm, kneading and pressing the mound. His thumb circled her nipple, finding it already sharp and tight, crying out for attention. Relief. His body was all too eager to oblige.

She moaned. "Yes." Her other hand had escaped his weakened hold and found its place at the base of his head, guiding and urging him on. She shifted, arching her back, offering more to him.

The movement pulled Ash from what he was about to do. He cursed under his breath. This was insane.

He reached like a madman for his sanity. Damn, it sucked being the good guy.

She stiffened beneath him. Her hands moved to his chest, palms covering each pec. Her thumbs mimicked the motion he'd done to her nipple. "Please?" she begged in that soft bedroom voice. "Please. I need you."

His body needed her more.

But he knew it was the drug talking. She'd take anyone right now.

When he didn't move, breathe, or speak, she bit off, "What's the matter with you?"

Gone was the adorable blue-eyed creature. In its place was a mean she-monster with furrowed brows and puckered lips. She was beginning to feel the severe effects of withdrawal. A pull so intense, Ash knew she'd never experienced anything like it before in her life.

"Get off me!" Her hips bucked against him.

He remained in place, gripping her wrists tighter to remind her of his strength.

"Now!" she said, practically spitting in his face.

"No." He was in control of himself, and she damn well better take notice.

"Ahhh!" She writhed beneath him. "I need— I need—"

"What you need is to lie still," he said. "You want another hit, but you're not going to get it. So be quiet."

Her face filled with blood, and her head whipped from side to side.

Since her eyes hadn't changed color, he knew she hadn't ingested the drug. His body relaxed with relief. She'd make it through the night. They just had to wait it out. He was prepared to hold her all night if that's what it would take to keep her safe.

"You're an asshole," she spat.

He chuckled. "Yeah, I've heard that before."

Ash held her, determined to keep his promise. All night if that's what it took.

• • •

Warmth. All Sam wanted was to be warm again. An odd need, given her AC had been broken for a week.

Her body shivered as if she'd been dipped into the icy waters of the Chesapeake Bay. Then all of a sudden, she was scorching and happy, enveloped in the most delicious heat imaginable. Like lying next to an open campfire.

"Mmmm," she murmured, snuggling closer.

Her head pounded at her temples. A few minutes longer and she'd have to give in to the migraine and search for Tylenol. But for the time being, she smiled in satisfaction—

Why was she naked?

She never slept naked.

Ever.

And why was the delicious warmth hard as a rock?

Something tightened around her stomach. It gripped, straining her ability to breath.

Her eyes flipped open.

In the early morning light, she made out the shapes of trees and power lines outside. But they looked different. Their positions were wrong. There wasn't a telephone pole in front of her bedroom window. No, no, it was in front of—

Oh God.

Her eyes adjusted to the shadows in the room. She was face to face with the silhouette of an angular jaw, broad shoulders, and a dark symbol with wings tattooed on a neck. In this light it appeared to be a bird in black silhouette. An eagle.

Her neighbor's eyes were closed, and his breaths regular.

Why the hell was she in his bed? Why the hell was his shirt off? And—*again*—why the hell was she naked?

Sam quickly peeked underneath the covers and exhaled a soft sigh of relief at the sight of dark shorts covering his bottom half. Okay, so hopefully they hadn't had sex. Though, who knows, because last night was a complete and utter blur. Nothing at all was coming to mind. Or at least nothing that would explain her current state of nakedness and location. First order of business was to get dressed. Then he'd have some explaining to do.

She lifted her head and surveyed the room. Next to the window was a chair with her clothes draped over it.

Slowly, so as not to wake the sleeping beast, she slithered toward the edge of the bed. She managed only a few inches before his strong arm locked tighter and pulled her until her nose was within inches of his bare chest.

She froze. When his deep, steady breaths blew across her skin, her body relaxed. He was still asleep.

A mixture of sweat and musk invaded her nostrils. She didn't think sweat could ever smell good, but with him, it was like an invigorating cologne. An essence of rugged maleness and brute strength designed to awaken all of her female senses.

She closed her eyes for the briefest moment, enjoying the sensation of being surrounded by him—*all* of him. It had been so long since she'd lain this close with a man, the heat and scent of his skin floating around her. She'd forgotten how amazing it was. How comforting. The tighter his hold, the safer she felt. A complete stranger; and yet at that moment, she was at home with him.

How was that possible?

He stirred, grumbling into her ear. The sizzling air against her skin roused things inside her she didn't recognize. Nerve endings all over tingled and came alive. It was overwhelming, lying next to a man who possessed such a powerful presence.

She moved, daring to press the full length of her body against his. Just once she wanted to feel safe and protected. Forget about the worry of losing Grandma Rose—a never-ending concern after having lost everyone else she loved. No, just this once she needed someone else to shoulder the burden of keeping Sam and her loved ones safe. This man, holding her in his capable hands, made her feel like she could let go. Allow someone in. To shelter her. Take care of her. The way she'd never let anyone else before.

He grumbled softly again.

She stilled, holding her breath for fear of waking him and ruining this perfect moment of contentment.

Calm, deep sounds reverberated against her ear.

She inched closer to him until their bodies touched with nothing between them but the thin, cotton bed sheet. His large warm frame overshadowed her small naked one. She nuzzled her face into his neck, enjoying the mouthwatering shivers overtaking her body because of the contact.

Suddenly, a hand stroked her hair, trailing down the middle of her back and continuing the journey of her spine all the way to her rear end. It was a firm, skilled hand, one that had experience traveling a woman's contours, knowing just the right spots to invoke the most stimulating response. He squeezed her right butt cheek in his large palm. Her stomach did somersaults and her muscles melted. He murmured incoherently, pulling her closer, positioning her against his hardness.

If she wanted heat, well, she got it. Between his body temperature and the flames igniting inside her, the bed was sure to catch fire at any second. She was surprised it hadn't already.

His hand gripped her thigh, forcing her leg to hitch over

his hip, yanking it along with the sheet. Then he traveled up her back again. His hand grabbed the base of her neck and dragged her on top of him.

Was he still asleep? Or was he awake and thought she was asking for this?

She didn't know. Nor did she have time to find out.

Before she could react, before she could attempt to refuse her neighbor, she straddled him and he hastily pulled her face toward his. By their own accord, her eyes dropped closed and she waited.

Then their lips touched.

Chapter Twelve

"Samantha?" Her weight rested on his midsection, and her image appeared above him. Her face was inches from his, eyes closed and lips parted. Unexpected, but an incredible image for a man to wake up to.

He licked his lips, tasting sweetness only a woman could leave behind.

Had they—?

A look of alarm covered her face as her eyes opened and her body shot up. Perfect form for riding in a saddle. The bed sheet had fallen to her waist. It took everything he had to lie still and only look into her eyes. But damn, those tight, perky breasts called to him. She cocked her head, suddenly cautious. "How do you know my name?"

He shouldn't enjoy the warm sensations against his stomach, but hell, he was a guy. He didn't move a muscle for fear she'd realize their position.

"You told me last night," he said. "I'm Ash, by the way. I know we didn't have much time for introductions. What, with air conditioners falling on my head and overgrown bartenders trying to kill me."

With her chest still naked and uncovered, she surveyed him through the early morning light. Her eyes narrowed as her fingers traced the outline of his Special Forces tattoo.

A shudder rolled through him. Jesus. In any other situation he'd be inside her so fast.

He'd been dreaming about her moments ago. She'd been in the same position as she was now but rode him with a fierce need that blew his ever-loving mind. She was loud and vocal, making him feel like a motherfucking god.

When her light touch traveled from his neck to his nipple, his damn stomach muscles clenched and his dick jumped beneath her spread legs.

Damn it.

She leaped off him and scrambled for the bed sheet, throwing herself onto her back, covering every square inch of her naked skin from neck to toes.

She stared at the ceiling. "What happened last night?" The jumble of words rushed out.

He fought the smile desperately wanting to break free. "Nothing you're thinking."

She managed a glance his way.

"You had a little episode. A trip, really."

Her wide, worried eyes were adorable. "Meaning?"

"You were high on Vamp."

"*What?*" She propelled into a sitting position. "How did I…how did you…why did it…what?"

"Slow down." Ash sat up and placed a hand on her shoulder. She didn't slap it away, so he kept it there, relishing the soft feel of her skin beneath his fingers. "You got a residual high. Luckily, you weren't exposed for long, so your body burned it off quickly."

"A what?" The soft despair in her voice cut right through his gut.

"Residual high. Pretty common, actually."

"How?"

"Did you drink anything? Smoke anything?"

She shook her head and fisted the sheet against her chest.

"Did you have any contact with the people in the club?" He cleared his throat, a rush of sudden anger rising, though he didn't know at whom. "Bodily fluids and the sort?"

She wrinkled her nose. "No." There was a pause and then she asked, "Why?"

"We learned that's how Vamp can be passed. It's—"

"We?"

Shit. He blinked. Twice. "Yes." He lowered his hand from her shoulder, balling it into a fist at his side.

She crossed her arms, keeping the sheet tucked neatly over her breasts. "Elaborate, please."

How to explain without blowing his reason for being in Baltimore? For all he knew, she worked for Heinrich. She may not be a cop, but she had access to things at the precinct Heinrich would have use for. He'd learned his lesson with Lorena. A beautiful woman wasn't going to take away his common sense this time.

"I'm waiting." She tapped her finger on her arm like a strict nun. He might be convinced of it if she wore a stitch of clothing beneath that sheet.

"Why were you there last night?" he asked, imitating her stern voice.

Her eyes narrowed, as if to spear him in the dimly lit room.

He leaned over to the nightstand and flipped on the lamp.

She clung tighter to the sheet. "Don't try to distract me. I want to know who 'we' are and why you know so much about Vamp."

"You first," he bit back. "Tell me what you were doing at a place like Club Hell and then maybe, if I like your answer,

I'll tell you."

Her mouth dropped open in fury.

Knowing a lecture was on its way, he held up his hand to silence her. "Let's compromise. You tell me something, and I'll tell you something in return." He wanted to know more about her, and he figured she wouldn't give up much without him doing the same. In one aspect, he feared that she was like Lorena—putting on a sweet front to fool him, then she'd flip once she'd gotten what she wanted from him. But, deep down he couldn't believe Sam was anything like Lorena. She wouldn't use him to get the information she needed and then leave him.

She thought about his proposition. Her thirst for knowledge must have outweighed her ability to negotiate further. "Fine. I went to Club Hell looking for someone."

"Well, you found him." Ash shot her a disapproving look.

"Not you," she said, rolling her eyes. "Well, okay, fine, you. Sort of."

When he raised an eyebrow, she said, "I…I, uh, followed you." She muttered it so low and quick, he almost didn't catch it.

"Why?"

"Oh, no you don't. It's your turn."

He let out an aggravated sigh. "I was at Club Hell because I was looking for someone, too." His lips twitched and he couldn't help but add, "Not you."

They glared at one another with warring expressions. She looked pissed because he reflected her words back at her, and he gloated for having evaded her question.

"Who were you looking for?" He felt about as impatient as she sounded, so he let her tone slide.

"You first," he demanded.

A muscle ticked in her jaw. "Viktor Heinrich."

His eyes expanded for a second before he composed

his expression. "And that has to do with me how?" At her puzzled expression, he added, "You said you followed me to Club Hell. How am I connected with Heinrich?"

She gave him a direct look. "That's what you're going to tell me."

His head fell back, and he laughed. "Oh, I am, am I? I don't know what you're trying to get at, Blondie, but—"

"You gonna deny you're connected?"

"What—"

"Tell me how you know about Vamp."

"I'm not going to—"

"What is your involvement with Viktor Heinrich?"

"I'm not—"

"Tell me how you knew he owned Club Hell."

"Damn it, woman. Let me speak!"

She stopped long enough for him to take a breath.

"I want to know—" she started before he shot her a menacing look that would have scared even Tyke.

"If you'll be quiet for one minute, I'll answer your questions," he spoke slowly, daring her to interrupt him again.

Wisely, she zipped her lips and nodded once.

"I need to know one thing first." Before she could bitch about his request, he asked, "What do you want with Heinrich? Just answer me that."

Samantha nibbled on her lower lip before responding. "I need information from him. Then I'm going to haul him to jail and lock him up for good."

"But you're not a cop."

She pulled back with scrunched eyebrows.

"Last night," he said, answering her unspoken question.

Her voice wavered when she asked, "What else did I say last night?"

He waited a moment, letting her sweat. The blood rushed to her face, a pretty pink color taking over her porcelain skin.

He fought back a grin. "Nothing much," he finally said, saving her head from exploding. "Unfortunately." A hint of a smile peeked at the corners of his mouth. "Your weapons were... interesting."

"Uh-uh." She wagged her finger. "Your turn. Tell me about Heinrich."

He did an eye roll of his own and took a deep breath. "Heinrich's getting ready to bring a large amount of Vamp into Baltimore." Simple statement. Nothing alluding to what his role would be.

"Oh God." Her face lost all its lush color, and her breath exited in a *whoosh*. "I have to stop him." Her words were barely a whisper.

"Come again?" There's no way he heard her right.

"When? When is he making the drop?" She looked like a ghost—her face a sheet of pure white, matching the one she clutched to her body.

He paused. "A few weeks." Not an exact date.

"How—" She swallowed hard. "How do you know?"

Another deep breath. Shit. He was going to get fired for this. *Bye-bye promotion. Bye-bye getting my team back. Bye-bye life as I know it.* "I've been tracking him."

She nodded as if he'd told her something she already knew. "So you're what? FBI? CIA?"

His gaze dropped to one of the white pillows on his bed.

"If you don't tell me, I'll still find out. It's easier this way, trust me."

"I'm sure," he muttered, resisting the urge to roll his eyes again.

"What's that supposed to mean?"

He laughed without humor. "After that sad display of recon you put on—"

"You—" Her eyes flared, then simmered. "You knew?"

"A blind man could've spotted the five of you. Why were

you watching me? And how did you know I went to Club Hell?"

"We…" Looking away, she muttered, "We GPS-ed your truck."

"You, *what*?"

She flinched but didn't apologize.

"I'm the last person you need to worry about. I'm a federal agent for Christ's sake!"

"How were we supposed to know?" She met his eyes with a look of doubt that cut right through him. "You looked like a threat."

He waved his hand toward her in an up and down motion. "Are you safe?"

She didn't say anything.

"Are. You. Safe?" He managed through tight lips.

She gave a stiff nod.

"You're naked in my bed. Did I touch you in any improper way?" He didn't consider the kissing inappropriate. If he'd acted on the thoughts that had ran through his mind, *that* would have been improper.

She didn't comment and must have sensed his anger brewing—maybe it was his nostrils flaring and his chest heaving—because she snapped, "I don't remember."

Her doubt in him as a man, a protector, caused a sharp pain in his gut as if he'd been stabbed. He slowed his breathing and unclenched his fists. Changing gears, he said, "Let's talk about your weapons. Where exactly did you get the air horn? The pepper spray was nice, too."

She shrugged. "A family recipe."

"You mean to tell me that pack of women across the street made them?"

She hesitated. Then nodded.

He laughed, unable to believe his ears. "So what's the story? You all moonlight as crime-fighting superheroes at night?"

"Neighborhood watch—"

"Neighborhood watch!" He swiped a hand over his short hair.

"We've had a few incidents on the street, so Grandma felt it best to arm ourselves."

"With pepper spray that gives third-degree burns and air horns that make ears bleed. What else have they come up with?"

She readjusted the sheet, lifting it damn near to her ears, and crossed her arms. "I don't think I should tell you."

"You better, Blondie. I want to know what I'm dealing with. I have to make sure one of you isn't hiding in my bushes, waiting to spray me with something that'll blind me. I'm rather fond of my vision." Grinning, his eyes raked over her body.

A rosy flush bloomed on her cheeks, but she didn't turn away this time. "No, it's your turn. Tell me who you work for and what it has to do with Viktor Heinrich."

His gaze locked with hers for a full minute before he realized he'd have to give her something. He took another deep breath. "DEA. I'm on assignment to watch Heinrich's operation here in the city until he makes the drop. We have a team ready to bring him in."

Her shoulders relaxed. "Good. I'll help."

"No."

"But—"

"I work alone." For now, until he got his team back. *If* he ever got them back. His head pounded at the thought.

"But you said you have a team—"

"Not *my* team! *A* team!" He rubbed his temples. "Jesus, woman. You would try the patience of a saint. Can't you just sit quietly and do as you're told?"

Her face twisted away.

"Look, Samantha, we've got this handled. I'm monitoring

Heinrich's movement around Club Hell and reporting back to the team." He gritted his teeth, preparing for the next statement. "They'll be ready to bring him down. They're professionals. The best." He personally trained each one, so he knew they could handle anything.

She turned back to him. "I'm coming with you whether you like it or not."

Damn, she was pushy. "Didn't you just hear me? It isn't my choice!" He was losing control. The rage building from the latent pain his fuckup with Lorena had caused—the bullet he had to dig out of his chest, the loss of his team, his best friend, the demotion, and the death of the little boy in the village—had finally come to the surface. Her insistence wasn't helping. "Damn it, Sam! I'm not going to be there!"

"Well, I will!" she said just as loud, crowding into his personal space. "When is the team going?"

He had to laugh. "Are you fucking kidding me right now? You're neighborhood watch. Your job is to make sure people don't let their dogs shit on the sidewalk without picking it up, or remind your neighbors to lock their goddamn doors at night. This isn't baby games, Samantha. This is serious. Viktor Heinrich is fucking serious."

Her face, turning an unsettling shade of red, scrunched up like she'd just sucked a lemon. "I'm—"

"No!" he burst. "No! No! No! And that's final! You're not going!" Goddamn it. He had to close his eyes and concentrate on breathing before his head exploded. This woman was the most stubborn person he'd ever met.

"I'm going."

Did she have a death wish? Because he was seriously thinking he'd help her out. He wouldn't even need inventive weapons. A good strangling would do.

"You'll never know when it's going down."

She gave him a smug smile.

"You've lost the element of surprise, babe. Now that I know you're watching me, I'll be more careful. Like I've been doing the last two days. Get anything on that audio device of yours lately?" His smile was smugger.

Her teeth were grinding into powder, he was sure of it. "How?"

"How, what? How have I been able to do my job without you pains-in-the-ass getting into my business?" He crossed his arms, the muscles in his back burning from the tension. "That's for me to know."

At her determined pout, he asked, "Why does it matter so much to you anyway? What's your beef with Heinrich?"

A grave shadow fell across her face.

He didn't expect that reaction, and he sure as hell didn't like seeing it. His arms dropped to his sides. The anger drained from his body. "Samantha?"

Chapter Thirteen

She turned to the plain white wall, staring blindly. "My father went missing while working with Heinrich. He was a cop. Undercover. And just one day stopped communicating with his handler." Her jaw shifted to the side and one corner of her lip lifted grimly. "It's been years and no one's heard from him. Everyone at the station thinks he's either ashamed because he turned dirty or he's...dead."

"Jesus." Logic clicked as he swallowed the large ball in his throat. Baltimore. Drugs. Cops. The port. Heinrich. "Your father was Davy Harper."

She turned back to him, her eyes bright as sapphires. "You knew him?"

"I knew *of* him. Read the case file."

Everything he'd studied about the case rushed into his mind. There'd been nothing in there about Harper being dirty. The file suggested he'd been killed by Heinrich, who hadn't been convicted because they never found Harper's body. Heinrich wouldn't be so lucky this time around. His sorry ass would rot in jail for the rest of his life when the team got hold of him.

Survived by his daughter, the file had said. The realization hit Ash hard, erasing any remaining anger, replacing it with understanding.

"What do you know about my dad?" she asked. "Anything specific? Anything I can use to try to find him?"

To find him? Christ. The woman had balls of steel and the stubbornness of a mule. What person willingly searched for a family member who'd been associated with a dangerous drug kingpin like Heinrich? Especially since she didn't have resources at her disposal like Ash and his teammates.

"Like you said, he was undercover," Ash said, "working for Heinrich, who was trying to smuggle a new drug into the port. The file suggests it was an early version of Vamp. Your father managed to uncover Heinrich's plan for the new drug before"—he lowered his voice—"before he was killed. Samantha, I'm sorry. The file said Heinrich killed your father." He looked her over, so small and fragile in the moment. She stiffened at his comment and jerked her pale face to him. Her lips quivered. She did her best to fight off the onslaught of the shock, but a single tear dropped down her cheek before landing on the cotton sheet. "He died a hero." He had to make sure she knew that.

"H-how do you know? How can you be sure he's gone?" She swiped her hand across her cheek. "Everyone at the station is sure he was dirty. Why would the DEA automatically assume he's dead?"

"No one can be a hundred percent sure. They never found…" His throat constricted to the point that he almost couldn't get the words out. He inhaled deeply and then thrust the words past his lips. "They never found his body."

She didn't react, which told him his revelation wasn't news to her. "Then no one knows for certain," she said, her expression hardening. "He might still be out there. Heinrich might have him locked away somewhere. At his mercy."

Aaaaaaand he just gave her the push she needed to start looking for him. "He might, but Samantha, the chances of that are—"

"Possible. It's still possible, Ash. It is."

Sure, anything was possible, even if it wasn't probable. But he wasn't going to tell her that. Whatever lingering emotions she'd had about her father, whatever suppressed pain she'd endured, Ash wasn't going to make it any better by telling her to lose hope. To give up and move on. Even though that's exactly what she needed to do.

What about you? You're not so different with your pain. Why don't you give up on that shit with Lorena and move on?

"Tell me more about Vamp," she said. "What's Heinrich's play?"

No sense keeping his cover at this point. She obviously wasn't working for Heinrich. And she deserved to know what her father had been wrapped up in. "It's in paper form. Small and virtually undetectable. Which is probably how they're smuggling it in and getting people hooked so easily. I watched a bartender at Club Hell drop it into a woman's drink. It evaporated instantly. No trace at all. I imagine the same is true if you smoked a cigarette wrapped in Vamp paper. It doesn't take much. The shit's potent. Just a small portion would do it."

"He has to be stopped," she said softly.

"It's not that simple."

Determination gleamed in her eyes. "Just go and burn it. The paper."

He shook his head. "There's a good chance by breathing in the fumes, everyone around would become addicts. And not in the way you were last night. I'm talking about becoming vamps. Like that maniac who held you at gunpoint. It would take years of treatment just to ease withdrawal. And that's if we don't die from it first." His stomach cramped at the thought of Viktor Heinrich succeeding in his plan. "It's too risky."

"But I have to do something. He can't get away with this. What he did to my dad. What he's trying to do to my friends and neighbors."

"Heinrich isn't the mastermind behind this operation. He's got guys below him, sure, some are even on the force. You probably work with some of them." He shot her a pointed stare, and at her look of surprise, he continued, "But he's working for someone big and powerful. A ghost. We watch long enough, whoever's pulling the strings will make a mistake. And then we can nail him." Ash's fists tightened, imagining it was Heinrich's neck.

"I can't wait." Her shoulders rose and fell with determined breaths. "I know where Viktor Heinrich is. I'm going back to Club Hell to interrogate him. I'm going to find out what happened to my father."

Ignoring her overuse of the pronoun "I," he tried to calm her down. "It doesn't work that way, Sam. We have to hang back, wait for him to make a move." Something Ash found hard to do himself.

"Oh, screw that! I'll go and—"

When he gripped her wrist a little too hard, her eyes widened. "Promise me you won't go back there." She opened her mouth like she was going to argue, so he hardened his stare. "*Promise* me." He wouldn't be able to endure another night of worry. Watching the crowd descend on her last night had been more than he could handle. A primitive need to protect took over. If he'd been able to free his hands, he would have demolished everyone in the room for even attempting to look at her. If Die Hard III—or was it IV?—hadn't taken his gun, Ash would have placed a round between all their eyes.

"I can use my resources to look for your dad," he said. "I'll call my teammates and ask them to keep an eye out. If Heinrich is holding him somewhere, then I should be able to find out pretty easy. Give me some time. We're so close to nailing Heinrich. We just need—"

She was already shaking her head. "I have to find out if my dad is still out there. He needs me. I can't sit here and wait."

"You have to," he snapped. The thought of her in danger mixed with the possibility she'd put herself back in it made his words harsh. "Whether you like it or not, you're going to go about your regular business while I do my job."

And in the meantime, he'd have to come up with a menial job to keep her occupied. Something enticing enough for her to think she was involved in the case when she really wasn't.

Her lips puckered and she said, "You don't know me very well if you think I'm just going to—"

There was only one way to keep her quiet. Only one thing could take her mind off the suicide mission she had in mind.

He crushed his lips to hers, silencing her of everything, even her breath. She clawed her nails into his shoulder, probably to invoke pain or push him away, but it was a futile attempt at best.

Seizing a handful of her hair, he forced her head back as his mouth devoured hers in raw power. His tongue sliced between her lips, and he was surprised to find hers dashing out to meet it. She gasped, probably from the shock of her own willingness, and let out a moan of—Resistance? Pleasure?— before she dug her nails deeper, nearly drawing blood from his shoulder. She withdrew her tongue and bit down hard on his lower lip. He pulled back from the sharp pain, but couldn't blame her.

Her palm cracked across his cheek.

He didn't even see it coming. How was she able to do that to him?

"How dare you." She scrambled to the edge of the bed, trying to drag the sheet with her as she stood.

He was still lying on top, anchoring it in place as he wiped drops of blood from his lips with the back of his hand. His subconscious smiled at the thought of allowing her to draw more blood from him. Would she like it rough?

She looked at him, and then down to the sheet, which barely covered her front. The slight swell of her breasts broached the line of cover, and her right hip and leg were bare and exposed. A smooth porcelain canvas just waiting to be completely uncovered...

One pull and it would all come down.

"What's it going to be?" he asked, more than amused at her predicament. "Quick getaway naked? Or retreat back to bed all covered up?"

She slinked toward the bed. "You are a horrible, horrible man."

"Eh." He shrugged. "I've been called worse." He stroked his chin in thought. "By you, actually."

Her mouth dropped open.

"Last night. Did I forget to mention that? Hmm, I guess I did. Now, let me try to remember..." His finger tapped his chin. "Ah, yes, 'asshole.' I think that's what you called me."

Her lips pinched as she yanked at the sheet again, hardly moving it an inch. "Would you please lift your big, *oafy* body?"

Pondering again, he said, "No. I think you're going to have to come back to bed." He sent her a satisfied grin. "You didn't seem to mind it last night."

"You're a pig."

She glanced around the room, noticing her clothes hanging on a nearby chair, out of reach. Her gaze fell to her feet and then darted back to the chair.

"You'll never make it," Ash said, still grinning. He rested his spine against the headboard, his arms bent and hands clasped behind his head. He hoped like hell she'd drop the sheet. "But, please, try."

After a moment of hopeless staring at the chair, she turned to him with a pleading expression. "Be a gentleman and turn around."

"Now what fun would that be? Besides, I didn't hear you ask nicely."

Her cheeks flinched and lips flattened into a tight line. "*Please* turn around."

"See, that wasn't so hard, was it?" He closed his eyes. "Go ahead."

"I don't trust you."

A rustle of movement sounded, then the sheet pulled from under his leg. He peeked one eye open.

"Close your eyes!"

Lowering his lid, he chuckled at the sight of her tiptoeing toward her clothes like a naked cat burglar. What a cat burglar she'd make. Long, sculpted legs, tight, curved ass, slender back. Why had he given her the option to get out of bed? He readjusted to ease his sudden discomfort.

"You done yet?" he asked, listening for movement. Thoughts of her naked would lead to nothing but trouble. He needed her fully clothed, and he needed it fast. Otherwise, he wasn't going to allow her to get dressed until much, much later.

"Almost!" The sound was muffled.

When he opened his eyes, the room was empty.

Chapter Fourteen

"You okay?" Ash shouted.

"Yes!" Sam yelled from the safety of the locked bathroom. She was already dressed. She'd accomplished the task in lightning speed for fear he'd bust in.

She plastered her ear to the door, imagining what he was doing on the other side. Hopefully putting a shirt on. Staring at his chest and tight abs made it impossible to keep her cool.

Sounds of movement thumped around the room, then footsteps neared the door.

He knocked gently. "Almost done?"

"Yes, yes. Almost." She sank onto the side of the porcelain tub, her shoulders drawn forward.

"Okay, I'll be downstairs." He grumbled, and then the bedroom door closed.

How had she gotten herself into this situation? Getting high on the latest street drug, sleeping naked next to her new neighbor, and straddling him in the morning was definitely not her idea of ladylike behavior.

And Ash mentioned her weapons. Had she actually used

them last night? Had people gotten hurt? She swung her head down and placed it between her knees. Her breath came at a rapid pace, and she worked to calm herself.

It's okay. Obviously you had to do it. Something must have happened for you to use them. A vague image of Ash being held by men much larger than he was flashed through her mind, then it was gone. She'd had to save him. It was self-defense. She wouldn't have used her weapons otherwise. Only if she'd needed to.

She growled through clenched teeth. Why couldn't she remember any of it? She remembered walking into Club Hell and trying to save Ash. Then nothing. It was like a black void in her brain.

From now on, she would be more careful in her investigation. No more slipups. If she was going to find Dad, then she needed to bring her A game.

At least Ash had agreed to contact his teammates for their help in looking for her dad. With their resources, she'd have a much better shot at finding him. And she *had* to find him.

Sam had every reason to believe what Ash told her about his involvement. There was something in his eyes, shining with conviction when he spoke. He wanted to nail Heinrich. She still didn't understand why he would allow other people to get all the credit for the work he'd been doing, but that was his business. If it was her, she'd demand to be included. Wear them down until they agreed to let her help. Which was what she was doing to him.

For so long she'd felt alone in her pursuit of the man who had taken her father from her. Her heart swelled at the thought of having reinforcements.

She nibbled on her nails. How could she convince him to let her come along while he did his surveillance on Heinrich? Sure, he wasn't technically in charge of his investigation. And yeah, okay, it was against the rules to have a civilian tag along. She might not be a cop, but she knew that much. But, damn it, she was desperate to get close to Heinrich. He was the one with answers.

After minutes of pondering, she poked her head out of the door into the bedroom.

Empty.

She scanned the room to learn what she could about its owner. A bed with only cotton sheets, a dark wood nightstand with a lamp, and a club chair by the window. All she could discern was that her neighbor was a minimalist.

Continuing through the bedroom, she entered the hallway.

Empty. And the walls were white and bare.

The layout of his house was identical to hers—three bedrooms in the back, stairs in the front—so it wasn't difficult to find her way around.

When she went down the steps and entered the kitchen, the sweet aroma of coffee hit her like a splash of cold water on a hot summer day.

"Not so fast." Ash maneuvered her hand toward a jug of purple Gatorade. "You're going to be dehydrated. You need to drink something other than coffee."

"But I love coffee."

"Too bad. Vamp dries out the organs, no matter how little you've had. You need to recoup what you lost last night."

"But—"

His features twisted, giving her an amused face she thought was meant to be stern.

"Fine, I'll drink the Gatorade."

"Good girl." He stood at the oven, flipping pancakes onto a plate.

A naked back, low-slung shorts on narrow hips, and calves leading to bare feet stared back. Was this his normal "at home" attire? She wanted to kick herself for hoping it was.

He appeared more foreboding, more dangerous, in the light of day. Shoulders exaggerated in size, legs mean and defined, and a tight rear just asking to be grabbed. His butt. Grabbing his butt would be—

He turned with a stack of pancakes in hand. "Hungry?"

"Starving," she said, sweeping her eyes up to meet his. "Is that a side effect too? The munchies?"

He laughed. "Nah. That's just weed. Vamp isn't your first experiment with drugs, I see."

"No, that's not what I meant—" She'd never done any kind of drug before. Not even a puff of a cigarette. She slouched in her chair and tapped her fork on the plate he'd just laid in front of her.

He sat across from her, offering a full view of his bare chest. She did her best not to stare as they ate in companionable silence. They both smiled and chewed, chewed and smiled.

When he glanced down to stab another bite on his plate, her gaze lingered a bit longer, traveling down to his tattoo. An eagle in flight. Its wings spread across the base of his neck, the tips of the feathers reaching up, and the eagle's body rested along the bulge of his pec. The beast's beak opened as if screeching a war cry. Its sharp talons extended toward an unsuspecting prey. Exquisitely drawn in all black, it was strong and menacing. Much like its owner.

Her eyes trailed further across his chest, admiring his spatter of dark hair and heart-shaped pecs. Her eyes caught something unusual on the left side. A small, round scar. Not even an inch and a half in circumference.

A bullet hole.

How had he gotten that? And in such a distinct place— just above his heart.

Ash cleared his throat and shifted in his chair. He stood, the chair skidding a few inches across the floor, and he vanished down the hallway. He was back moments later covered in a T-shirt.

"So," he said, as if he hadn't left, "I've been thinking. You want to go after Heinrich in order to find out what happened to your father. I get that. But, Sam, I can't let you get anywhere near that psychopath." He dropped into his chair and propped an elbow on the table.

"But—"

He held up a hand. "Let me finish."

She debated whether to tell him to go shove it, but her curiosity won out. "Fine. Go ahead."

He nodded as if satisfied by her quick obedience. Ugh. She definitely should have told him to suck it.

"I'll make you a deal," he said. "Remember how I mentioned some of your BPD coworkers were on Heinrich's payroll?"

She gave a small nod. She'd remembered all right. Didn't believe it. But she remembered.

"Well, why don't you see if you can find them? Do a little recon and let me know if anyone's acting out of the ordinary. Or seems to be hiding something. It could lead somewhere big." He leaned in, staring into her eyes. "It could even lead directly to Heinrich himself."

Heinrich? She could definitely live with that. Whether she went back to Club Hell and confronted him there or she found another route, it didn't matter. As long as she found out what happened to Dad. Plus, if she kept Ash happy, giving him some tangible info, then maybe he'd soften and give her something in return. Maybe he'd let her tag along to some meetings with his teammates. It was best to cast a wide net at this point.

Her excitement must have been written all over her face, because his expression changed, and he leaned even farther across the table, his chest hovering over the wood. "But do not, under any circumstances, take matters into your own hands. You come right back here and tell me what you found. Do you understand?"

"Yeah, sure," she said, smiling. Yep. Absolutely. Uh-huh.

He lounged back in his seat, but his expression stayed firm. "I mean it, Sam," he said. "I don't think you're taking Heinrich seriously enough. I know you want to find your father, but don't let that cause you to make stupid decisions."

"Okay, okay," she said. "I got it."

His eyes narrowed, and he waited. Maybe to see if she'd argue some more. But she knew better. Quit while you're ahead. Poker with Grandma Rose and the ladies had at least taught her that.

When she didn't respond, his expression softened and he asked, "So what's on the agenda today? Do you have to work?"

Desperately wanting to invade his privacy and ask about the scar he'd covered up so quickly before, she instead nodded. "Night shift tonight. You?"

"I have some work around here I could do."

She followed his eyes, surveying the room. It was plain and downright masculine. Not even a spice rack on the counter. Just the linoleum floor, a simple table with two chairs, and low-grade appliances. The cabinets were probably bare. The guy obviously didn't ever have guests over. Or hadn't made Baltimore a permanent place of residence. "How long are you here?"

He paused, his expression blank as he finished chewing. "For as long as it takes. A few more weeks probably. Once the assignment is over, I'll be relocated to another city. Another assignment."

A few more weeks. Why did a small pang of unpleasantness jab her heart at the thought?

What did it matter how long he was here? A few weeks, months, or years, she didn't care as long as he helped her find out about Dad.

But where would he go? What would he do? She hardly knew anything about him.

As if reading her mind and wanting to avoid the topic, he asked, "So what should we do today?"

Huh? Now he wanted to hang out? "Look," she began, "I really appreciate what you did for me yesterday."

"I appreciate what you did for me, too."

"I don't want to even think about what would have happened if you hadn't been there."

She thought she heard him groan in agreement.

"But I should get going. My grandma will know I didn't come home last night, and she's probably beside herself right now."

He shook his head. "She knows you're here."

Sam cocked her head, confused. Grandma Rose and the girls went to the church fund-raiser last night.

"The red light," he said, popping another forkful in his mouth. "I thought the same thing about your grandmother worrying, so I looked across the street this morning. The light was still blinking. No one was in the room, but the recorder was definitely still powered on. You should tell them to put something over it. Black electrical tape usually works." His jaw worked as he chewed. "Should be interesting to watch what they captured last night, huh?" Then a mischievous toothless grin slid across his face.

Ah, shit. "Sorry," was all she could say when the rush of embarrassment hit her. She groaned and wanted to drop her head into the plate of remaining syrup when she thought about how Grandma would react when she watched the tape this morning. "We'll stop watching your house. It's not necessary now that we know who you are."

He rested the fork on his plate and eased back in his chair. "I appreciate that. It'll make things easier. Communication with the team, for starters." He smiled into his plate. "My workout routine, for another."

She grimaced as her face heated. And it wasn't because his house was about a thousand degrees.

They again fell into comfortable silence, munching on their pancakes. But silence—no matter how pleasant—was something Sam never could tolerate.

"So when did you join the DEA?"

"Five years ago."

"What did you do before that?"

"Military for ten years."

"Do you like it?"

He shrugged. "Can't complain. I got to see the world while busting bad guys. How about you? You like working for the City Police?"

She mirrored his shrug. "Not my dream job. But I can't complain."

"Really?" He set his fork on the table and clasped his hands in front of him, leaning toward her. "What's your dream job?"

"I don't know." She glanced away, staring at the butcher-block counter.

"Oh, come on. I've seen you high. That makes us friends. And friends talk about this kind of stuff." He gave her an adorable lopsided grin.

She waited, deciding what she'd lose by revealing her secret, and then just said it. "I want to be a cop."

"Then you should do it." Simple and matter of fact. Easy for him to say.

"I can't."

"Why not?"

How could she admit her problem to someone like him? Someone so competent. She took a deep, encouraging breath and then squared her shoulders. "I've taken the police exam six times, and I can't pass it."

"What?" He coughed twice and then cleared his throat. "Is there a certain part that gives you the most trouble?"

"Shooting," she admitted. She traced her fork through the syrup. "I ace the written and physical parts every time, but I can't hit the target to save my life."

Just as she started to regret telling him, Ash surprised her by saying, "Easy to fix."

"You don't understand. I've worked with experts, and it hasn't helped. Actually, I think I'm getting worse."

"You just haven't had the right teacher." He offered a wide smile, showing almost all his teeth. "How's tomorrow?"

"Really? I don't know if—"

"Come on, Samantha. You've proven yourself more than capable."

"But—"

"I could use the practice. Plus, I owe you for saving my life last night."

She glanced down at the oak table. Would it be worth the disappointment? She'd miss. She always did. And it would ruin the rest of her day.

But what if she didn't?

That question hung in the air. A rushing river of emotions coursed through her body, before he added, "It's the least I can do."

• • •

See if anyone's acting suspicious.

It was still hard to believe that any member of the BPD would work for a man like Viktor Heinrich. Especially since most of them knew her father had disappeared. But more because she couldn't understand why anyone would willingly betray his brothers and sisters of the badge. His family.

She breezed down the hallway, past Major Fowler's office, keeping her eyes straight ahead and feet moving. Her eyes slanted to the side, catching Fowler hunched over behind his desk. She kept going. It wasn't that she wasn't allowed in other parts of the precinct, it was that she had no reason to be anywhere but her desk. Her job was simple: sit at the front, answer phones, and log in reports for the major. Nothing that used much brainpower.

She fisted her hands at her sides and picked up the pace. If this little covert assignment would help her find Dad and clear his name, then she'd do it and a hell of a lot more.

The end of the hallway opened into a wide room, desks lined along the walls, beneath windows with large, white slatted blinds. The clamor of phones, footsteps, and chatter filled her ears.

Throwing back her shoulders, she stepped into the room and acted as though she belonged. She scanned the left side of the room, then the right.

She walked the length of the left row of desks, glancing down occasionally to observe what everyone was working on. She peered at the papers on Detective Voight's desk. His dark head was tipped forward, his forehead propped against his hand. He must have sensed her, because his head snapped up, revealing suspicion-filled eyes and a creased forehead.

"What do you want, Harper?" The sleeves of his white dress shirt were cuffed, revealing his thick forearms, which he used to cover most of the report.

She shrugged. "Just checking on something for the Major."

He hitched a thumb over his shoulder. "Well, check on it somewhere else. Some of us have real police work to do."

She ignored the jibe and gave him a brave smile. "Sure, Voight. We've all got important things to do."

He harrumphed and dropped his head forward, ignoring

her.

She continued up the lane to Detective Branham's desk, her cautious footsteps in contradiction with her racing heart. Not that she thought anyone around here would have incriminating information in plain sight, but she could hope.

She sidled up to his workstation and placed her hand on the back of his vacant chair, then leaned in. She retrieved a pen and notepad from the corner of the desk and acted like she was leaving him a note, while gazing across the surface.

A frame with a picture of his wife and kids. A crapload of No. 2 pencils in a mug. And a bunch of standard reports in an orderly stack.

With a finger, she nudged one paper after the other to see what lay beneath each layer. Still standard reports, damn it.

But something caught her attention. Chatter from two detectives in front of her. One was a female she didn't recognize, the other was a veteran cop from her dad's days. Marcus Lyons. She caught him saying "Heinrich" and then some mumbling about "drug testing."

The female said something low Sam didn't catch, then asked Lyons if he knew where.

Sam tilted her head, trying to listen. She kept her eyes down as she scribbled a few circles and squiggly lines on the paper.

"Yeah," he said. "Or at least I think so. Some place in Upper Marlboro. Still trying to find out where. The dicks from the DEA aren't giving me much. Something about us compromising their investigation or some shit."

DEA? Ash's team?

She leaned straight-armed on Branham's desk with her ear pointed at the pair.

The female scoffed and thrust a hand into her pants pocket. "What about—?"

"Harper!"

Sam shot upright and spun toward the voice.

Captain McGrath stood behind her with a scowl on his tanned face. He wore a navy suit with a white shirt and dark-print tie. The jacket was unbuttoned and held open by his hands braced on his hips. "What the hell are you doing back here?"

She twisted to glance around. Heads lifted from their desks and looked at her. So she crossed the room and stopped about a foot from the captain. Her voice was low when she responded. "I'm just checking on something for Major Fowler. No biggie."

His brown eyes creased in the corner as doubt filled his expression. "Checking on what? He didn't tell me he needed anything."

"He didn't want to bother you." She sliced a hand through the air. "It's no big deal, really. I'll just be on my way."

She managed one step before his hand clamped on her upper arm. She looked into McGrath's direct gaze and gave it right back. He wasn't going to intimidate her.

His face lowered so his nose rested an inch from hers. "Get the hell out of my unit," he said in a low voice. "You're distracting my team. Next time Fowler needs something, you can pick up the phone and ask me directly."

Yanking her arm from his grip, she scrunched her expression. "We're all on the same team here, McGrath."

One dark eyebrow lifted into his salt-and-pepper hair. "Not from what I heard," he said.

When she gasped, a tiny smile played at one corner of his mouth. "Back to work, Harper." His long finger pointed to the hallway. "That way."

She tried to act casual so McGrath wouldn't have the satisfaction of knowing he'd gotten to her. Putting one foot in front of the other, she smiled and offered a wave to her coworkers as she passed.

Her plan had been to visit CID—Criminal Investigative Division—next. But, the rest of the day was spent answering calls, dispatching units, and reviewing reports for Major Fowler. McGrath must have said something to Lou about her visit to his unit, because every time Sam got up from her desk to see what else she could learn about Heinrich, Lou popped his head into the hallway to ask where she was headed. There were only so many times she could say *the bathroom* before Lou had suggested Sam leave work early because of "the serious digestive issues" she must have been experiencing.

It sucked because she wanted to find out more about Heinrich, her father, and the drugs, but the early release allowed her to get home, eat, change into a pair of comfy clothes before meeting Ash at the shooting range. She wasn't giving up on her assignment. Not yet. Her coworkers knew more, and she was going to get them to talk.

Chapter Fifteen

"So the first thing to remember when shooting a handgun is how to grip it," Ash spoke. He stood against her back, the heat of her body scorching through her thin cotton top. He didn't need to stand this close. If this had been Calder, Tyke, or Reese, he definitely would've kept his distance. But it was Sam. He needed to be close to her. Needed to know she was safe and within his grasp if shit went haywire.

It drove him crazy how quickly she'd gotten under his skin. Her irrational way of jumping into everything without thinking was dangerous. And exactly what he didn't need given his track record. But damn if he could stay away from her.

His thigh brushed hers. He worked to steady his breathing. Getting an erection right now wouldn't help either of them.

"Most people grab a gun and squeeze the life out of it." He held his own in front of her, gripping it until his knuckles turned white. "This is wrong. And you should always use point index." He stretched his index finger along the frame of the gun. "Never put your finger on the trigger unless you're ready to shoot."

"Got it." She nudged his body away as she positioned herself in modified weaver stance—one foot in front of the other, her dominant arm straight, other arm bent and her weight forward. "I've heard all this before."

He laughed, taken aback by her snappy response. He pressed the button to send the target to the back wall, about seventy-five feet away. "Okay, Ace, show me what you've got, then." He stepped back, readjusting the cover on his ears. "Whenever you're ready," he shouted.

As she'd said, she stood in perfect form. He couldn't find fault in anything she did prior to pulling the trigger.

The *after* was the problem.

Once she'd emptied the bullets from her magazine, he stepped next to her.

He brought the target forward, and they both focused on the body pictured.

Her face said it all—eyes creased and lips pulled down in the corners. Her shoulders had lowered almost to her waist. "See. I told you." She turned away as if she couldn't bear to look at the disgrace.

He'd never seen anything like this in all his years in the military or with the agency. He'd seen people who were horrible shots, missing their targets by miles. But this, he couldn't understand.

He slid an ear free of the cover and waited for her to do the same. Constructive criticism was always best. How to make what she did a positive... "This is definitely a first for me." He scratched his head. "Uh, you did technically hit the target. If he was human, he wouldn't be happy. And if he had a gun, he wouldn't be able to use it against you."

"I shot off his fingers!" She threw her hands up in the air. "His *fingers*! All that big, open space of his chest and I shot his fingers."

Ash wasn't sure he'd be able to shoot off someone's fingers if he tried. With his sniper rifle and plenty of time, yeah. But not with a handgun. "It's pretty remarkable, actually."

She shook her head. "No, it's not. I'm a disgrace. I don't deserve to be a cop."

"You'll get better. We just need to work on it."

"Better? I'm not getting any better. I'm getting *worse!*"

"Do you know how many people in the world can make that shot? A small handful." She scowled, and he rushed to say, "No pun intended. And most of them could only do it once. You did it"—he glanced at the paper to count—"nine times. Really, it's impressive." He wasn't just trying to make her feel better. What she'd done was quite a feat. His body simmered with desire at the thought of this woman making such an impossible shot. Repeatedly. "Can you do it again?"

At her sad blue eyes and jutted bottom lip, he changed his approach.

"Want me to show you? I guarantee I won't be able to do what you just did." Without waiting for her answer, he sent the target to the back wall and placed the cover over his open ear.

"You better not miss on purpose," she said behind him.

Ha. Fat chance. He didn't do anything unless it was all the way. Just because she pouted, didn't mean he'd give in.

Peering through his back sights, he concentrated on the appendages at the target's right side. He took a deep breath, relaxing his body as he'd been trained.

POP. POP. POP. POP. POP.

"Shit," he said under his breath, knowing he didn't even nick the target.

Pulling it forward, he saw he'd managed to clip the target's pinky finger once. The rest of the bullets hit wide right.

He turned toward her with a look that said, *see?*

"Shooting someone's fingers isn't something to brag

about," she said. "I bet if you wanted, you could hit him square in the head, neck, and chest without even blinking."

She was right, but he wasn't going to show her.

"Okay, let's try a shorter distance." He held the button down just long enough to send the target back about ten feet. There's no way she'd miss from this distance. She wouldn't even have to aim.

She glanced down at the pistol in her hand and back up at him.

"Humor me," he said.

She hesitated. "Fine."

Gripping the gun, she raised it. Her shoulders lifted as she inhaled and then exhaled long and slow.

The shot went about six inches wide of the target's throat.

Shaking her head and looking at the ceiling, she said, "I can't even do point shooting." She signaled with the gun at the target—a picture of a man holding a revolver in one hand and the other at his side. "He's only a few feet away for crying out loud."

"Maybe we're going about this all wrong," he said.

She tilted her head. "What do you mean?"

"Well, you obviously know how to shoot. Your form is perfect. Maybe it's not so much mechanical as it is mental."

Holy shit. For once, she didn't comment. Her lips remained in a tight line as she thought over his logic.

"What do you think about before you pull the trigger?" As a sniper, he'd learned more than enough about mental toughness. Sitting alone with only your spotter, sometimes for days, with nothing to do but watch your target. It could make a lesser person crumble from boredom. The key was to keep one's mind clear and ready at all times. Calm breaths and a slow pulse was a sure-fire way to coax the bullet into doing what you wanted.

When she paused a moment longer, he knew she was

holding something back. "I don't know."

"I think you do. Samantha, this is important. Shooting is instinctual. Like baseball pitchers throwing a fastball. After so much practice, they tell their brain to do it and it obeys. They don't over analyze; they don't change their tactics. They just throw. You have to train your brain to listen. Block out everything and do it. Eventually it becomes habit."

"I can't."

He placed his hands on her shoulders and looked her in the eyes. "You can. You need to —"

She pulled away on contact, rolling her shoulders from him. "I can't! I've tried. Okay? It doesn't work. Holding this metal in my hand is terrifying. Yeah, I said it. *Terrifying*. I want to be a cop, and I'm afraid of guns. It's ridiculous. Why do you think I was armed with things like pepper spray and an air horn? Huh? You don't have to be accurate with those, do ya?"

Shit. "I see." Because really, what else could he have said? He blinked a couple times, but nothing ingenious came to mind.

She slammed the gun onto the counter and turned her back on it. "Most of the time I squeeze my eyes closed and just hope I hit the stupid target." She peered over her shoulder at him. "Tell me how safe that is. Who would want to be my partner if they found that out?"

No way was he letting her give up.

He sent the target toward the back wall. "You can do it." He cupped her shoulders and lowered his face to look her in the eyes. "And you will. You can beat this. It's fear, and it's restricting, but that doesn't mean it's debilitating."

She reluctantly allowed him to nudge her shoulders around.

When she faced the target, he slid his hand down her arm, a jolt of energy erupting from the contact. *Calm down*. His right hand covered hers, forcing her to pick up the gun and aim. He slid the cover from her other ear so he could talk to her softly.

"Clear your mind," he whispered into her ear. Her breaths were short and loud, and her hand shook the tiniest bit beneath his hold. He slid his left hand up the length of her side, slowly as not to startle her, resting it over her heart. "Sam, calm down. Your heart's racing. You have to relax." So did he. It took effort to keep his hand pinned against her heart when all it wanted to do was travel two inches lower to those receptive breasts.

"I—I can't," she said.

"Take a few deep breaths. Do it with me." He inhaled two overexaggerated breaths, knowing she'd feel his chest against her back. Her lungs expanded and contracted beneath his palm, her heart rate slowed, and her hand stopped shaking. "Better. Now, close your eyes."

"Close my—?"

"Just do it," he commanded softly.

"I don't see how—"

"Sam."

"Fine."

"Closed?"

She nodded.

"Okay, when I tell you, pull the trigger. Got it?"

She paused, probably ready to argue again, but then she nodded.

"Imagine the target. See the outline of his body." Ash slid his hand away from the gun, up her slender arm toward her bare shoulder. He rested his palm on the thin strap of her top.

"What are you—?"

"Shhh, just relax and picture the target in front of you. Block out everything else." His hands kneaded her shoulders, working loose the knots of anxiety. After a few moments, her shoulders released. He moved lower to the strain in the middle of her back.

"Got your visual?" His fingers pressed deeper, and she made a sound, maybe a sigh. He smiled at the thought of hearing that sound over and over as he pressed deeper and much lower. Without being able to stop, he dropped his mouth to his favorite spot at the back of her neck. At the contact with her soft skin, she sucked in a sharp breath.

His eyes closed, taking in the moment, her body pressed against his, her back to his front. He inhaled, smelling her warm, feminine scent. His lips touched the spot one more time before he whispered, "Pull the trigger."

One shot sounded.

He didn't look, didn't even care to see the path of the bullet. All he noticed were flushed cheeks and gleaming eyes of the woman in his arms as she turned to him.

She smiled, so proud of herself, so sure she'd succeeded this time. He wanted her to be right. Wanted her to feel nothing but happiness from here on out.

When he didn't move, she brought the target forward. Anticipation was so intense it circled them like wild fire.

She turned from him, and he finally dragged his eyes to the target. A single shot through the head, perfectly distanced between both eyes.

He had to clear his throat. Pride in this woman stole his ability to speak. "Nice shot. See, I knew you could do it."

Something stirred deep inside, making him feel stronger, better. He knew Samantha Harper was the reason. His heart beat a bit faster. Nerves and happiness warred for dominance inside him.

What was she doing to him?

He was scared as shit this woman was getting too close. He was letting her.

What would happen if he let her in?

Chapter Sixteen

"Do you want something to drink?" Ash called from the kitchen, his head buried inside his refrigerator. "Don't have much. You have your choice of beer or OJ. Oh, and I've got tap water." He poked his head around the fridge door, giving her a teasing smile. Her heart leaped in response.

"Beer's great, thanks." Sam settled onto his sofa, her legs curled beneath her as if she belonged there.

"I haven't been to the store," he admitted as he entered the living area. He handed her a dark bottle and sat close enough that her body hummed in response. "To the soon-to-be Officer Harper."

She tapped her bottle to his, then placed the bottle to her lips. Joy and nervousness rolled in her stomach.

"I'm proud of you," he said. "You did really well today."

She smiled. "I think it was because I had a good teacher."

They had spent four hours at the range, trying various techniques to improve her shot. Only one method worked. As long as Ash's body pressed flush against hers, his hands caressing her skin, she didn't miss. Once he stepped back and she felt the loss of his touch, she overthought her shots and couldn't hit her target. She hadn't been as disappointed when she missed this time. What mattered was the man sitting next to her.

Ash had been patient and kind as he gave instruction, never once showing sign of frustration or anger. Even when she missed, he'd encourage her to regroup and try again.

She stole a sideways glance at him. His mouth drew her eyes. A shiver ran through her body as she remembered the feel of it pressed against her. She'd like to feel it again right now. Flutters started in her belly and moved lower as she imagined his lips traveling the path the quivers were heading. Light stubble peppered his chin and cheeks, drifting into the hint of sideburns. Tanned skin glowed under the sheen of sweat from their earlier exertions.

He turned, catching her gaze, staring back with pale blue eyes almost the same shade as hers.

"What?" he asked.

She lifted one shoulder. "You."

The corner of his mouth quirked before he took another drink. "What about me?"

"You're not what I expected."

Both corners lifted. "What did you expect?"

"I don't know. Someone more dangerous. Intimidating."

He nearly spit his beer out. A small trail of beer slipped out the side of his mouth, and he swiped the back of his other hand to wipe it away. "And I'm not?"

"Oh, please. " She laughed. "You're far from it."

With a frown, he responded, "Some people would say I'm scary as hell."

"Then they don't know you very well."

He paused, seeming to think that over. "Well you're not what I expected, either."

"Oh, really?" So he was going to play that game. "And

what did you expect?"

His eyes warmed as he gathered his thoughts. "Not you," he said, his face suddenly serious. He stared at her, taking in all of her features at once. From the awed glint in his eyes, he seemed unable to believe the sight.

She shifted from the intensity of his stare. "Well," she said, her face growing warm. "I'm still mad at you for letting that vamp get away. Next one we encounter is mine."

His jaw clenched in an instant. "There won't be a next time."

"What if another one shows up? What am I supposed to do? Call big bad Ash to rescue me?"

He grinned, sitting up straighter. "That's exactly what you should do."

She rolled her eyes and slouched against the back of the sofa, before taking a sip from her beer. "Has anyone ever told you you're conceited?"

"Let me think." He stroked his chin. "Yeah, probably."

"What about overbearing?"

He chuckled. "Yes."

"Egotistical?"

"Sam, they all mean the same thing."

She looked at him pointedly.

"Okay," he conceded, "so we've established I'm arrogant. What about you? You're stubborn and bossy as hell."

Her mouth dropped open. "I'm offended!" She swatted at his shoulder. "I'm only that way around you. Everyone else loves how I am. You seem to bring out the worst in me."

"Right back at you," he said. "Oh, and speaking of stubborn, you need a new car."

"Hey! I love my Honda!"

"Good brand," he agreed. "Not as reliable as a Ford or Dodge, but you're driving it. Not me. Just get a newer one."

"What's wrong with my girl? She's dependable and gets

me where I need to go without any issues." Most of the time.

Ash continued laughing. "What about the smoking engine, grinding gears, and squeaky doors? It's so old I guarantee it doesn't have air conditioning. And I know firsthand it doesn't have power steering."

She didn't have a rebuttal for that.

He gave her his *that's-what-I-thought* look.

"Seriously though. Why the hunk of junk, Sam? I'm sure your job pays you enough to get a newer car."

She took another sip and shook her head. "I don't deserve it. Not yet. Not until I pass."

His face was blank, and then contorted when recognition dawned. "You won't buy a new car until you pass the police exam?"

She nodded.

"Your stubbornness is worse than I thought. It's a disease, really. What if that contraption breaks down?"

"Then I'll fix it." Duh.

"Wouldn't it be easier—and cheaper—to get a new car?"

She shrugged, refusing to give in to his logic. "I don't deserve to."

He shook his head. "You're something else."

Her pulse kicked up. "Something good? Or something bad?"

Grinning, he eyed her a moment without responding. Ugh, it was killing her.

"Good," he finally said. "Frustrating, but good. I don't think I've ever met anyone like you. Samantha Harper, you are one of a kind."

She dropped her gaze, peeling the label off her beer bottle. Her insides shouted in excitement.

"Sam, look at me."

When she didn't move, he placed his hand under her chin and tilted her face up to meet his eyes.

Holding her chin between his thumb and index finger, he gave her that now familiar probing look. "You're hard as nails when you're threatened. Ballsy, even. But the second I compliment you, you back away. Why?"

She shrugged.

"I mean it," he pressed, his eyes darkening. "You're one of a kind."

She tried to drop her head again, but he held her in place.

"Thank you," she murmured. "For everything."

"You're welcome." He nodded, as if supremely satisfied she accepted his compliment.

Keeping her chin in his hold, he searched her eyes once more, giving nothing away as to what he searched for. She hoped when he came back up for air that he wanted whatever he found in her depths. She felt strong and important, higher than when she'd been on Vamp, and sick to her stomach all at the same time.

Only with this man. She'd never experienced it before Ash. She couldn't turn away, didn't want to.

They were drawn together by force. Now connected, they were captive. There was no escape.

His knuckles ran along her cheek, before his palm cupped the side of her face, his thumb caressing. He leaned toward her, his head tilting, eyes focused on her lips.

She moved forward, offering her consent for what she knew they both craved.

His lips brushed hers, softly, naturally. Her eyes closed, and she sighed. It was like free-falling without a chute, but knowing Ash would be there to catch her.

Her hands went around the nape of his neck, holding him in place. The stubble of hair at the base of his neck tickled her fingers. Never had anything felt so good. So right. She smiled against his lips.

"Ash…" She pulled back to see his face.

He met her gaze straight on. He opened his mouth to say something, but his phone buzzed on the table beside them. Ash stilled, and that quickly the moment was over.

He dropped his hand from her face and shifted away. "I-I have work to do. I'm sure you do, too."

"Ash?" Her gut clenched. "Ash, what's wrong?"

When she reached out, he stood and paced in front of the window. Then he turned to her. "I have to make a couple of calls."

Her heart dropped when she caught his meaning. He wanted to be alone.

She got to her feet and placed the empty bottle in the kitchen sink. He continued to pace. She approached and reached out to place her hand on his shoulder. "Ash, if I did anything—"

He spun away before she could touch him. "You didn't. I'm sorry, Sam. I…I shouldn't have…I—I can't do this. It isn't a good idea."

"But—"

"Look, I'm sorry if I gave you the wrong impression. That was a dick move. I didn't mean…I just…you have to go."

She obeyed. At the door, she turned again, imploring him to change his mind.

The muscles in his body remained stiff. His cell phone was already in his hand. He offered her a tight resemblance of a farewell smile.

• • •

Great idea, dickhead. Take her to the range. Hold her body against yours. Imagine what it would be like to let her in. Kiss her. Then kick her ass to the curb.

He raked his fingernails over his buzzed scalp and dropped onto the sofa in the front room. His head fell back, and he closed his eyes. She must think he was mental. He'd felt the attraction. Couldn't ignore it. She felt great in his arms. Right. And her lips pressing against his were like heaven and hell all at once. It made him high, and it made him crazy. It made him want to lay her down on this couch and forget all about his past. About his team. About Heinrich and this goddamn assignment.

And that scared the hell out of him.

Because that was almost the exact thought he'd had with Lorena. They could've made a go of it. Been happy. Lived out the rest of their days lying on a beach somewhere, her beneath him wearing nothing but a smile.

Before she'd shot him, of course.

Nope, he wasn't doing it again. He wasn't going to soften for a woman. Not this time. He didn't give a shit that this one was hard as nails. That she stood toe-to-toe with a Vamper and didn't back down. That despite losing her father she refused to give up hope he was truly gone.

Not. Gonna. Do. It.

But his gut didn't agree. The thing cramped like his appendix was about to burst. He leaped to his feet and searched for his keys. He needed air. Needed to clear his head. Otherwise, he'd walk his sorry ass next door and open up to her like a fucking pussy. He'd spill all his secrets before he could stop himself.

Finding his keys on the kitchen counter, he hustled for the front door. He ripped the thing open, stepped through the doorway, and slammed it shut behind him. Then sprinted down his front steps.

He hit the concrete landing and froze.

There she was. Her lithe body making its way across the street as the sun radiated off her bared skin. Those long legs and arms of hers swishing back and forth on a mission—to get as far away from him as possible.

Good. It was best.

She turned and met his gaze, and even from thirty yards he could see the devastated expression. It nearly brought him to his knees. When an explanation for his actions wormed its way up his throat, nearly choking him, he severed their connection and snapped his gaze to the ground, hauling ass to his truck. He jumped in without a destination in mind. Only to get away as fast as possible.

He'd driven about ten minutes, making his way down the narrow city streets, tailgating anyone who had the nerve to get in his way, when his cell phone rang. Keeping one hand on the wheel, he dug in his pocket with the other.

Ash pressed a button on the screen to place the call on speaker phone. "Yeah."

"What the fuck were you thinking, you stupid, arrogant asshole?"

"I'm not really in the mood for games, Tyke," he said. "Get to the point. What did I do this time?"

"What did you do? I'll tell you exactly what you did," he blasted into the receiver. "How about racking up a body count of more than a hundred people? Let's start with that. You know I'm supposed to take that shit to Landry. And what's that gonna do? It's gonna piss him off, which is only going to prolong this torture. The more you fuck up, the longer I'm stuck being team lead. Jesus, man. Now I gotta cover for you. Get Your shit. Together, Cooper." He grumbled a string of words, huffing gruff breaths into Ash's ear. Ash let him go on, knowing he needed to get it out. When finished, Tyke said, "But you know what? That's not enough. I also have to cover up the fact that you promised that woman your team—a team that's not even yours anymore—would take time from their critical mission of tracking a drug dealer to look for her missing father. How's that?"

"Her father was Baltimore Police, Tyke. He was

working—"

"Undercover, trying to stop Heinrich. Spare me. I know the story. What I want to know is why you're telling her we'll try to find him. You read the file, man. The guy's dead."

"Christ, Tyke." His heart thumped against his ribcage, his fingers tightening on the steering wheel. He jerked the wheel to the right into a lot for an automobile repair shop and threw the truck in park.

"It's in the file, Coop," Tyke said in a calmer voice. "Just repeating what I read. We're taxed already with everything that's going on. Your little episode at Club Hell set us back big-time. We can't risk deviating from the plan. Intel's suggesting the drop's going down within the next two weeks. We need to be ready to move, and that's not gonna happen if we're worried about an ex-undercover cop."

He closed his eyes, then pressed his fingers into his sockets. "Fine."

"But lucky for you," Tyke said in a slick tone. "Calder, Reese, and I know how to multi-task. Must've been something we learned from an old team leader."

A smile slid across Ash's face in response. "What did you get?"

"We think the son of a bitch is actually alive," Tyke said. "But you're not gonna like how."

Chapter Seventeen

What was that? Sam ambled down Ash's front steps, her tennis shoes smacking the cement with each step.

Everything had been going great. They laughed and joked, and then all of a sudden it was as if someone pulled him from a dream and reminded him where he was. *Oh no, that's Samantha Harper. Steer clear of her.*

Sickness filled her stomach, and her heart wanted to rip open. What had she done to turn him away? Had he not felt the pull? That insane attraction? She didn't have much experience with guys, but she'd never experienced something so off-putting. How could she not take it personally? All she'd done was sit there and wait for him to kiss her.

She'd heard around the station that some of those macho-men types liked strong, gutsy women in the bedroom. Ones who gave as much as they got. Was that what Ash wanted? Her to take control? Make the first move as she'd done at Club Hell? He sure as hell reciprocated then.

But wait, had she really done something wrong? He's the one who acted like everything was great and then flipped on her like a switch. *He's* the one with the problem. Maybe he was one of those guys with a relationship phobia.

Ugh, men were so confusing.

One would think working in a male-dominated profession she'd have it figured out.

Grandma Rose opened the front door for Sam. Ash's tires screamed behind her, but she didn't turn to watch him drive away.

"He's not who we think he is," Sam said. "He's DEA and after Viktor Heinrich, too."

She stopped short when she caught the other members of the 19th Street Patrol sitting in the living room, sipping lemonade. They sat next to each other hip-to-hip on the dated velour couch.

"We know," Maybel spoke. "His name is Ashland Cooper. He's deep undercover. We're lucky we got that much."

"But…when…?"

Rose patted Sam's shoulder. "This morning, sweets."

"It's a big relief if you ask me." Maybel lifted the glass to her mouth.

"I told you so," Celia added.

"I knew a man that fine couldn't be bad," Estelle said, fluffing her hair.

"Sam, are you expecting anyone today?" Celia asked, gazing out the front window.

"I don't think so. Why?"

"There's a man walking in your front yard."

The ladies craned their necks to peer out.

A short man in his late thirties with dark features, wearing a bland tan uniform paced in front of Sam's house.

Must be someone from the HVAC company to fix her main air conditioning unit.

"Finally," she breathed. "Took 'em long enough. I can't put up with another night of soaked sheets." She started for the door. "Be right back."

She hopped down her grandmother's cement steps, crossed the street, ready to hug and kiss the wonderful man. Air conditioning! She couldn't believe it. She was going to have working AC. And not a crappy little window unit. A full-fledged full-house unit. Finally.

"Hey there!" She'd be turning the system down to thirty degrees and smiling as frost gathered on her windows tonight.

When she reached the sidewalk on the other side of the street, the man looked up and his eyes widened.

Everything happened in slow motion.

He moved his arm, and she caught a gleam of metal in his waistband.

Gun!

She turned toward Rose's house, spotting the women on the porch.

"No!" She took off in a dead run toward the armed man. "Get inside!" she shouted to the women.

On the sidewalk, his hand at his waistband, he took determined steps toward her. They were a foot apart when he clasped the gun and raised it in her direction. She used her forward momentum to lunge at him and shove his hand upward.

One shot fired into the clouds.

She smashed her right palm up and onto the tip of the man's nose, causing his head to snap back. Gripping his nape, she plunged his head forward, doubling him over, then kneed him in the face.

His hold on the weapon loosened enough for her to disarm him with one twist on the slide. He fell into a heap on the pavement, looking up at her with a stunned expression, blood dripping from his nostrils.

She pulled the slide, ejected the bullet from the chamber, and tossed the gun a few feet away.

Sam turned to make sure Rose and the women were unharmed, but a female shrieked and footsteps stomped behind her. Then an arm clamped around her neck.

He squeezed enough to make her vision darken at the corners. She fought and struggled, no way would she let him win, but he squeezed even tighter. Her feet dangled off the ground, her back plastered against his hard chest. More and more of her eyesight decreased, complete darkness imminent.

She tried to suck in a breath, but all that came was a slow *wheeze*. Her lungs filled like heavy weights, bloating in an effort to conserve whatever oxygen she had left.

Her arms swung wildly around, not hitting anything.

Female voices screamed for her to hold on.

In a final attempt to free herself, she gritted her teeth and threw her fist down like a jackhammer, connecting with the man's balls. His arm slipped enough for her to suck in a quick gasp of air, and her vision cleared.

She prepared to slam her head backward into the man's face, but instead his hold released. A scream sounded as he fell to the ground and shook in intense spasms.

"You okay, sweets?" Rose asked, holding a Taser aimed at the man's back.

Sam nodded, rubbing her neck as she looked around.

Still running on heightened adrenaline, she grabbed the first man's collar and hoisted him into a sitting position on the pavement in front of her house. "Who are you?" She lowered her face toward his. "Why are you here?"

Tires squealed. Her head jerked up. A black sedan barreled down the street, headed straight for her and Rose. The driver stuck a gun out the window in their direction.

"Grandma!" Sam pushed Rose onto Ash's front lawn. Sam hit the concrete sidewalk, her knees dropping first, then her cheek as two rounds went off.

No searing pain, so Sam lifted her head to see the two

injured men leap into the sedan. The scent of burnt rubber wafted through the air as the car sped down 19th Street.

She was sweaty, out of breath, and her knees seethed in pain from their brush with the concrete. Those factors, combined with the fact that someone shot at her grandma, really pissed her off.

Sam turned to Rose. "You okay? Sorry about the spill." She bent to help the older woman to her feet. "At least I pushed you into the grass."

Rose stood, dusting herself off.

Sam turned, making sure her friends were all right. The women scowled. No one came into their neighborhood and threatened one of their own.

"DJR 714," Sam repeated to herself as she and Rose trudged up the porch steps. "DJR 714...DJR 714..."

"Maybel," Sam huffed, grabbing the porch railing for support, "Can you look up a plate?"

The woman had her cell phone up to her ear. "Already on it."

. . .

He sent people after her. Viktor Heinrich sent his men after Sam, and her grandmother could have been injured. Or worse.

Rage and impatience pumped through her veins, filling her insides to the max. Her body vibrated with the need to protect her family. The need to do something to keep them safe. Heinrich had taken her father from her. And he could've taken her grandmother.

Heinrich knew where she lived, and he would try again. She was sure of it. After the death and destruction she'd caused at Club Hell, it seemed Heinrich wanted revenge. She'd been in sticky messes before, but being on a dangerous drug dealer's hit list was about as bad as it got.

Whether her life was in danger or not, her priority was still to find out what happened to her father. To clear his name. Which was why she stood on Ash's front steps, waiting for him to answer the door.

It didn't matter what he thought about her or how he'd treated her before. In fact, he'd made it easier on her. If their kiss had gone any further, had developed into something more, then things would get messy. Feelings would surface and hearts would be on the line. No, she was facing him today because she needed information about her father. So she'd do her part and report back to Ash on what she'd found about suspicious activity within BPD. Anything to get on his good side so he'd help her in return.

She'd knocked twice and raised her hand for a third time, when the door swung open.

Ash appeared, taking up most of the doorway with his large frame. Small streams of afternoon light glittered from the kitchen window behind him, illuminating the outline of his body. The dips and valleys of his shape, his wide shoulders and trim waist. He wore only low-slung workout shorts and a white towel draped over his bare shoulder. His short hair was darker, the droplets of shower water trailing down to his naked chest and abs. Her gaze roamed all the way to his bare toes, and a zing raced up her spine. Why the hell his bare feet did anything to her, she had no idea. Maybe because he was normally so buttoned up, so severe, and his bare feet made him seem approachable. Human.

She brought her attention up to his crossed arms and waiting expression.

"Something I can do for you, Sam?" he asked.

"Yeah," she said, clearing her throat. "I, uh, came to give you an update on my assignment."

He lifted a dark brow, then it dropped and he said, "You mean looking for any dirty cops."

She nodded. "I started in the Narcotics unit, figuring that would be the most likely place. It was, after all, where my father worked."

His posture remained guarded, arms still crossed, weight evenly distributed on both feet. "Find anything?"

"A little." She turned her head to peer down 19th Street and clenched her jaw. "I was interrupted." She brought her attention back to him and said, "But I'm going to try again. You can bet on that."

"Good," he said. "I appreciate the help." He unfolded his arms and braced one hand on the doorframe.

She was ready to ask him about Heinrich's place in Upper Marlboro, the one Lyons mentioned, but he said, "Since you're here, I have something to tell you, too." He glanced to the floor, then his eyes flicked up to meet hers. His body swayed as he shifted his weight from one foot to the other. "Why don't you come inside for a minute?" He gestured with an outstretched arm, his biceps lengthening from the motion, and he followed her into his living room.

She sat on the edge of the couch at a loss over what he had to tell her. When he settled on the opposite end, she turned to face him.

"What is it?"

He didn't meet her stare, choosing to keep his attention on the television. Though given the distant look in his eyes, he didn't seem to be watching it. His jaw worked as if he was trying to form the words.

"It's your father," he said, turning to look at her. "My teammates think they might've found something."

A surge of electricity zapped her body upright. "What? What did they find? Did they find him? Is he all right? Is he—?"

"Calm down, Sam," he said. "While I'm here surveying Heinrich's movements in Baltimore City, the rest of the team is farther south monitoring Heinrich's compound. My teammates think they spotted someone who resembled your father." He stared at her, as if he was unsure what to say next.

"Okay," she said, drawing the syllables out.

He cupped the back of his neck. "This guy, he, uh, works for Heinrich."

"Yeah," she said. "My dad was working for Heinrich undercover."

"No, he *works* for Heinrich. For real. He's the business manager for Heinrich's entire drug operation."

She paused and let what he was suggesting sink in. Her brain seemed to reject what he'd said as the truth, so her only reaction was to repeat his words. "So my dad's there, and he's Heinrich's right hand man."

"It looks that way, but he's going by Jonah Michaels now. Does that name mean anything to you?"

"No." A mammoth headache crept its way into the front of her brain, pounding for a way out. She closed her eyes and rubbed her forehead. "What does that mean?"

"It looks like your father took on another identity when he started working for Heinrich in earnest. That's why there's no record of him in the recent files. It's probably also why the DEA assumes he's dead."

"No," she said, shaking her head. "Impossible. My dad wouldn't do that. He must still be undercover." Which also meant that he was still alive. She could save him.

His eyebrows lifted into his hairline. "And not communicating with his handler?"

"Maybe something happened, and he can't send word."

"It's been a pretty long time with no communication, Sam."

Two long and grueling years. "I don't care. My dad would never work for Heinrich. It's a mistake. What your team saw isn't what's really going on."

"Think about it, Sam. Why would your dad stay there if he didn't want to?"

"Maybe Heinrich's holding him against his will," she said. "Maybe he can't leave. Did your teammates think of that before they started throwing accusations around?"

He laid a hand on her shoulder. "My teammates are expertly trained. They know what they're looking at."

"They're still human. They can make mistakes. And this is definitely a mistake. So you go right back to your team and tell them to reevaluate."

"The evidence doesn't lie. I'm telling you—"

Anger clamped on to her lungs, thrusting her words out like missiles. "No, I'm telling you. They're wrong."

A muscle in his jaw flinched and he said, "They watched Heinrich's business manager physically hurting other people. Does that sound like something your father would do?"

He what? "No," she croaked, hugging her arms around herself. "He wouldn't. Even if he had to. Even if Heinrich held a gun to his head. He wouldn't do it. It's a mistake."

Ash's expression softened, and his fingers tightened on her shoulder. "Or he's not the man you thought he was."

She yanked her shoulders away from him, and his hand fell to his side.

He scrubbed a hand down his face, his skin stretching with the motion. "Look, I only told you to try to spare you. The team's bringing down Heinrich's whole operation. Everyone involved will be indicted. I thought you'd want to hear it now, from me, rather than from someone else afterwards."

She doubled over, shoving her head between her knees. *Concentrate on breathing. In and out. In and out.* The DEA was going to indict her father along with Heinrich. They were going to publically shame him. Put him on display for all his BPD coworkers to ridicule. To laugh in his face and say how they knew all along that Davy Harper was a liar. A cheat.

A dirty cop.

She wouldn't be able prove his innocence. She'd never save him. He'd rot in jail for the rest of his life because of a stupid mix-up that no one seemed to care to clear up. Ash's teammates were so sure it was him. So sure he'd willingly work for Heinrich and hurt other people.

"I want you to be prepared, Sam," he said. "The evidence is pretty damning. For once, BPD seemed to get something right. Your father's dirty."

Breathe. In and out. "How do they know?" She slowly unfolded herself to sit upright. "What exactly did your teammates see him do? Why are they so sure?"

Ash's lips twisted as he seemed to think over what he should say. "He's been keeping people in the cellar and doing things to them."

Her lungs squeezed to the point that pain sliced through her chest. "In the cellar?"

His nostrils flared, and he looked to the ceiling again. When he brought his gaze back to hers, he said, "Yeah. The cellar. He's using Vamp to..." He looked past her like he didn't want to finish.

Detective Lyons' words came back to her with a vengeance.

"Do drug testing?"

Ash's eyes widened before getting control of his reaction. He adjusted himself on the sofa, sitting up straighter, then said, "Where'd you hear that?"

She shrugged. "Something I heard around the station."

"Who did you hear it from?"

She nibbled on her bottom lip. Should she tell him? What if Ash went back to Lyons and told him not to share information with her? Or what if Major Fowler or Captain McGrath found out?

"Who, Sam?" His voice was serious and immediate.

"A detective in Narcotics. I was going to tell you about it, but then you started talking about my dad. He mentioned Heinrich had another place in Upper Marlboro. He didn't call it a compound. But he did say Heinrich was doing drug testing there."

Ash laughed, but it wasn't a happy sound. He looked away and shook his head. "Fucking BPD." He turned back to her and speared her with his gaze. "You don't repeat that to anyone, do you understand?"

She nodded on instinct.

"I'm serious. No one. This is the breakthrough we've been waiting for. We can't risk anyone from Baltimore Police screwing this up. We get one shot at this."

"I understand. But what does this mean for my dad?"

"I'll tell my team to make sure without a doubt that this Jonah guy is your dad."

"So they're not sure? But you just said they were going to indict my dad. Accuse him—"

He cursed under his breath. "They're sure. But if the DEA is gonna indict a Baltimore Police Detective, then we're gonna be one hundred percent before we make public accusations."

"How not sure are they? Because if there's even the slightest doubt, then we need to go check it out right now. Before things get out of control."

"The rest of the team *is* checking it out."

"Well, what are we doing sitting here?" she asked. "We should go help them." She started to stand, but he latched on to her forearm, yanking her back down.

"What the hell's the matter with you?" he asked, his face igniting into a disturbing shade of red. "Do you get off on putting yourself in danger on a daily basis? Are you an adrenaline junkie or something?"

She ripped her arm from his hold. "Of course not. But I'm not someone who sits around waiting for bad people to do bad things. You said my dad's at that compound, so I need to rule out the possibility that he's not being held there against his will. I'm not going to let him be prosecuted with Heinrich and the rest of his goons when I know for a fact he's innocent."

Panic slithered its way through her body, working up her throat. Dad could go to jail. He would be locked away for the rest of the life as a traitor. She needed to get him out of that compound. Needed to save him before Ash's team went in and cleaned house. "When?" she asked. "When is your team going in?" *How much time do I have to save my dad?*

"Whoa, whoa," he said. "I see that look in your eyes. Don't go getting that let's-go-break-down-the-door attitude. I told you, my team's handling it."

"But if Heinrich's taking people against their will and forcing them to take Vamp then we shouldn't wait. We need to—"

"We are. That's what the other guys on my team are doing. They've been watching the compound for a while. But this stuff takes strategy. We need more information. Something solid to nail Heinrich with. Something his lawyers can't get him out of this time."

Frustration bubbled inside her, causing a ragged grunting noise to blow past her lips. "I hate that logic." It made sense, but it still made her angry. People's lives were being ruined. Likely her father's too.

"Just be patient," he said. "I know that's impossible for you, but I need you to do it. The team's going to the compound in two weeks. That's when the next shipment of Vamp is coming. That'll give them plenty of time to investigate whether your father's really working for Heinrich or if he's being forced."

Or enough time for them to condemn him.

If only she could figure out where the damn compound was. She had no idea who Ash's team members were or a way to get in touch with them. But she did have the GPS. She and the ladies stopped monitoring Ash's house, but they never removed the tracker on his truck.

"Are you going?" She tried to sound uninterested, but failed. Especially after he cocked his head to the side and lifted both eyebrows. She shrugged. "What? I'm just trying to figure out the dynamic of your team, that's all."

"The team's making plans to move in and apprehend Heinrich and his supplier, once the supplier shows his face. I won't be at the compound. But if your dad's there, my teammates will report it back."

Her lips thinned, and she nodded. Damn. So he was a part of a team but excluded from the team at the same time.

Arguing was useless. She was stubborn, not stupid. They could spit words back at one another all night, and they still wouldn't see eye to eye. He cared more about his job, where she cared more about her family.

"Fine," she said through a heavy sigh. "I'll sit and behave myself, waiting for your teammates to gather information on my father. It's not something I'm happy about, but I'll do it."

He gave her that skeptical, squinty-eyed expression again, then nodded once. "Good."

It was good. Now she knew where she stood with Ash Cooper. If he wouldn't help her, then she'd go to someone who would. Someone who cared about her father almost as much as she did. Good thing she was due into work in another couple of hours.

She was going to find out where that compound was, and she was going to get her father out of there before the DEA team captured him.

• • •

As usual, Fowler was hunched over his desk, head hung, staring at what looked like a report. Sam knocked on the doorframe of his office and waited for him to look up.

"Sam," he said, smiling. "How's it going?"

"Good, Lou." She sat in the chair across from his desk. "Paperwork's never done, huh?"

He released a small, weary laugh. "Nope. Not as long as there are criminals in my district who think they can get away with anything." He slapped his palm on top of a tall stack of papers on the corner of his desk. "These are ready to be entered into the system." Then he glanced down, scribbling something on the paper in front of him.

She fought back a groan rising in her throat. Yay. More reports.

"Listen, Lou," she said, crossing one leg over the other. "I was wondering if I could ask you something. It's about my dad."

His hand froze, the ballpoint tip resting idle on the paper. After a moment of charged silence, he placed the pen down, and clasped his hands on his desk. "Sure, kid. What is it?"

"It's just, I miss him," she said. "A lot. Every day, in fact. And I know you do, too. I mean, he was your partner for a long time before…" She bit her bottom lip. "Before he went away. And I wanted to know if there was a chance to see him again, if you'd take it."

"Of course," he said with all seriousness. "You already knew that. I'd do anything to have your old man back here, cutting it up with the fellas"—his gaze flitted to the tall stack of reports—"taking over some of this paperwork for me."

She did know that. Which was why she came to him. "What if I told you Dad is still alive?"

Fowler's expression didn't change, he only blinked and his chest rose and fell with each breath. "What are you getting at, Sam?"

"I think I know how to save him. And I need your help to find the location of—"

"No," he said. "No. No. No." It was almost lyrical the way the word came out. "Whatever you have brewing in that stubborn Harper brain of yours, get it out now. Forget about it. We're not going down this road again. Your father's gone, Sam. I know it hurts, but you need to let it rest."

Let it rest? No way, no how. Not until she had closure. Not until she knew once and for all what happened to her father.

"But he isn't," she said, hating the childish whine in her voice. "He's still alive."

"What's your proof?" he asked.

She hesitated. She couldn't tell Lou about Ash and his team. It would ruin their investigation and their chances of nailing Viktor Heinrich. She wanted her father back, but she didn't want a man like Heinrich free on the streets of Baltimore. She trusted Lou, but Ash made it clear BPD can't be involved.

"I can't tell you how I know, but I do. You have to trust me."

Lou closed his eyes, and his lips curled inward so his thick mustache was all that showed. He opened his eyes and leaned across the desk, the corner indenting against his full stomach. "Sam, listen to me very closely. You're not a cop. You can't take the law into your own hands because you have a personal vendetta. We sent men out looking for him. You know we did. But we didn't find anything suggesting he was still there. He's gone."

"But I'm telling you, Lou—"

"No, kid, I'm telling you. Forget it. Don't go out looking for trouble."

Her bottom lip trembled in frustration. If there was one person she thought she could rely on, it was Lou. He'd lost his best friend, his partner. He should be jumping for joy that she came to him with information. He wanted to clear Dad's name as badly as she did. If he wouldn't help her, she didn't know what to do next. Even if she corralled the 19th Street Patrol to help, she still didn't know where the hell Heinrich's compound was. She knew the city, sure. But not the exact location. And it's not like she could stroll up to Detective Lyons and ask him. Even if he knew he wouldn't tell her.

"Your grandma needs you," Fowler said with soft brown eyes squeezing her heart like a vice. "Don't make her lose her son and granddaughter in one lifetime. Go home. Be with her. Take care of each other."

It was slick, but effective. Lou knew exactly where to hit her for the most impact.

She shifted her gaze to the floor beside his desk, glancing at a scuffed tile with a chipped corner. She stared at that imperfection until her insides hollowed and angry tears welled from deep inside, climbing, reaching for a way out. Not today. She blinked a few times and snapped her attention back to her father's oldest friend.

She'd find another way. And she had a hunch her only option was the man next door. He'd given her more information than anyone else so far, so maybe she could sweet-talk him into giving up more.

Chapter Eighteen

Sam carried the deck of cards to her grandmother's dining room and placed it on the antique cherry table. "I don't believe it," she said. "It just doesn't seem right."

Estelle stood at the kitchen counter, craning her neck to peer out the doorway into the dining room. "Sammie, I'm tellin' ya. When a man has an erection, not only does the blood rush downstairs, but all his common sense does, too."

Estelle pulled a bottle of vodka out of the freezer and poured the liquor into her tumbler until it was nearly full, then tipped the bottle again to let another rivulet drizzle out. She reached into the fridge for fresh-squeezed lemonade and splashed about an ounce into her glass. Turning, Estelle joined Sam in the dining room, sipping the concoction and licking her lips. "That's a woman's greatest opportunity. Corner a man when he's got a hard-on, and he'll tell you anything you want. He can't help it."

"I don't know about this," Rose said, taking her seat at the head of the table. She picked up the deck and shuffled the cards as fluidly as a Vegas dealer. "There has to be another option."

Celia was already in her lucky spot, in the chair to Rose's right. She cut the deck when Rose signaled. "I agree. A woman shouldn't have to expose herself in such a way."

"Of course there are other options," Estelle said, dropping into the chair at the opposite end of the table from Rose. "But none as quick and effective."

"I don't know if I can do it," Sam confessed. She sat between Estelle and Celia, leaning against the back of her chair. "What if I screw it up?"

"Screwin' is the main objective here, hon," Estelle said through a grin.

Grandma sent Estelle a disapproving look.

Estelle shrugged. "Do we wanna get Davy outta there or not? My idea is the quickest way. Seduce Ash and get him to give up the info he's got. We find out where the compound is, and we go get Davy."

Sam sighed and rested her hand under her chin. "You make it sound so easy."

Estelle fluffed her medium-length brown hair. "It is."

Grandma Rose remained quiet, her gaze on the table as she dealt cards to each player.

Sam wanted her father home more than anything. She just didn't know if seducing Ash and tricking him into telling her where the compound was located was something she could do. Physically or morally.

Sure, she'd had boyfriends. But sex wasn't something Sam was comfortable with. Or good at. In fact, her ex had commented often how sucky she'd been the few times they'd done it. "I don't know…"

Estelle slapped her cards facedown on the table. "In two weeks, the team's goin' to the compound and arrestin' everyone involved. Isn't that what Ash said?" She looked at Sam for confirmation. When Sam nodded, she said, "We need to find out where. This is our best option. It's gonna take at least that long to plan a strategy to get him out." She took a breath and picked her cards up. "Unless any of you Einsteins have a better idea." She peered over her cards, surveying each woman.

Heads shook in the negative.

"That's what I thought." She placed a one-dollar bill in the center of the table.

Maybel entered the room, carrying a bucket of popcorn. She set it next to Estelle's dollar and then positioned herself in the chair to Rose's left. "I'm with Estelle. We need the information Ashland has. I asked Jackson. He couldn't find anything on a compound in Upper Marlboro." Maybel turned to Estelle and said, "I'll see your one and raise you two." She added three dollars to the pot.

"I'm out." Celia shook her head and placed her cards facedown on the table.

Maybel eyed Sam, who nodded and placed three dollars on the pile.

"We could go to Club Hell. Wait for Heinrich there," Celia said, smoothing the floral tablecloth with her hand. "Make him tell us where his compound is." She gave Sam a sympathetic smile, like she was trying to save Sam from a fate worse than death by offering an alternative to seducing Ash.

Sam shook her head. "Dad was spotted at the compound, not Club Hell. It would be too much work to try to interrogate Heinrich. Besides, he might not even be there."

"Show 'em," Estelle said.

The four players turned their cards over. Rose beat the group with three of a kind.

"Damn," Maybel said.

Sam snapped her fingers in disappointment.

"I still don't like it," Rose said, reaching toward the center of the table and pulling the bills toward her. "You're playing with emotions."

"Emotions won't be a problem if she does it right," Estelle said.

Maybel lifted one eyebrow.

"I'm serious," Estelle pressed. "It's purely physical. No need to get all misty-eyed over it."

Rose began dealing the second hand.

"He doesn't even like me, Grandma," Sam agreed, remembering the way he'd turned away from her. "There's no risk of breaking his heart. I'll just get the info we need and then get out. I don't even have to see him again."

Easy peasy. No problem. If the other women believed she could do it, then Sam did too. She could totally do casual sex without commitment.

Rose stilled with her arm extended but didn't release the card to Sam. She met her granddaughter's gaze and said, "It isn't *his* heart I'm worried about, sweets."

Sam fidgeted under her grandmother's honest stare. She'd be a fool to deny her attraction to Ash. What red-blooded woman wouldn't be attracted to a man like him? But what scared her were the feelings deep inside threatening to come to the surface. Trust, admiration, passion. All qualities to build a relationship on. A strong foundation to be nurtured into deep-rooted feelings of forever. And that couldn't happen.

First, Ash was leaving. When this deal was complete, he'd be relocated to wherever the DEA relocated people after a job well done. Second, he didn't feel the same way about Sam. He'd made it perfectly clear this was a job and Sam was in the way.

Her heart thundered in her chest, roundhouse kicking her ribcage, but she kept her gaze trained on Rose's. "I can do it, Grandma. I can. Don't worry about my heart. It's locked up nice and tight." Yep. Absolutely. Definitely. 100 percent.

Rose hesitated, her expression giving nothing away. Then

her lips thinned, and she dropped the card in front of Sam. "I still don't like it. You're in too deep. I don't want you doing this."

"But Grandma—!"

"No," she said, jolting to her feet. The table rattled from the impact. "It's too complicated. You're going to get hurt."

"I won't," Sam said, desperate. She didn't have anything if she didn't have Rose's support. "I'm telling you. Trust me. I can do it. He's already told me stuff he shouldn't have. What's a little more?"

"And what if more men show up to kill you?" Grandma rounded the table and approached Sam's side. Rose placed her palm on Sam's cheek. "I couldn't bear it, sweets. I couldn't."

The other women at the table didn't interfere, choosing to keep their attention on their cards. The normally raucous room was silent except for the sounds of each woman trying not to pry on the private moment. Estelle's nails tapped the tabletop. Celia shuffled her cards. And Maybel breathed deeply.

"That won't happen. I'm going to—"

"Sam," Rose said. "Viktor Heinrich has already shown how far he's willing to go. Hasn't this family lost enough to him?"

What was she saying? This was all they'd wanted since her father's disappearance. Now they had their chance to find him and Grandma Rose didn't want to see it through? Inconceivable. "But—"

"He can't take you away from me. Not like he did your father." Rose placed her other palm on Sam's face and turned her attention toward her. "You don't understand what it's like to lose a child, sweets. What it does to you. Day in and day out. Knowing there was nothing you could do to stop it. Or bring your baby back."

Sam tore her face out of her grandmother's grasp. "But

I do know what it's like to lose a parent." She picked up her cards and tried to concentrate on her hand, but the damn cards blurred to a mish-mash of red and black.

Rose paused, her hand frozen in midair. Then it dropped, and she stepped away. "You're right. I'm sorry." She retreated to her seat at the head of the table. With her back to Sam and her head dropped forward, she whispered, "It would tear me apart if I lost you, too."

Sam nodded, clenching her jaw to fight the sting of tears. "My thoughts exactly."

Which was why she had to see this plan through. Her father was out there. And she was going to bring him home.

• • •

Strands of loose blond hair danced in the hot breeze across his front window. The owner's trim body stopped at his door.

Don't answer. Don't answer and he wouldn't get tangled in the mess she was sure to put him in. Everything would go as planned: he'd gather more intel on Heinrich, pass the info on to Tyke, get his team back, and then go to Buenos Aires to track down Lorena and her father. Ash could finally go back to the way things were—before Samantha came into his life.

He'd helped Sam shoot, and with more practice, she'd be on the force in no time. They'd both be living their dreams.

But, there she was. On his porch. Turning his insides out and scrambling his head like a goddamn blender, not allowing him to form a rational thought. On more than one occasion, he'd thought blowing this mission and being marooned in Baltimore wouldn't be such a bad thing.

But he knew it was.

A knock came at the door.

"Just ignore her." He kept his gaze fixed on the O's game and took a long gulp of Natty Boh. "Ignore her and she'll go away."

Knock, knock, knock. "I know you're home," she shouted.

He sighed. "Who am I kidding?" Ash stood and opened the door, keeping his arm across the entryway so she didn't take it as an invite.

"Hi-ya." She smiled.

At the sight of her pink lips, hair down, and bare shoulders, his heart beat a few thumps out of sync. She was in another one of her tiny spaghetti-strap tank tops. The hot weather in Baltimore was a fantastic thing. The small crease peeking above the top of her shirt highlighted where her petite breasts nestled. He gave silent thanks he hadn't been on assignment during the dead of winter. All conviction to avoid her flew out the window.

"Samantha," he said, dropping his gaze to the floor. He immediately regretted it when he got a front-row view of her long, lean legs. A man could get lost between those legs.

She stepped forward. "Can I come in?"

God, I want you to. But he remained in place. "I'm kinda busy today, what do you need?" *That's it. Remain strong. Don't let her in. It's just cleavage. They're just legs. Every woman has them. Don't be fooled. Once you let her into your house, then you'll let her into your heart. Just like you did with Lorena.*

He growled.

"Are you okay?" Sam stepped back as if he looked ready to puke on her sandals.

"I'm fine," he recovered. "Just tired. What did you need?"

"Oh, right." Her features relaxed, and she looked down at the items in her hand. "Grandma and the girls wanted me to bring some food over as thanks for"—she cleared her throat—"helping me lately. You know…with my little trip and shooting and all."

"I see. Well, tell them thank you." He reached out to take the containers from her.

She pulled back. "Can't I at least come in and have a bite, too?" She flashed a sweet, but cunning smile. "Please?"

Damn, she was good. When she popped the lid and raised the container to his nose, his stomach lurched in joy. The scent of garlic and spices lifted into the air like perfume. Women and food were two things he never could refuse.

He shifted. "Come in." *Weakling*.

Making herself at home, she carried the containers into the kitchen, opened each one, and then offered him a full plate.

Once seated on his worn sofa, plates in hand, her body close to his, she spoke over the sound of the ballgame in the background.

"There was a short dark-haired man walking around outside the other day. You wouldn't have seen him since you weren't home. I thought he was here to fix my AC. It's been out for weeks…"

He scooped a large spoonful of lasagna into his mouth, half-listening as the incredible flavors invaded his taste buds.

"I've been calling and calling, but no one at the HVAC company seems to care. I thought they finally sent someone today…"

He doubled the helping of food on his fork this time, shoveling a huge amount into his eager mouth. He hadn't eaten this well since he lived back home, before he joined the military.

He wasn't making much sense of what she was saying. All he'd gathered was that someone came to fix her broken AC unit. Maybe he could give them a call to fix his, too.

When they finished eating, Sam took their plates into the kitchen and returned a moment later. She settled beside him again, but this time she turned to face him. He didn't miss— nor mind—the seemingly deliberate press of her breasts to his shoulder.

"Sam. What are you doing?"

Her arm went around his shoulders and her hand skirted under the neckline of his T-shirt. The soft skin of her palm burned like fire as her fingers played with the hair on his chest. He was stunned—baffled, even—by the quick turn of events.

His body came alive at her touch, surging and simmering beneath the surface as if charged with electricity. He closed his eyes and pictured her naked, begging him to do whatever he wanted.

Her lips were at his ear, her breathing ragged, when she whispered, "So I've been thinking…"

"Mmm-hmm." So had he. A firm image of her hand stroking his length came back to him. His shorts tightened in anticipation.

He'd been more frustrated in the past few days than he'd ever been in his life. This woman drove him insane. Just one press of her willing body was enough to make him want to agree to anything. No questions asked.

What about Lorena? his subconscious asked. *Forget about her already?* She pretended to love him and then shot him. His hopes, his dreams, his love—all of it gone with one single bullet.

But Sam seemed different. He didn't even think the woman knew what the word betrayal meant. Could he trust his gut?

"Sam." He placed his hands on her shoulders, nudging her away.

She pushed forward, landing a kiss on his ear and running her tongue along the lobe.

"Sam," he gritted out.

"Mmm, Ash, you taste so good. I think I need another bite." She slid her tongue along his jawline, nipping and purring.

His eyes closed as a stream of scorching lava shot from his

neck straight to his cock.

He was done. He could take caning across his bare back or bamboo under his fingernails, but he sure as hell didn't stand a chance against this kind of torture. A man's resolve was only so strong against a woman like Sam.

Telling his subconscious to take a hike, he hitched her leg over his lap. She drew a quick breath, but then settled astride him as if her body was made to fit his. Her legs cradled his thighs, and the center of her heat married flawlessly over his growing erection.

Imagining what it would feel like to be buried deep inside her, he shifted to encourage more friction. Her body went rigid, her spine as straight as a damn board, then she relaxed and trailed her hands along every piece of his available skin. Up under his sleeve to his biceps, where she squeezed the muscles; across his chest and stomach; his back. The impression of her touch lasted even after her hands moved on to their next location.

His shirt was off in seconds, and he was doing his damnedest to remove hers just as quickly. Would she be upset if he ripped it from her body? It was a mere scrap of fabric anyway.

She breathed a path of hungry kisses down his neck and chest. "As I was saying, there was this guy—"

When he unlatched her bra, her breath hitched. Damn. What other noises could he coax from her?

"You're sexy as hell, you know that?" He tossed the garment behind him. "And you're going to be so fucking delicious." He took one of her taut buds into his mouth, licking and sucking like a kid with a lollipop in a race to reach the creamy center.

"Ash," she breathed, gripping hard to his neck, her back arching. "Oh God, Ash."

He chuckled under his breath. He loved a vocal woman.

Had his hair been longer, she would have ripped it out by now. He'd have to give considerable thought to letting it grow.

"Ash, I want to…I came to…"

"Me too," he said, bringing her mouth to his. "Me too."

He devoured her, licking and sucking, taking her lush lips hostage. Christ, she tasted good. It was a mix of lasagna and a flavor purely her. His heart rate picked up when he skimmed his tongue along the bottom edge of her nipple. She shivered in his arms.

"…talk to you," she tried again.

He grasped her breasts, their slight weight cradled in his palms, and ran his thumb over the wet tips.

When he lifted her hair and kissed along her neck, her head fell back, giving him greater access. Heavy moans replaced her words. His nose nuzzled her throat. Breathing in her invigorating female scent, it made him crazed with lust and wanting her. His tongue came out and tasted the soft skin on her neck. His blood boiled.

His free hand gripped her waist so she couldn't escape. She was his prisoner and he was determined to make her want more. With his mouth, hands, and body, she'd know just how badly he wanted her. Needed her. It consumed him.

"Can I—?" she tried to speak again.

"Whatever it is—yes. *Yes, Samantha, yes.*"

She didn't say anything else once he stood, her legs wrapped like a clamp around him, and hurried toward the stairs. Ash wasn't sure he'd make it as far as the bedroom, but he was for damn sure going to try.

Chapter Nineteen

Is this what heaven feels like?

Ash grabbed and pulled at her, reaching for anything he could stick in his mouth. She helped by bending and contorting her body.

The sensations shot through her like fireworks. Damn the cliché. Truly, she had fireworks exploding inside her, stretching, expanding, and rushing to be released. They sizzled in her belly and then blasted to her heart, down her arms and legs, and especially in the crux of her sweet spot, where the sensations began to build again. She had no idea her body could feel like this.

Good Lord, the man had magic hands, eyes, mouth—everything worked in tandem to ignite her most elemental flame. She wasn't sure how much more she could take.

Her purpose for seducing him was…

Wait, what was it?

She couldn't think of anything but getting this man inside her. Which was not at all supposed to be the plan. Moisture pooled between her legs with each touch. The evidence of his arousal pressed against that moisture, calling to it, welcoming it home. It felt normal. Natural. Not at all like Estelle said it would. No feelings or emotions—that was supposed to be the plan. But something deep inside needed him. A burning she'd never felt before.

He guided Sam down on the bed and hovered above her, his gaze thoughtful as he studied her. A wonderfully playful curve appeared on his lips. It seemed to promise more enjoyment. And she was A-okay with that.

When he unbuttoned her shorts, it came to her: *Seduce him so he'd tell her the location of Heinrich's compound.*

Estelle taught her the fine art of seducing a man, but she never told Sam how to ensure she wouldn't lose her own brains in the process.

Yowsa. She was in big trouble. If he managed to remove her shorts, there would be only one thin layer between her sanity and oblivion. Her cotton panties weren't going to withstand his raw power.

"Goddamn, I want you," he said through a heavy breath. "So fucking bad."

Yep, definitely big trouble…

"Like no one else. You hear me? No one else, Sam."

His lips pressed against her stomach, crossing the sensitive skin of her abdomen. She giggled at the soft, ticklish touch. His hands roamed, kneading her breasts and butt. She squirmed and wiggled, melting with every touch.

He tugged her shorts down, down, down…

And they were off.

She was screwed.

Or at least she would be in about five minutes.

There was no way she was going to regain control of this situation. She craved his touch too much.

Hungry eyes stared into hers as if she was the only woman he had ever looked at that way.

Something changed. A charged connection that hadn't been in the room minutes ago. There was no hesitation between them. No inhibitions. Her body thrummed in anticipation of what his look meant.

"I'm gonna make you feel so good," he promised. "Will you let me do that?"

She nodded again, like a moronic bobblehead. Man, what he was doing to her.

His gaze went to her breasts. "So perfect." He cupped one and then the other. She resisted the urge to turn away. To cover herself. With him, she wasn't self-conscious. She was beautiful.

When his hand traveled between her thighs and slipped beneath her panties, her heart stopped. He placed his warm fingers on her. *Holy hell.* She was supposed to be the one in control. The one doing the touching. But her brain didn't seem to want to get with the program. And her body smirked in response.

"Shit, Sam, you're so wet." He closed his eyes, the corners crinkling in approval. "I love how receptive your body is to everything I do. Let's see what happens when I—" He slid one finger inside.

She damn near catapulted off the bed.

His grin was enormous.

"Ash," she moaned.

"Tell me."

"I…I…" God, he felt amazing.

"You what?" His grin widened, his blue eyes sparkling.

She squirmed and twisted under his touch. It was impossible to talk. At this point, she didn't know what she wanted. She came here with a purpose, but now she wanted nothing more than for him to continue his ministrations on her body.

His fingers retreated and his gaze met hers. Without his

hands on her body, her heart returned to a more regular pace and she could think clearly, and breathe easier.

She reached out to brush away a tiny bead of sweat from his brow. Her eyes met his and held. It gave her a surge of confidence.

With little effort, she pushed against his shoulders, flipping him onto his back. Straddling his hips, she tortured him with her mouth. Following his example from earlier, she pressed her mouth all over his chest and stomach. Loose tendrils of her hair brushed his naked skin, his muscles rippling in response. His diaphragm rose and fell with each breath, and she rode the wave with pleasure.

He moaned deep in his throat, confirming that this brute man wanted a pushy woman in his bed.

She bit and sucked on his lower lip. Domination was euphoric. He was hers for the taking. Boldly, and not knowing where it came from, she slid her fabric-covered folds against his shorts-covered rock-hard length. His eyes darkened. Excitement. Intensity. Anticipation. And she was the cause. Her pulse raced in response. Dying to extend this power, she took one of his nipples into her mouth and nipped with her teeth.

He sucked in a sharp breath. "Jesus, Sam. What are you doing to me?" It was his turn to squirm.

Grinning, she dragged her tongue down the center of his chest. He tasted even better than she'd imagined. His stiffness pressed against her body as her mouth traveled toward it.

Loud and ragged breaths erupted from his lungs, speeding up with each movement she made. His hands pressed against her back, holding her against him.

She kissed his stomach and slipped her fingers inside the waistband of his pants. Pausing, she met his eyes, increasing the suspense. Dominance over this man had gone to her head.

"*Now*, woman!" Ash cried out. "What are you waiting

for?"

She couldn't suppress the chuckle bubbling up. He was putty in her hands. Well, most of him. The important part strained against his shorts, screaming for release. Estelle was right. Sam seemed to have the power to make Ash do whatever she wanted.

As she pulled his shorts down, she spoke in a soft voice, "Ash?"

"Yes." The sound rumbled from deep in his chest.

"How do you feel?" His shorts were off. She placed a kiss on each muscle of his chest, and then dipped her fingers into his waistband.

His head lifted from the mattress, and his breathing stopped for a brief second. His gaze sharpened on hers. "Frustrated. Horny as hell. Why? How should I feel?"

She needed him crazed with need before she could accomplish what she came to do. Currently, he seemed too with it.

"You need to relax," she said in a soothing tone, circling a nipple with her finger. "Let me do all the work."

He shook his head. "Sorry, babe, that's not how this works. I'm always an active participant. Always. Most of the fun is knowing I got you off." He started to sit up, probably to take the foreplay reins, but she shoved him back against the mattress.

Surprise flashed in his eyes, then hunger.

Yeah, he definitely liked pushy women.

"Just lie back and enjoy," she said.

He laced his fingers behind his head, his biceps flexing.

Her fingers glided along the elastic of his boxer briefs one final time. One yank and he'd be bared to her. Once she let the tiger out of its cage, she'd have no way of taming it. He would take her, and she wouldn't try to stop him.

She wanted this. She wanted Ash to make love to her.

Only he would satisfy her body's cravings.

Slipping her hand under his waistband, she closed it around his bare flesh. His moan and closed eyes only encouraged her. She began to slide her hand up and down the silky shaft in a steady rhythm, eliciting additional moans.

Her tongue darted out to moisten her lips as she thought about Estelle's lesson. She had to get it just right. This was crucial.

"Ash?"

His body appeared so relaxed he could be asleep—eyes closed, hands locked behind his head, his muscles at ease. "Mmm-hmm," he murmured.

She tightened her grip. *Up and down. Up and down.* Then, as she gathered her thoughts, ready to broach the subject, his eyes snapped open. Those baby blues flashed and a growl erupted from his lungs.

Oomph.

That quickly she was on her back, looking up at a very turned-on male. His face was red, which was funny since all the blood in his body was supposed to be somewhere else. His muscles were taut and spine straight. His nostrils flared with each breath, the warm draft blowing against her already heated skin.

He was untamed. Wild. And all because of her.

"I can't stand not touching you," he said. "I thought I could, but it's not possible." He leaned back and looked down at her, his gaze roaming her body. He shook his head. "Yeah, I definitely can't keep my hands off you." No sooner had he said it than one of them stroked down from her throat and cupped her breast. With rough fingers, he teased the nipple, coaxing it to attention.

Pleasure ripped through her.

So much for keeping emotions out of it. So much for locking her heart up. She wanted this. All of it.

What about your mission? What you came to do? It was a fleeting thought, passing out of her brain just as fast as it came in. At the moment she was having difficulty holding on to any single thought. She'd badly underestimated Ash and his ability to hold her in his arms and make her feel like the only woman who'd ever matter. His ability to make her body come alive under his touch and yearn for more.

She'd underestimated the depth of her feelings for him.

"Say it, Sam. If you don't want this, now's the time to speak up."

Say it. You're in way over your head. Say it, Sam.

When she didn't say anything, he paused, hand still on her breast. "I need to hear it. That you're into this, too. That it's not just me." A hint of vulnerability crept into his face, and it pulled at her. "Please tell me it's not just me."

It wasn't. It couldn't be. Not with a man like Ash. A protector. Enforcer. Lover.

No hesitation at all, she nodded. "Please. I want this. I want you."

A quick rush of air escaped his lips before he slid off her to remove his bottoms. Her panties skated down her legs just as fast. He rolled on a condom, then crawled back onto the bed and positioned himself over her. His straining arms bracketed her head. His hips tilted forward and stiff pressure nudged against her opening. He stared into her eyes with an expression so open she almost gasped. He was bared to her. His tough-guy armor stripped away. She cupped his cheek as her lips lifted into a soft smile. He was vulnerable. It didn't happen often. He didn't let his guard down for just anyone. He trusted her. That realization alone was enough to send her flying. But then he pressed his hips forward, nudging in and out. By the third time he was halfway in.

She gritted her teeth in frustration and opened her legs wider, urging him on. *Just a little farther.*

His head tipped forward, his forehead resting on hers. "Christ, Sam," he mumbled, eyes closed. "It's like you're squeezing the goddamn life out of me." The muscles in his shoulders bunched as his body shook slightly. He was holding back. Fighting the urge to drive into her.

She shifted, twisting her hips enough for him to slide to the hilt.

They both stilled and released a long, slow exhale, taking in the delicious feeling of his body joined with hers.

He lifted his head and opened his eyes. Holding her gaze, he began to move. Slowly, carefully he pulled his hips back, then glided forward.

Her body responded, following his lead, answering every swivel of his hips with one of her own. Warmth sparked and spread through her lower abdomen, filling her with need. Desire ignited so strong and demanding she might never find relief, at least until he gave her more. Until he pushed her body to its limit.

"Ash, that's…that's so…"

"I know," he murmured. "Jesus Christ, I know." He gripped her backside, which forced her left leg higher, creating a whole new angle for him to explore. He must have sensed the change, the possibility, because his eyes widened. He pulled back almost enough to pull completely out, then he thrust forward in one quick motion. Pulled back. Thrust forward. And again. Each time harder than the last. He increased his hold, his fingernails piercing her skin.

"You have no idea what you do to me, Sam," he rasped. "No fucking idea. None."

She was getting the idea, because he did the same thing to her. She arched her back, begging for more. Her insides clenched in an attempt to keep him inside. To prolong the exquisite torture.

But he kept up his motion, assaulting every last shred of

willpower she had to regain control. He was possessing her, forcing her to his will. And she reveled in it.

"Shit," he said. "Tell me you're getting close. I wanna hold off, but—"

She raked her fingernails down his back, scoring his naked skin.

A rough groan rumbled from his chest. "Fuck. Yeah, tell me what you need. Right. Now."

She wrapped her legs around him, hooking her feet behind his back. Heat exploded inside her. The uphill climb came quick, building and ready for release. "Nothing," she said, panting. "Just. Don't. Stop."

"No way that's happening," he said through a choked laugh.

He was getting close. His body enveloped hers like a steel cocoon. He increased speed. "That's it," he said. "I can't—I'm going to—"

"Me too," she said. "I'm right there."

She barely finished her statement before she exploded, crying out. He groaned and his head fell forward. Heavy breaths blew against her ear.

"That was..." she started. *Incredible? Amazing? More than she ever could've imagined?*

"Yeah," he said. "It was."

Chapter Twenty

They lay in each other's arms for what seemed like hours. It might have been minutes. It might have been days. Happiness was funny that way. It stretched everything around you into endless contentment where you had no concept of the outside world. And that's exactly what she'd needed. To forget about what she'd lost. What she still might lose. Or at least *who* she might lose. In Ash's arms, she let go. It was the escape she craved in order to regain her strength. To regroup and plan her way forward. She was stronger with him by her side.

But she'd come here with a purpose. She was never going to find her father if she didn't convince Ash to tell her where he was. And she'd never get the answers if she didn't reclaim some of the ground she'd lost. It was time to take back control.

With her head on his shoulder, her leg kicked over his, she played with the soft hair on his chest until he opened his eyes and looked at her.

"So, I've been thinking," she said.

He grinned. God, that mouth curled like that. She was ready for round two seeing the damn thing. "Me too." His hand trailed down her back and over her hip, nudging her leg farther over his, and urging her on top of him.

Her body melded closer to his, holding on to the last few moments of bliss, because she was about to sever it. "Not about that."

"Why not?" He nuzzled his face in the soft spot under her ear. Warm wetness flicked against her skin, sending a jolt of white-hot desire through her.

Concentrate, Sam. Forget what his body feels like against yours. How good it feels to move in rhythm with his.

She gave his shoulder a weak swat, but thankfully he laughed, breaking the tension. She slid away from him, creating enough space to think straight.

His head cocked to the side and eyebrows gathered in the center of his forehead. Before he could question her actions, she said, "You remember how I told you about the dark-haired man in my front yard the other day?"

Ash's eyes slid closed, and he nodded.

"Well, I figure now we really don't have a choice." She inhaled a slow breath, giving her brain a second to formulate the words. "How about you tell me where Viktor Heinrich's compound is."

Ash sputtered and coughed, his eyes snapping open to reveal a haze of fury. "Absolutely not. I know what you're thinking and the answer is no."

So apparently Estelle was wrong—some men *can* think about two things at once.

"Come on, Ash." She sat up and folded her legs into her chest. "It's important to me."

He sat up and leaned against the headboard. "Sam, I told you—"

She raised her hand to stop him. "I know what you said. Just hear me out."

He made the mistake of catching his breath. She used the

pause to continue.

"Things are different than they were when you originally told me to butt out."

His skeptical expression was back. "Different how?"

"Some of Heinrich's people came to my house and fired off a few rounds." She sent him a look of, *Duh*.

"*What*?" he roared.

Completely undeterred by his outburst, she placed her hand on her hip. "Did you hear anything I said about the dark-haired guy?" She thought he'd taken it a little too well when she recounted the story over lasagna. She didn't realize he hadn't been listening.

Either not hearing her query or choosing to ignore it, he said, "This is exactly why I told you to stay out of it. This is *my* case, therefore it's *my* concern. Not yours."

"But you said it wasn't *your* case, it's another team's case."

A mask of crimson overtook his face. It was nothing like the lust-induced shade of red he'd been sporting earlier. This color boiled under his skin, making him seem ready to explode. His chest rose and fell in exaggerated heaves, his nostrils flaring with every breath.

Obviously a sore subject. She backed away, hugging her legs. "Ash, I'm…I'm sorry. I just thought…I thought since it wasn't technically your case that I could…you'd let me…"

"Let you what?" He smacked his flat palm onto the mattress. "Tag along? Are you fucking kidding me? You're a civilian, Sam. You, of all people, know I can't do that."

"Yes, you can. I'm involved now. Just tell me the location and—"

"The location?" An evil bark of laughter erupted. "You're out of your goddamn mind if you think I'm telling you the location of that compound. And you're *involved* because you showed up at Club Hell—like you weren't supposed to—and caused a fucking scene."

"Caused a scene?" How dare he throw that on her! "I don't remember being the one thrown out the back door and pummeled by a bunch of Germans on steroids!"

His gaze turned to the nearby window. "And now Heinrich knows who you are, and he's coming after you." He skimmed a hand over his short hair before leaping off the bed. He snatched his shorts from the bed and yanked them on before pacing the room. "They shot at you! Jesus Christ, Sam, they *shot* at you!" He stopped and stared at her from head to toe, as if to assure himself she was unharmed. Once satisfied she was, he continued, "I told you to stay out of it." He rubbed his neck. "How in the hell am I going to protect you now? What if they come back?"

Touching, but an unneeded gesture. "I can take care of myself, Ash."

Like a cat pouncing on its prey, he leaped at her.

She fell, her back landing on the mattress in a *whoosh*. His hands claimed space on both sides of her head, caging her in. His naked chest was only inches above hers. She gripped the bed sheets so she wouldn't reach for him, her fingers throbbing from the strain. Something about his intensity in trying to protect her fueled her heated blood.

She arched slightly...

Her nipples ached, crying out for more attention. His heat, his strength, everything drew her to him. Her arms moved by their own volition, wrapping around his waist, drawing him down. When he collapsed on top of her, the span of his bare body against hers, moisture gathered once again between her legs. Definitely ready for round two.

"You don't know who you're dealing with," he said in a challenging tone, his eyes never leaving hers.

She gave him the sinful smile she'd practiced. Her fingers stroked his back, the striations of muscle jumping beneath her touch. "I know exactly who I'm dealing with, Ash."

He looked down at their position. "Damn it, woman!" He propelled himself off the bed and toward the window. "This is serious, Sam. Stop touching me like that."

She followed him. "Like what?" Clasping her arms around his waist, her cheek pressed against his back, his abdomen muscles clenched. Now that she'd had a taste of how to harness his lust, she couldn't get enough. If she broke the connection, she feared she'd lose it forever. Having the carnal power of a man like Ash at her disposal was more than heady. It was incredible. She wanted him to break free. Throw her down and take her with all the enraged passion he possessed.

He groaned. "That." Turning, he removed her hands and held them firmly at her side. "I'm sure you've noticed, but I can't think straight when you do that. Please. Stop."

She grinned.

He looked down, his line of sight directed at her breasts. "Christ, cover yourself!" He faced the window, grumbling.

She did some grumbling of her own. "You're the one who undressed me." She grabbed a worn-out white T-shirt from the nearby chair and pulled it over her head. The hem brushed against the top of her thighs. "Happy?"

"Yes." He breathed a sigh of relief. "Now what were we talking about?"

She lifted her hand toward him.

He jumped back about ten feet. "Don't."

"Fine." She raised her arms in surrender. "You think you need to protect me. And I said you don't."

"These people are dangerous, Sam."

"I realize that now. But I can't sit around and do nothing. This is the closest I've come to getting real answers about what happened to my dad. I need to see this through. I need to save him."

"I get that, but—" He froze, his gaze on her sharp as razors. "Did you...when you came over with that food, did you do it on purpose? Did you sleep with me so I'd tell you where the compound was?"

Shit. Shit, shit, shit. She swallowed the enormous ball in her throat. That was the intention, yes. But it wasn't what happened.

Her silence must have given him the answer he wanted. "You're unbelievable, you know that? Un-fucking-believable."

"Ash, wait. I—" She reached for him, but he spun away from her.

"Don't touch me."

"That's not what happened. It wasn't. I swear."

"Oh really?" He let out a dark laugh. "Tell me how it was then. 'Cause from where I'm standing that's exactly what it looks like. You fucked me to get what you want."

She recoiled from his words. He was technically right, but she hadn't planned to go through with it. She was only going to push him far enough to get the information she needed. But she'd botched it big-time. She'd let her emotions run away with her, and she'd given in to the need still coursing through her body.

"Ash, please," she said. "I'm sorry. That wasn't supposed to happen."

"What? So now sleeping with me was a mistake?" He tossed his hands in the air. "That's even better. Keep going, Sam. I don't think you pierced my heart yet."

"I'm sorry," she said. "I'll say it a million times if you need me to. But you don't understand how much this means to me. I'll do whatever I have to do to find my dad."

He shook his head again, still not looking at her. "I thought we might've had something. That maybe you felt it, too. But as usual, I don't know shit about women. No, scratch that," he said, meeting her gaze, "I know you're all the same. Lying and conniving and you only care about yourselves. You know what? Whatever. Just tell me what happened. When they came after you."

She paused, deciding whether to give him *all* the details. When he gave her a severe look, she said, "I disarmed the first guy, and Grandma shot the second with a Taser."

His eyes darkened. "There were two?"

"Three, actually. The driver had a gun, too."

A muscle in his cheek ticked.

At least he wasn't scolding her. "Grandma and the girls—"

He looked at the ceiling as he paced the room again.

"—did some recon, and they think—"

"They *think*?" Ash turned on her, giving her a look that made cold currents rush through her veins. The pool between her legs dried up instantly. "No. No. No! What part of 'don't get involved' made you think you could invite the Granny Squad?"

Her insides lit up. "Does that mean I can help? As long as I don't bring them?"

"Oh, no you don't." He shook his head from side to side as if watching a game of table tennis at supersonic speed. "Don't try to turn my words around. This is official law enforcement business. You're a civilian, Sam. You're obviously not a cop—"

That hurt. A lead ball dropped into her stomach, making the food she'd eaten slosh and rise back up her esophagus. Her eyes filled with tears. She held them at bay, but the stupid things pooled, ready to spill over. She wanted to be brave, but it stung too much. After everything she'd learned over the last week or so, she was lucky she hadn't broken down earlier. She turned away as one stupid tear broke loose.

"Damn it," he said through a sigh. "Sam, I didn't mean—" He closed the distance between them in two strides. His hands clamped on her shoulders. "I didn't mean it like that. Oh Christ, you're crying." He swiped a hand over his scalp again. "Please don't cry, Sam. I'm sorry. I just meant—"

"You're right." She shrugged him off. "I'm not a cop."

She bent to pick up her clothes from the floor. Once she buttoned her shorts, she stepped toward the door. "I'm sorry for bothering you."

"Sam, don't go. I—"

"It's fine," she spoke over her shoulder. "Just like you said, I'm obviously not cut out to be a cop."

He was at her side in an instant. "I didn't say that and you know it." He might as well have. Stupid, stupid woman for letting her emotions take over. For trusting him.

She laughed, but it lacked the emotion to make it a happy gesture. "I gotta go. Early day tomorrow."

"Sam, please. Can't we talk about this?"

"What is there to talk about? You obviously don't see how important this is to me." She stepped into the hallway.

He wasn't the man she'd hoped he was.

• • •

Damn it, he had to make this right.

"Sam, I never said that," he said, chasing her down the hall. The wooden floorboards creaked beneath his bare feet. She neared the top of the stairs when he said, "Are you listening to me? I think you'd make a hell of a cop. You want to know why?"

She paused, her eyes slanting once in his direction.

"When you were faced with danger not once, but twice, you ran toward it. That takes guts. It's human instinct to be afraid. There are very few people in the world who look danger in the eye and go after it. You're brave in a way the academy will never teach you. It's instinctual. It's in your blood."

Her head turned enough for him to see a slight smile. "Major Fowler said my dad was the same way. There wasn't a dare he wouldn't take or a life he wouldn't try to save. Even if it seemed impossible, Dad still tried. Lou said my father wasn't scared of anything. They got into some pretty hairy situations, but they always came out of it together. Said my dad must have had nine lives. Didn't know how he got out of some of the things he did." Her smile faltered. "Well, except, you know…the last time."

His hand reached out to stroke her back. "I'm sorry, Sam. I can't imagine what it's like to lose a parent."

She leaned into his touch. "Thank you."

They stood in silence, listening to each other breathe. The air was hot, but tempers were cool.

She straightened her spine, facing him with determination in her eyes. "You know how much this case means to me."

"He's dangerous, Sam. You've never dealt with someone like Viktor Heinrich. If you get in his way, he won't hesitate to kill you."

Her gaze dropped to the floor.

He brushed a stray blond hair behind her ear. "Can you see why I don't want you there? If something happened to you…" That damn unfamiliar stab of worry pierced his gut. He didn't ever want to see Sam hurt. He wanted to pull her to him and hold her there so he was sure she'd be safe.

"But what about you?" Her gaze fell to his chest, and her eyes zeroed in on his heart. His scar. Her finger traced the outline of the circle.

He shivered slightly at her touch. "What about me? I can take care myself. It's what I'm trained for." When she gave him a *look*, her finger slowing its motion on his skin, he gave a small laugh. "Okay, except air conditioners falling out of windows and Germans on steroids."

Her finger circled his scar again. "What happened?"

He knew what she meant. "Sam, I don't think—"

Sam's gaze lifted, full of softness when it met his. "Tell me. Please. I want to know you. All of you. This wasn't an accident, was it?"

Most bullet holes weren't accidents, but he didn't point that out. Her expression was too sincere. "No, it wasn't. It was very intentional."

"Tell me." Her palm flattened over his heart, covering the scar as if she could erase the memory of it for him.

Chapter Twenty-One

Ash sighed, but deep down he wanted Sam to know about his past. For so long he'd kept it locked away, fighting to forget. But now, with her blue eyes pleading, he realized he needed to tell her. It was a part of who he was, and he wanted to share it with her.

"When I said the team going in to extract Viktor Heinrich isn't mine, I meant it." He hesitated. "But what I didn't say was they used to be."

She kept her hand over his heart, her thumb stroking his skin. Her eyes warmed to a bright, comforting blue. He could trust her. He saw that now.

"I…" Christ, the emotions flooding him made him sick. Reliving all this shit again was torture. He'd trusted Lorena and she'd shot him. Left him for dead. Now he was trusting Sam, opening up to her, and it scared the shit out of him. "I was the team leader, responsible for the lives of my men and the citizens in the town where we were stationed in Argentina. José Serrano is a major supplier of most of the world's drugs. He's from that area. Never been caught. He's got lawyers that would make a pit bull cry." Ash laughed without humor. "We'd been there six months. It was a small town, so we knew just about everyone. But then—" He rubbed his neck, trying to ease the tension.

"Here." Sam reached for his hand and led him to his bedroom.

They lay on the bed, his arm around her shoulders, her head nestled on his chest. At once, it became easier to talk.

"Our intelligence officer told me a local woman would be meeting us. She had information about Serrano. She supposedly worked at his estate as a housekeeper. The plan was for her to give us the layout of his property and help us apprehend him."

Her head jerked up. "But why? Why would she help if she worked for him?"

His lips thinned. "According to my intelligence guy, her family had been killed and Serrano was holding her captive as an indentured servant. Keep in mind—this was a remote part of the country. Very low income. These kinds of things happened all the time. The story was plausible. I didn't question it." His gaze narrowed on her. "Nor did I question her once she walked into the bar to meet us the first time." Closing his eyes, he thought back to what Lorena had looked like that day. He'd never seen anything more perfect in all his life. Long, dark brown hair, full sensual lips, cat-like brown eyes, and a curvy body that would send any man to the Promised Land.

When he met Sam's earnest expression, he knew he'd been an idiot. Lorena's beauty didn't compare to Sam's. Sam was twice the woman Lorena would ever hope to be. Open. Honest. Giving. Lorena was none of those things. "I guess you could say I was a bit thunderstruck. I took one look at the woman and fell. Hard."

Sam's hands roamed his bare chest, softly caressing. It

was so soothing, his eyes grew heavy and started to close.

After a minute of silence, she asked, "Then what happened?"

He took a deep breath. "She knew things. Too many things. Those who lived in the area were either indebted to Serrano or terrified of him. No one ever came forward to help turn him in like Lorena had."

"Lorena." Sam spoke the name as if it held some significance.

"I should've known. Should've listened to my team. She started giving us information we hadn't asked for. I was greedy, so pleased that this beautiful creature was so forthcoming. I never imagined it could be a trap." He shook his head at his own foolishness and ignored the pressure building in his temple. "I was so stupid. Blinded by her sex appeal. But I guess that was the point."

"How could you have known?" Sam asked. "You thought she was trying to help."

"My team warned me. They saw what I couldn't. They knew something wasn't right and I didn't listen. Luke—" Ash swallowed in order to mention his best friend's name out loud. "Luke tried to talk sense into me, and I didn't listen."

"Luke? Was he one of the members of your team?"

Ash nodded. "Luke Calder. Tyke and Reese are the others."

Sam perked up at the mention of the names. Her head rose from his chest, and her hand halted its motion.

Ash gave her a questioning glance.

She shrugged and snuggled back against him.

Her soft cheek nuzzling into his shoulder felt so good. So right. It took the sting away from finally getting the words out.

"They all tried to warn me. But I took everything Lorena said, and I made plans to raid Serrano's estate. I was overconfident." He gave her a sideways glance. "*Arrogant.*

Tyke went to the director, told him of my plan. Director Landry gave me a direct order to stand down. Said we didn't . have enough evidence to extradite Serrano. My intention was to use Lorena to testify against him. But the director still didn't buy it. I gave the order anyway."

He swallowed again, preparing for the next part. "I told Lorena when the mission was over, after we caught Serrano, I was going to leave the agency for her. We were going to travel the world together. No more danger for either of us."

Sam's fingers froze. Ash wasn't sure if it was because he'd said he'd quit so easily or if she felt a twinge of jealousy.

He stole a glance at her. She remained quiet, hiding her hesitation behind a smile.

"Turns out, she didn't work for Serrano." His fists clenched, and his hold around Sam's shoulders tightened. "She was his daughter."

Obviously not expecting that, her words gelled together. "But—how—she—what—"

"He'd sent her, knowing we were there to get him. He used his daughter for his own selfish fucking needs. And she did it. Whether it was from fear or love, I don't know. She and I were together for months. We got close. I brought her to meetings, rendezvous with the team, and she reported back to her father on what we were doing the whole damn time. He knew we were coming from day one. And we—no, I—played right into it. And the laughable part? Serrano wasn't even there. He'd hightailed it to one of his hideouts weeks earlier."

"But, how could you have known?"

He jerked away from her. "I could have, damn it."

She fell against the mattress from the surprise. She righted herself, placing her back against the headboard.

"I should have," he said more calmly. "But I didn't listen. Luke was my best friend. Above everyone else, I should have listened to him. He warned me, and I wouldn't fucking listen." His chest heaved in a large rush of oxygen. "On the day of the raid, a little boy was killed." He glanced at Sam for her reaction. He wanted shock, disappointment, and horror. He needed to feel shame for his actions. But she kept her expression hidden, blanketed by a barricade of softness and sympathy.

Slowly and through clenched teeth, he said, "It was my fault." She asked for this, so he'd make damn sure she knew *all* of it. Every last fucking detail. "Do you hear me? I killed him."

Her eyes widened a bit, but still she didn't give in.

"I did it. And I have to live with that for the rest of my miserable life."

Her hand went to his cheek. "Ash, you did what you had to, I'm sure of it."

He brushed her hand away. "Bullshit. The kid wasn't even supposed to be there. Lorena was supposed to get everyone out."

"Ash—"

"He was there when we went in. We caught movement, something flashed, it was too fast to tell what it was. We should have waited. Should have given it a few more seconds. But when you've got a gun in your hand and your life's on the line, you make sure you and your team get out no matter what. That's what we did. When the bullets started flying, we shot back. Anything that moved. The same was true on the other side of the battle lines. The boy was caught in the crossfire. If I hadn't called the raid—"

"Oh, Ash…"

She reached for him, but he pulled back, determined to suffer for his sins. "Then Luke went down."

Her breath hitched.

"He'd gone after the kid. Tried to pull him away. They both got hit. Calder dropped and fell on top the kid. Blood poured from everywhere."

Her throat bobbed as she swallowed.

"The Kevlar did its job," he said. "Luke only suffered a cracked rib from the bullet's impact. Tyke and Reese stayed with him and the boy, trying to get them out. I kept going. I had to find Lorena. I needed to make sure she was safe." A sour taste invaded his mouth. Blood pounded in his ears. "She was throwing things into a bag when I found her. I practically pulled her down the stairs. And that's when we saw him. The still, lifeless body lying on the floor. Tyke and Reese had gotten Calder out, but it was too late for the boy. They had to leave him. When she saw him, Lorena screamed and dropped to her knees. She held him against her chest and sobbed. I didn't have time to feel. My only thought was to escape. It didn't matter that her father wasn't there. I'd go after him another day. She and I were getting out of there alive. I yanked her from the floor and carried her as she kicked and screamed.

"Once we were back at the safe house, I held her, so thankful she'd made it out alive. We finally passed out around dawn. When I woke up, she was sleeping, so I went and checked on my team. No one was happy to see me. Barely got a nod from any of them. Contempt was so thick it nearly choked me."

He paused, lost in his thoughts. His body sagged against the headboard. "When I…when I went back in to check on Lorena, the bed was empty. Of course thinking something had happened to her, I rushed into the room. Then heard the door close behind me. When I turned, she stood with my service pistol in her hand, aimed at my heart."

Sam had stilled next to him. He wasn't sure she even blinked.

"*Por asesinar a mi hijo*," he said in Spanish. "Do you know what that means?"

With an unfocused gaze, she shook her head.

"For murdering my son," he whispered.

Her eyes cleared and a tiny rush of air escaped her lungs. "Ash—"

"She pulled the trigger and that was it. Next thing I know, I'm staring at a white ceiling, hooked up to monitors."

Sam settled herself against him, her head on his chest. Wetness touched his skin. "It wasn't your fault."

His body stiffened at her words. "You're wrong."

"No—"

"It was my team. My decision. And that boy paid the price."

"But, you couldn't—"

He jerked away, severing their contact. "I could, damn it. I could have prevented it." After a few breaths, he said, "But I didn't. And I have to live with that."

"You were only doing what you thought was right." He opened his mouth to rebut, but she cut him off, "Ash, listen to me." She grabbed his face and none too gently turned it to hers. Her eyes blazed as they bore into his. "It wasn't your fault. You got played. That's what Lorena wanted. That's what her father wanted. And it worked. It would've happened no matter what."

"But—"

"Stop it!" she shouted. His blood roared in his veins at her boldness, and his stomach tightened. "I won't let you blame yourself. I won't." Her expression was fierce, her cheeks flushed with purpose. "What's done is done. All you can do now is learn from it and move on."

Thinking back to his life after the mission, he recalled those awful months of recovery. How he'd felt—lying in that hospital bed, useless and used up. Lorena had seen to it. She couldn't do it all the way though. No, she'd missed his heart, leaving him to remember everything he'd been responsible for.

"You don't think we've all had shit to deal with?" The acidic tone of Sam's voice burned through him. "You don't think I feel remorse or regret for the way my life's turned out?"

He stared at her, unable to respond.

"All I've ever wanted to do was help people. I've wanted to wear that badge for as long as I can remember. Never wanted anything so bad in my life. And I can't do it. But you can. You have the power to change things, Ash. To make them right. And you're choosing not to. You're choosing to let her win."

"Sam, I can't—"

"Bull." She crossed her arms. "You *won't*. There's a difference."

Unable to bear her honesty, he looked away, ashamed at the man he'd become. She was right. He'd blamed himself for so long, choosing to ignore his options. It was easier to be pissed off than take responsibility for his actions. That hurt worst of all—showing Sam how weak he'd been. Having her point it out was like a fatal stab through his heart.

No one had ever been able to get through to him. He'd never let anyone in. Then this woman came along, turned his world upside down, and punched him in the damn gut.

"Sam, I—"

"You need me, Ash," Sam said, as if hearing his thoughts. "As much as I need you. So we'll do it together. We'll make this right together."

He didn't comment. He couldn't, because she was right. He did need her. Her smiles, her confidence, her body.

All of it.

His draw to Sam was nowhere near what he'd experienced with Lorena. It was stronger. Much stronger.

But if something happened to her... If Heinrich's goons came back. If they shot at her again and this time didn't miss.

Or if she went to that compound and something went wrong. If Heinrich found out she was there. What would Ash do then?

Blame yourself. The answer was plain as day, echoing in his brain, taunting him.

He couldn't bear it. Wouldn't. He wasn't going to bring another woman into his life and get her or her family killed. She'd already lost her father. There was no way he'd allow her to lose her grandmother, too.

No, the best place for Sam was as far away from the compound as possible. The farther he could keep Sam from Heinrich, the better. Until Heinrich was apprehended. It was the only way to keep her safe. No way he was giving her the location.

"Come on, Ash. Admit it. You need me."

Nothing.

"Ash…"

More silence.

"Ash, come on—"

"I don't," he said, the words passing his lips in a rush. "I don't want or need you, Sam." His stomach clenched, but this time it wasn't even in the ballpark of pleasant.

This was the best way. Otherwise she wouldn't leave it alone. She would've kept pushing and pushing until he finally broke. Which he would have, given time. She had that effect on him. He would've looked into those sad blue eyes and told her the location of the compound, the floor plan, and the exact place Tyke and the boys had spotted her father's look-alike.

Because he had fallen for this woman, and he wanted nothing more than to make her happy. See to it she never cried another day in her life. He'd tried to fight her off, but the attraction was too strong.

Even bracing himself for the heartbreaking look he knew was on its way, it didn't do a damn thing to help. When her hand dropped and those beautiful eyes filled with tears, she speared his heart to the core. Tiny cracks formed and spread like fractured ice on an open pond. Fast and furious it stretched, threatening to take him under and suffocate the life out of him.

"I'm sorry," he said, reaching for her.

She spun out of his reach and stood from the bed. "Me too." She walked toward the doorway without looking back. "Me too."

The door clicked closed.

Then silence.

Chapter Twenty-Two

At her desk, Sam didn't pay any attention to her fingers flying across the keyboard. She typed reports, but her thoughts were far, far away from work.

Seducing Ash last night had originally been about getting what she wanted so she could find her dad. But along the way, what she also wanted turned out to be Ash.

It snuck up on her. An intense emotion she never thought she could experience. He made her feel safe and dangerous, hot and cold, outgoing and timid all at once.

She wanted her next-door neighbor in the worst way. She wanted to lie in his arms in the morning, talk about their day over dinner, watch the ballgame at night, and then make love until dawn.

It was amazing and exhilarating—wanting a man so badly.

And yet, crushing when that same man thought she couldn't take care of herself.

She'd trusted him with the information about her father and her reason for not passing the police entrance exam, only for him to crush her trust with one fatal blow.

The way he'd looked at her, eyes blazing as he spoke the words—*You're obviously not a cop.*

Obviously.

Like it was so easily explained. *Obviously,* she couldn't hack it. *Obviously,* she'd never be able to. *Obviously,* it was *obvious* to everyone but her.

Resigned, she shook her head. Maybe he was right. Maybe she couldn't hack it. She probably wasn't good enough. She'd failed the exam six times, for crying out loud.

When that familiar despair crept into her subconscious, she squashed it.

No. She refused to believe it. Whenever she thought about busting bad guys and keeping the streets safe from lowlifes like Viktor Heinrich, she sizzled with determination. It's all she'd ever wanted to do. She wasn't about to let Ash, Viktor Heinrich, or anyone else tell her she couldn't.

"You okay, Harper?" Martinez asked, holding a coffee cup. "Looks like you could use this."

A smile started at the corners of her lips. "Thanks."

After a sip, he asked, "What's going on, Sam? You've been moping around all day. It's so bad Hanson and Michaels bet if I brought you that coffee, you'd throw it in my face."

She wanted to laugh, but she didn't have it in her.

His smile faded. "Wanna talk about it?" He propped his hip on the corner of her desk.

Her shoulders went up and her chest expanded once. "It's my neighbor."

Martinez's body tensed, his eyes intent on hers. "What did he do? Did he hurt you? Your grandma?' He cradled a fist in the opposite palm. "You want me to rough him up a little? You know I will." '

She did laugh then. "No, no. Calm down, Rocky. He didn't hurt me. Well, not in the way you're thinking. Just said some things. Mostly true, but it still hurt."

"You two getting close, then? He moved in, when? A week or two ago?" The protectiveness in his voice was hard to miss.

Had it really only been a week or two? What a turn of events her life had taken since Ash moved in next door.

He waited, seeming to want an explanation, so she said, "I'd rather not talk about it. Thanks for the coffee though."

"You sure? I mean, I'm here." He grinned. "I've been told I'm a great listener."

"Nah, I'm good." She turned her attention back to her computer screen.

"Sam?"

She looked up, catching his worried expression.

"You're doing okay, right? You aren't getting involved with anyone who isn't right for you? I mean, you're hanging out with good people?"

She blinked. Where had that comment come from? "Uh, yeah."

He glanced around the room, checking if anyone was listening to their conversation. Webb had just walked out, Michaels was on the phone, and Hanson sat behind his computer with a pair of headphones, but Dan lowered his voice anyway. "'Cause I'd hate for you to start hanging out with someone and then fall for him, and have him lead you somewhere dark. Know what I mean?"

No, she had no freakin' idea what he meant. "I'm cool, Martinez. No need to worry."

He nodded once but didn't erase his worried expression. "I just…I mean, he's not making you do things you don't want to do, is he? If you need help… Or you feel trapped…you know you can come to me, right? I'll help you."

"Yeah," she said as if the word held ten syllables. This had to be the strangest conversation she'd ever had with her friend.

"I don't know about this new neighbor of yours. I'm getting a bad vibe from him."

One corner of her mouth drooped. "You've never met him, Dan."

"Yeah, but based on what you've said, how you've been acting lately, there's something going on. You're not yourself, Sam. He's not a good influence on you."

"Seriously. I'm good." Her gaze cut back to her computer screen. "There's nothing going on between me and Ash." Not anymore.

"Okay." He raised his arms in surrender. "Just thought I'd check. There've been some bad things going on downtown. I wanna make sure you and your grandma are okay."

"Downtown?" she asked. "Like what?"

He eyed her a moment. It was the most serious she'd ever seen him. "Club Hell. That place on 27th Street. It's all over the precinct. Didn't you hear? Someone killed a bunch of bartenders and patrons. Blood everywhere."

Oh no. It was all over the precinct. Did anyone know she'd been involved? That *she'd* been responsible for taking all of those lives? "Oh, that," she said through a forced laugh. "Yeah, of course I heard. Man, what a mess that must've been, huh?"

"Yeah," he said, still serious. "Just be careful who you're hanging out with, okay?"

She nodded once. "Sure. Got it. Thanks for the tip."

As he turned to head back to his desk, she said, "That was Viktor Heinrich's place, right?"

He paused, his body locking into place. Then he craned his neck and nodded at her. She couldn't discern anything from his bland expression.

"Was that his only place?" she asked, making sure it came out cool and even. "Does he have any other locations around town that might've been hit?" *Like a compound?*

"Nah," he said. "Not that I heard." And he walked across the room to his workstation.

Gritting her teeth in frustration, Sam continued to type reports. Nothing was more monotonous than deciphering Major Fowler's chicken scratch.

No matter how much she tried, she couldn't stop thinking about Ash. So he didn't want her involved. She understood to a point. She wasn't a cop. Yet. But she felt like one, deep in her heart. She'd wanted it so bad for so long that maybe she'd disillusioned herself into thinking she was one. That to be a cop she didn't need a badge, she simply needed the will and determination. Sure, there were things legally she couldn't do until she joined the force, but she grew more and more impatient with each passing day. Especially since her father was out there, and no one would help her find him. No one believed enough in her abilities or heart.

But if she showed them she had what it took. If she found concrete evidence that her father was at that compound, maybe then Ash and Lou and whomever else would jump in and help save him. It was worth a shot. If Dad was being held against his will, possibly tormented, tortured, then she needed to do something. He didn't deserve to spend one more second in that maniac's clutches.

Was her plan reckless? Yes. Was it unplanned and a tad rash? Definitely. But if she was going to succeed, she needed to do what Heinrich wouldn't expect. She'd go back to Club Hell and see what information she could find. That was her only lead at this point. If she was lucky, there'd be someone there to question. It was better than nothing.

Chapter Twenty-Three

It was still dark and gross, but this time it wasn't packed. In fact, Sam was the only person in the room.

She dragged the large steel door closed, which eliminated most of the light she might have used to navigate the empty floor of Club Hell. The place looked different during the day without any patrons — er, Vamp addicts.

Bottles had been stacked neatly on glass shelves lining the walls. Small lights illuminated behind them, casting refractions of colored streams, giving the illusion this was just an ordinary run-of-the-mill Baltimore bar.

It was quiet and empty. Which was good. She wouldn't be able to interrogate anyone, like she'd originally planned, but she would be able to keep her presence a secret. That was a hell of a lot better. She could be impulsive sometimes, but she didn't consider herself stupid. Of course, Grandma Rose and Ash would consider her being here right now pretty stupid, but she ignored the thought.

Get into Heinrich's office. See what you can find. Then get the hell out.

Grateful she'd worn flats, she tiptoed across the sticky floor, not daring to look down to see if it was blood or grime that grabbed at the soles of her shoes.

Major Fowler had looked worried when Sam insisted she'd needed to go home because she wasn't feeling well. He'd watched her out his office window as she lifted her trunk and rooted around inside. He, of course, had no idea she'd been making sure her weapons were accounted for. She prayed he wouldn't call Grandma. Otherwise, her mission would be over before it began. Grandma Rose and the ladies couldn't know where she was. They couldn't come here. Not ever.

Taser in her right hand, and a spare in her purse, she moved with stealth, halting at the wall just before Heinrich's office door.

Voices spoke from inside.

Shit! She spun and smashed her back against the wall. Flattening herself as thin as possible, she remained immobile until she could decipher whether the voices moved to exit or remained in the office.

Staying put, from the sound of it. Deep voices reverberated off the walls. Footsteps clicked as if someone paced the room.

With her heart lodged in her throat, cutting off air supply, she tried to calm herself.

"You're not going to do this to me. No fucking way." A man's voice rose to intimidating levels, his footsteps now stomping on the concrete floor in the office. "You're crazy if you think I'm going to let you do this and get away with it. You can forget the whole fucking deal."

A female voice, calm but sardonic, responded. "Heinrich," it was said in a thick Spanish accent. Sam almost missed the name because of the strong inflection.

Sam leaned in, tilting her head toward the doorway. She couldn't help it. Curiosity made it impossible to turn away. Based on Heinrich's outburst, whatever this woman had decided was going to be detrimental to his plans. Sam liked whoever she was.

"I came to renegotiate the terms," the female said. "If you do not like it, then *you* can forget the whole fucking deal." With emphasis on the *F*s, her voice exuded authority, despite its soft velvet lilt.

"You bitch!" Heinrich shouted.

When she dared a peek through the small opening of the cracked door, Sam's breath caught. It was one thing to hear the woman say Heinrich's name, it was another to see him five feet away. Vulnerable. Reachable. *Taser-able*. Her fingers drummed on the device, itching to aim and pull the trigger.

He wore a finely tailored black suit with a dark, silk tie and a perfectly pressed white dress shirt. His hair was a bit longer than the normal fashion; the back, filled with varying shades of blond, touched his collar, and the shaggy top was bleached to almost white. His nose was severely pointed and cheekbones sharply contoured. Thin, almost non-existent lips and a cleft chin completed his Eastern European look.

Sam peered past him, searching for the woman.

"Now, Heinrich," the female spoke, still composed, "is that any way to speak to a lady?"

"A lady?" Heinrich laughed, showcasing his veneers, but broke off when a gun pointed at his face.

Three other men stood in the small office with Heinrich and the woman. They wore dark suits, positioned behind her, as if for protection. Only one raised his gun, the others rested their hands casually at their waists, just within reach of their 9mms. Judging from the menacing glint in the woman's almond-shaped eyes, this chick didn't need protection from anyone.

Her other features were just as fierce. Taller than average, dark skinned, and curvy to the point of being sinful. At the view of the woman's overabundant chest spilling out of her brightly colored wrap dress, a pang of jealousy hinted in the back of Sam's mind.

"As I said, Heinrich," the woman's sexy Spanish accent caressed his name, "we have decided to change the terms. You will agree, or we will take our shipment elsewhere. Your choice."

Heinrich remained silent.

"That is what I thought," she purred, smiling with her luscious red-painted lips. She sauntered up to Heinrich, leaning into his ear. "Remember who is in charge." Like a rattlesnake, her hand clamped onto his crotch and squeezed.

Sam gasped. Then threw her hand to her lips.

All heads turned to the sound.

"What the—?"

"Sven! Gunter! Heinz! Max!" Heinrich's voice rang out over the clatter and confusion of shouts and heavy footsteps. "Attack!"

Sam bolted to her left for the nearest bar, only turning once to see the hostile look on Heinrich's face. "You!"

Guns fired, but Sam didn't feel any pain as she leapt over a lacquer-covered wooden bar. She dropped behind it with a loud *thud* that sent a slicing pain down her right side.

"Holy hell," she squeaked, rubbing her shoulder and knee. Taser still in one hand, she braced her back against the bar and felt her body with the other, searching for holes. None. And no blood around her.

Shouts and slamming doors echoed. Doing a quick inventory of her supplies—two Tasers, a can of pepper spray, and one pair of handcuffs—she realized they were useless against bullets flying over a thousand feet per second.

Real smooth, Sam.

Additional shots fired. The *booms* pounded against the bar as the bullets dug their way into the wood. Glass and wood shattered, shards spewing all around her.

Covering her head with her hands, she sat and thought. Thought about Ash. About Grandma Rose. The ladies. Martinez. Fowler. Her father.

What had Dad always told her whenever she found herself in trouble?

When all else fails, improvise.

With what?

She glanced up at the bottles of liquor on the shelves above. Setting her Taser aside, she reached for a bottle of Bacardi 151 and a bottle of White Lightning.

This was ridiculous. There was no way Dad ever had cause to use liquor bottles in a gunfight.

Crouching behind the bar, she peeked over. The three men in expensive suits fired shots in her direction as they hurried for the door. The beautiful woman was nowhere in sight. Heinrich stood behind a gaggle of his Germans, who held nothing but their fists. Which, Sam knew first-hand, were all they needed.

She ducked each time a bullet whizzed by. Would they ever run out of ammunition?

Dropping back to the floor, she hugged her knees and rocked in place. With nothing but liquor and makeshift weapons to defend herself, she wasn't getting out of this unharmed. Ash was right. Heinrich was dangerous. He didn't care who he killed.

Suddenly everything was silent. Dead silent.

"Stand up nice and slow," Heinrich said in his thick German accent. "Do it now, and I'll spare your life."

Both bottles were still in her hands. Her Taser was on the floor next to her. "You-you promise not to shoot?" Her voice broke once, but she forced air into her lungs.

She could hear Heinrich's smile when he answered, "I promise not to shoot."

Just as before, she hesitantly lifted her head to peer above the top of the bar.

When she met eyes with one of the large Germans wearing a smug grin, his arms stretched out to grab her, and she shrieked.

She shot to her feet and slammed the bottle in her right hand on top of the German's head. It shattered into pieces, covering him, the bar, and floor in liquor and glass shards. He staggered back as his comrade leapt forward. Sam jumped out of his reach, then came forward and smashed the other bottle on top of the second guy's head. He shifted on his feet, a momentary dazed look on his face as he recovered, and then snarled at her.

Four additional men surged forward in full assault mode. Their chests heaved, stretching their massive chests against their short-sleeve shirts. Their faces promised murder.

She whirled, grabbing bottles and tossing them this way and that. She didn't have time to pick up her Taser or purse. Glass and liquor could keep the savages at bay for now.

A sudden burst of light filled the room as another group of massive Germans entered. Where did Heinrich find them? Was he harvesting them in the basement?

As the muscle-bound men moved in on her, she continued to pelt them with bottles, some slipping in the liquor and glass on floor.

"Get her goddamn it! *Get her!*" Heinrich screamed from behind the line of Germans. Not so scary and dangerous without them, was he?

Sam grabbed the final bottle on the shelf and chucked it at the nearest German. It didn't break; it bounced off his shoulder and landed on the floor with a *crack*. The top broke off and liquor poured across the floor.

Sam's eyes widened when she realized she hadn't done anything to deter the Germans' approach. Instead she'd only managed to anger them more, and they came at her that much faster.

She sank to her knees and scrambled for the Taser and her purse, then stood.

The Germans froze. They stared unblinking at the black contraption conveniently resembling a gun. Sam smirked at their stunned expressions.

"Back away now or I shoot."

"Attack!" Heinrich shouted. "Don't listen to her! Attack!"

None of the Germans moved. Then, after a moment, one took a hesitant step forward.

"I-I'm warning you," she said, "I'll do it. I don't want to, but I will."

The German grinned and took another step forward.

"Don't—don't do it. I'll shoot."

Another step.

She glanced at Heinrich. He grinned as if he sensed her fear.

Dad.

A black shadow filled her chest, making it difficult to remain composed. *Shit, here it comes.* The nightmare. The one that haunted her since Heinrich took her father from her. Dad's smiling face. It was the last time she saw him. He'd told her he'd be fine, and he'd come back.

But he wasn't fine. And he didn't come back.

Then his eyes widened and he mouthed, *Help.* He glanced down at his chest, where three red orbs spread. He looked up at her, his eyes misting. "Sam, help me," he said. "Help. Me."

She reached, but he slipped through her fingers. His body fell into darkness seemingly forever. Until a splash cut through the silence, then ice-cold water doused her body, swallowing her whole. When she surfaced, she frantically searched for him.

Dad floated beside her facedown in the Chesapeake.

"No!" she screamed, coming back to the present. Her

hand squeezed the Taser, her knuckles going white from the intense strain.

No. Dad was still alive. She'd get through this. She had to. She had to find him.

Another step. One more and the German would be on her.

Her gaze flitted to Heinrich. *Please don't miss. Not this time.*

With a tremble, she pulled the trigger.

Viktor Heinrich and his men threw their long blond manes back and laughed at the trajectory of the Taser's arc. It missed the man in front of Sam by a few feet, landing on nothing but the floor. Bright sparks shot from the end, dancing and jumping in the puddles of spilled liquor. A burning stench permeated as the sparks kicked up in intensity.

Once the German in front of her calmed his laughter, he reached for her arm to yank her forward. His stale breath blew in her face as his beefy hand clamped on her shoulder.

She still had one more shot.

Sam twisted and thrust her fist upward, connecting with his chin. He stumbled back enough for her to aim a second time. There was no way she could miss at this close range. Even with Heinrich laughing at her and with the nightmare of Dad threatening to resurface.

She aimed and shot. The arc curved and landed square on the man's broad chest and stomach. Textbook shot.

She held the trigger.

He screamed. Spasms from the amped up voltage caused the man's feet to fly off the floor. When he landed, his knees buckled, and he dropped next to where Sam's first shot had missed. Twisting and writhing worse than an epileptic episode, his body rolled to the side on top of the first shot. She didn't let up on the trigger. His eyebrows and hair began to singe from the heat. The burnt smell attacked her nostrils. His eyes rolled back, and his smile disappeared. Once peachy and pristine, his skin was now dark and charred as steam wafted from his body.

His pseudo-brothers grabbed for him, horrified. Then snatched their hands back as if they'd been electrocuted. They might've been. Maybel had increased the voltage on these babies enough to knock out a one-thousand pound rhino. The first missed shot still zapped on the floor, a sharp sizzle melding with the singed man's groans.

The Germans whirled on Sam with looks of anger and confusion. Heinrich glowered, but he took a small step backward.

She'd already reached in her purse and had the next Taser ready. "Anyone else?" She pointed the weapon at each man in turn. Her bones rattled, and her heart was ready to give out, but she shot them her best tough girl glare.

Her courage increased as the group took a step back. Then another. She reveled in the favorable shift of power.

Heinrich peered around the safety of the Berlin wall. "You created quite a mess for me during your last visit, Samantha."

"How do you know my name?" The Taser in her hand dropped a fraction of an inch.

He smirked and stepped over the scorched body on the floor, which still thrashed. Dense, dark puffs of smoke wafted off it.

"Oh, I know all about you," he said. "You're the apple of your daddy's eye."

"Where is he, Heinrich? I know you've got him."

"Now, why would I tell you that? Davy Harper is one of my best employees. Very diligent in his work ethic. With his help, I've become the sole supplier of drugs in the city and soon to be the East Coast."

Realizing the Taser had dropped almost to her side, Sam snapped it back to attention. "Tell me where your compound is." Shit. She hadn't planned on bringing that up yet.

An evil laugh blew past his lips. "My, my, you're feisty. I like that. If I'd have known, I would've bypassed your father and come after you years ago. I still might. I made a deal with your father, but I think I need to renegotiate the terms. How would you like to be a very rich young woman, Samantha? I could use someone with your youth and vitality."

"Heinrich, you—"

There was a sound. A *whoosh* so resounding all heads turned to the twisting body on the floor. Within seconds, it ignited and burst into flames as if someone had covered it in lighter fluid and thrown a match. The entire body, consumed by the blaze, rolled and turned in the large puddle of liquor. His screams of terror pierced the room.

Always ready and able to state the obvious, Sam screamed, "The alcohol! It's flammable!"

Loud *whooshes* mirroring the initial sound took off in rapid succession, igniting the back corner of the club in seconds. She watched the meaning dawn on Heinrich's face. He turned as if to lunge at her, but his sleeve caught fire. He desperately patted his arm and shouted orders at the men surrounding him.

As if someone had cast a spell, the fire created a line between Sam and Heinrich, blocking one from the other. Neither could cross. The flames wailed and screeched, torching everything in their path.

The smoke thickened, filling the already dark room. Sam coughed and dropped to her hands and knees and crawled in the direction of the exit. Every few seconds she glanced behind her to be sure no one followed and then continued to crawl, feeling the bruises on her knees growing from the rough contact with the cold cement floor.

"Where are you, you little bitch?" Heinrich screamed.

Keep moving, Sam!

She scurried in the direction of where the front door should be.

There was a faint line of light peeking from under the steel door. Just a few more feet, and she'd be free.

A clamp locked around her right ankle. It pulled, yanking her away from her escape. Her chin slammed against the hard floor, sending pain up her jaw and cheeks. Another burst exploded inside her brain. She squeezed her eyes closed.

The owner of the hand flipped her onto her back.

She got a quick peek at the German gripping her ankle, before she kicked her other leg out, connecting with his nose. He wailed and released her, covering his face.

Screw this. She rolled onto her knees, vaulted to her feet, and bolted for the door.

The stagnate air of 27th Street filled her lungs as she sprinted to her car. Jamming her key in the ignition, she pulled away in seconds.

She dared a glance in the rearview mirror. Angry flames punched out the warehouse's windows and screamed for the sky.

Chapter Twenty-Four

Ash needed sleep. He'd spent the last week at his bedroom window, keeping watch over the neighborhood. More specifically over Sam.

She'd spent most of her days at work and her afternoons at Rose's, doing God-knows-what those women did to pass the time. Probably sharpening their switchblades.

Today he purposefully worked in the front yard, wanting an excuse to run into her. He needed a smile or a simple hello. Even when his Humvee had crashed and he'd been stranded in the middle of the Afghani desert, bleeding, needing food and water, without any support in sight, he didn't hurt as much as he did now. It was as if a part of him had been ripped away. Vital organs torn from his insides, now on display for the world to see.

He had to make it stop.

Which meant he had to talk to her. Reemphasize his reasons for turning her away. Remind her how he was responsible for the death of that kid, loss of his team and his self-respect. She deserved all of him, not a shell of who he used to be. He needed to get himself in order. Straighten out the messes he'd created. Not make new ones.

Over the last week, she'd avoided him better than a well-trained spy, ducking and dodging her way into her house, locked securely behind a door. He could have easily picked the lock or broken the goddamn thing down. But he wanted her trust. He wanted her to *want* to talk to him.

It didn't seem that was going to happen. And well, Ash wasn't much of a patient man when it came to something he wanted. Waiting for Heinrich to make the drop was one thing. Waiting for someone like Sam to utter a single word in his direction was something he didn't have the strength with which to wait. That was something a man had to fight for. Die for.

She hadn't looked his way once since he turned her out. And he wasn't sure he'd even seen her smile. Not the way she had before he came into her life. God, that first day he'd seen her bouncing down her front steps wearing that smile. It had done incredible things to his insides. Each night since they'd parted, he'd visualized her body under his wearing nothing but that smile.

He had pulled an overgrown azalea bush from his front garden and dragged it to the curb, when a car pulled up. A flashy car. Much too nice for this neighborhood. It was sleek, red, and waxed to a pristine glossy finish, with low-profile tires and oversize shiny rims. It pulled behind his truck and slowed to a stop. There was only one person who would drive such a pompous car.

Luke Calder.

He and Luke had been best friends since Army basic training. When the DEA recruited Ash five years ago, part of the deal was that the agency took Calder, too. He was the first member of Ash's four-man team.

"Coop!" Calder shouted as he exited. As usual, Luke

wore his best attire when in plain-clothes. Tailored white linen shirt, designer label shorts, and flip-flops that probably cost three hundred dollars. Calder liked to impress.

But why he had shown up at Ash's house unannounced after so much time had passed was a mystery. "What are you doing here?" Ash asked when Luke was beside him.

Easygoing surfer-boy that he was, Calder chuckled. "Nice to see you, too, man." He ran a hand through his blond hair, which was longer than he used to keep it. More relaxed.

Maybe Luke hadn't taken their assignment in Argentina as well as Ash had thought. Maybe the guilt ate at Luke's conscience, too.

Ash gave him a doubtful look.

"What?" Calder said, "I can't pop in and say hi to my best friend?"

"Not when you haven't spoken to him in a year." Ash crossed his arms. "What gives?"

Calder removed his mirrored aviator sunglasses, folding them with careful slowness, then stowed them in his front shirt pocket. "We need to talk."

Ash knew Calder better than anyone. He used to think he knew him better than himself. So at Luke's vacillating expression, Ash had to calm his breathing and pulse. Whatever Luke came for, it wasn't because he wanted to talk about the good old days.

He'd been sent to deal with Ash.

Luke placed his hand on Ash's shoulder. "Maybe we should go somewhere to chat, buddy."

Ash nodded and dropped the dead plant still in his hand.

Before he turned, Sam's Honda pulled up. The hair on Ash's arms stood on end and a prickle rushed down his spine. The anticipation of seeing her crippled him.

Calder turned, following Ash's gaze. "Mmmm. And who might this pretty little thing be?"

Ash caught the sly smile in his tone and snarled. "Hands off." Ash met Sam's eyes through the driver's side window.

Terror and hesitation crossed her face. Though he knew Samantha Harper wasn't scared or hesitant of anyone, least of all him. But as her eyes darted from Ash to her front door and back, he started to sweat. Would talking to him really be that bad?

Biting her bottom lip, she drummed her fingers on the steering wheel, her eyes glancing between it and him.

"She better get out soon or she's going to suffer heat exhaustion," Luke murmured.

Ash frowned. Would she prefer that to forced conversation with him?

She finally exited the car but didn't acknowledge him, even though he knew she could feel him piercing her with his eyes. She lifted the car's hood. Thick, white steam wafted from the engine.

"What the—?" Luke said.

Ash kept his gaze on Sam.

She sidestepped the front of the car, still not turning to him.

You're not getting away that easy. "Hi, Sam." Offering a smile, he fell in step behind her as she looked straight ahead and hustled to her front steps. He remained close, hoping it would drive her crazy enough to turn around. "How are you?"

She nodded her half-assed greeting, keeping her eyes forward, picking up her pace.

"Lovely weather we're having today, don't you think?" He was fully aware of Luke behind him, watching the exchange with keen interest. "Really beautiful."

She grunted.

Luke laughed.

"I think we're in for another scorcher. At least that's what Channel Two says." He quickened his pace, almost stepping on her feet as she scaled her stairs. What an ironic turn of events since their first meeting had ended the same way, except Sam was the one chasing him up his front steps.

She didn't face him until she was through her front door and standing in her foyer. "What do you want, Ash?" She glanced behind him, toward the street, and then back to his face.

The only thing separating them was the thin screen door. He could easily push it out of the way or reach through it. And boy did he want to.

Calder stood next to him, rocking back on his heels and smiling like a damn idiot.

"To talk to you," Ash said, failing to hide the desperation in his voice. Luke's smile grew wider. Ash leaned closer to her and lowered his voice. "To make sure you're okay."

"I'm fine. Why wouldn't I be fine?" Her eyes filled with something close to regret, but it was gone in seconds. She glanced past him to the street again.

He glanced too. What was she looking for?

When her eyes came back to the porch, she zeroed in on Luke. "Oh." She shook her head as if to clear her thoughts. "Hello." She smiled at him, damn it. Not one of her special smiles, but a smile nonetheless.

Ash nearly stepped in front of Luke to block his irresistible pheromones from reaching her. No woman within thirty miles could resist him. He'd been here less than five minutes and already he'd worked his magic. "Sam," Ash growled. "This is Luke Calder."

Her eyes widened and her eyebrows shot up at the name. "Yes, *that* Luke Calder."

The man in question cocked his head at Ash, then gave Sam a ridiculous bow Ash had seen him do a thousand times. This time though, he wanted to kick his ass. "It's a pleasure. I'd kiss your hand if you weren't already inside."

Ash rolled his eyes. "Luke, this is Samantha Harper."

Calder froze and his head snapped up. The seducer's expression was wiped away and replaced with a look of utter shock. "Harper?"

"Yeah." Sam's eyes narrowed. "Why?"

Luke recovered, pasting that slick grin back on his lips. "No reason, sweetheart. Just repeating what I heard." His gaze slanted to Ash for an imperceptible second, but he caught it. Something was up.

Her hand rested on her hip. "Will you be in town long, Luke?"

Why the sudden interest in Luke's travel plans?

Luke opened his mouth to speak, but Ash stepped in front of him. "He's just visiting. Heading back to DC tonight. Isn't that right, Calder?" Ash could practically see the wheels spinning in her head, planning, scheming. If she thought Luke would be around, she'd sic her pack of undercover grannies on him.

Catching on quick, his friend nodded and remained silent.

Sam narrowed her eyes again. Always suspicious.

A car drove down the street, loud thumping music blaring from the open windows. Sam's breath hitched, and her head jerked in that direction. Her hand gripped the wood door preparing to close it. Her knuckles turned white, as did her complexion.

"Sam," he said, keeping his eyes on her. "Are you—?"

"I'm fine," she said when the car had disappeared down the street. "Thanks for your concern." Then she shut the door in his face.

He stood, staring, deciding whether he should stick his fist through it and pull the damn woman out by her hair.

Calder had the nerve to laugh beside him. "Wow. I see your talents with women haven't changed much."

Ash glanced at the now empty street in the direction the

car had driven. "Did anything about that seem odd to you?"

"You mean the part where a beautiful woman just shot you down without blinking? Or her aversion to loud music and cars?"

Ash bit the inside of his cheek as he pondered. "Both. And I want to know why."

• • •

On her tiptoes, Sam peered through the peephole. Ash stood on her front porch, most likely contemplating breaking down the door. Brute. Luke slapped Ash on the back and muttered something about going somewhere to talk. After a moment, Ash gave up and walked away. He and Luke walked down her front steps and got into Luke's sports car. Ash glanced once at her house, then turned to face front as they drove away.

She leaned her back against the door and slid down the hard surface. She landed on the floor and curled her legs to her chest, resting her forehead on her knees.

He wanted to see if she was okay. She let out a bitter laugh. She'd be okay if he would leave her the hell alone. Or if he'd stop looking so sexy without a shirt on, doing manual labor. Or if he wouldn't give her that I'm-so-sorry-puppy-dog look, eyes wide and sympathetic. She'd most especially be okay if Ash Cooper hadn't moved in next door or been involved in her father's case.

They could have cut ties and parted ways, gone back to being indifferent acquaintances. Distant yet cordial neighbors.

Not now. Not after the way he made her feel. Lying in his bed, his body coming alive under her touch. His patience at the shooting range. Laughing and joking in his living room. It was a connection she'd never had with anyone else and feared she'd never feel again.

She missed him.

But it was more than that. She had this relentless ache in her stomach that wouldn't go away. Emptiness left behind after Dad left. Ash filled that hole. Gave her life new meaning. Showed her there were things still worth fighting for.

His assignment would be over soon. Then he'd be gone. Out of her life forever.

She doubled over, clutching her midsection.

Gone.

Why the hell did it hurt so bad to think about Ash somewhere other than next door? Why did it feel like her heart would explode?

See, this was why she'd avoided him. If she'd just been able to wait in the car. Or think of somewhere else to drive. But no, he'd cornered her. Forced her to face this insane flurry of messed-up emotions.

Sitting up, she banged her skull against the oak door.

Idiot. You just had to go and get attached, didn't you?

Ash was the first person she'd thought of when the body at Club Hell caught fire. Despair and regret was immediate when she realized she'd taken a life. The bartender was probably someone's husband or son. Or someone's father. This time she hadn't had Vamp or anything else to blame it on. She'd taken the Taser and pulled the trigger. The ache turned painful, slicing through her stomach.

She'd overreacted when that car drove past her house. Like Viktor Heinrich would really speed down the road blaring rap music. *Ha!* But it still got under her skin. She'd foolishly gone after Heinrich under-armed and alone. Something everyone who cared about her would have scolded her for.

She'd made an enormous mistake. But there was no fixing it now. Only waiting. Heinrich would come for her. It was simply a matter of time.

Part of her wanted him to come. Then this toxic thing between them could be over. One of them would come out victorious, while the other one…well, at least it would be over.

Sam considered confessing everything to Ash when he got back. He'd be really pissed about the fire, but he'd get over it. She was still alive after all. That had to stand for something. If—no, *when*—Heinrich came for her, she could make Ash promise to look after Rose and the other ladies. He'd do it. Because he was an honorable man. No matter how he viewed himself.

"Just tell him." She massaged her temples. "He isn't any scarier than Viktor Heinrich." The pain in her head increased. "Why do you care what he thinks anyway?"

An incessant knock pounded on her door. She shot to her feet, heart racing, and looked through the peephole. Celia stood on the other side, grief etched on her pale face.

Sam threw open the door and rushed onto the porch. The older woman looked like she might collapse, so Sam grabbed hold of her shoulders. "What is it?"

"Rose." Celia's fist clutched at her chest as she gasped for air. Sam dragged the older woman to a seat on her porch. "He's got Rose. He took her." Celia closed her eyes as tears streamed down her cheeks.

All thoughts about Ash evaporated. Her eyes glazed over. Her ears couldn't hear any sound but Celia's cries. Her mind couldn't process anything but what Celia said. *He's got Rose. He took her.*

This was her worst nightmare come to life. Heinrich didn't come for Sam. Instead he'd hit her where it would hurt most. He'd taken her father from her, and now he was going to take her grandmother. "Where are they?" Sam shook the woman's shoulders when it seemed she wouldn't speak. "Celia! *Where?*"

She held out a note. "I stopped by to watch *Jerry Springer* with her…" The older woman wiped her tears as her shoulders bounced with each sob. "The door was propped open, so I let myself in." She heaved a deep breath and sniffled. "This was on her recliner."

Sam opened the folded piece of paper, noticing the beautiful script, as if the sender had taken all the time and care in the world to write the missive.

Just an insurance policy.

Once the deal is over at the port, I'll bring her back unharmed. If you interfere, I'll bring her back in pieces.

Your choice, apple.
V.H.

Sam reread the note twice before dragging her gaze back to Celia. The older woman still gasped for air, clutching hard at her chest.

"What...are we...going...to...do?" she asked through sobs.

"*We* aren't going to do anything," Sam said. "*I'm* going to the port." Heinrich had told her exactly where to find him. He was taunting her. Tempting her.

Celia's eyes cleared, and her head snapped to attention. "But he'll kill you."

"He's going to kill me anyway. I...I provoked him. He took her because he knows I'll come after her. It's me he wants. I have to go."

"But, Sam—"

"Stay here. And promise me you won't tell the others. I can't let anyone else get hurt." Sam pinned the older woman with a firm stare. "Celia, promise me."

Celia looked as though she might argue, but then her features relaxed. "All right. But at least take some ammunition."

Sam nodded, though she had a different idea about weapons this time. No more playing cop. This time she'd face Heinrich with some real firepower.

Even if she couldn't save herself, Sam was going to make sure her grandmother survived. She had to. Viktor Heinrich wasn't going to take anyone else from her. She'd kill him long before he even thought about it.

Chapter Twenty-Five

Ash and Luke found themselves at Ropewalk Tavern for a few beers. They sat at a table in the corner, out of earshot of others. Ash figured Luke suggested going out for a reason, so he didn't argue. Probably had news Ash wouldn't like, so it was better they were out in public where he couldn't make too much of a scene. At home he would break something important. Like his fist in the refrigerator. Or his foot through the front door.

"It's just…after Buenos Aires…after *Lorena*—"

"Don't start on that shit again," Luke said, popping the top off his beer. "Let it go, man. The longer you—"

"Let it go?" Ash leaned across the high-top table and said in a low voice, "I killed a kid, Luke. How can I let that go? Do you know what it's like to live with that shit on your conscience every day?"

Calder lifted one shoulder. "He was in the wrong place at the wrong time. Collateral damage. Did it suck that it happened? Hell yeah. But there's nothing you could've done."

"I gave the fucking orders to go in." Blood vessels strained under Ash's skin. Seeing Calder again brought all his demons back to the surface.

Luke propped a forearm on the table and leaned over it. "And we fucking followed you." His voice might have sounded calm, but his tight expression said he was anything but. "We followed you, Ash. Jesus. We'd do it again if it came down to it."

Ash started at the words. "What are you saying?"

"We fucked up. *All* of us. That boy died because we couldn't protect him."

"Luke—"

"No." He dropped his beer bottle down with the *thud*. "This shit's not yours to bear. We went in as a team; we came out as a team. Simple as that."

"Came out, shit," Ash huffed. "Do you hear yourself, Luke? The only thing I remember after that mission is losing my team and my best friend. We weren't a team. Not after that."

"That's because no one could stand to be around you, you son of a bitch. All self-loathing and pitiful. Taking full blame for everything that happened. Lorena was a bitch. You found out too late. Get over it." He picked up his menu, blocking his face from Ash's view. "They got any good grub around here? I'm starving."

Ash's fist tightened around the bottle, his knuckles screaming from the strain. "You're a huge dick, you know that, Calder?"

The menu dropped, revealing one side of Luke's mouth lifted. "One of my best qualities I'm told."

Just like old times. Ash allowed himself a small smile, then contemplated his friend's unannounced visit. "The others send you to smooth things over?"

Luke shrugged before opening the menu again. "They knew you'd be less likely to rip *my* head off."

Ash threw his head back and laughed. "Was I that bad?"

"A little more than an ass, just shy of a douche. We contemplated shooting you out of your misery."

The corner of Ash's mouth twitched. "It's a wonder you didn't."

"Tyke wanted to," he said, face still buried behind the menu. "But Reese said it'd involve too much paperwork. And you know how much he hates unnecessary paperwork."

Ash smiled over his teammate's notorious OCD need to follow protocol.

Luke lowered the menu to the table and signaled with a flick of his wrist to the waiter.

A college-aged guy approached with notepad and pen in hand. Luke ordered wings, potato skins, chili, and fries. Ash went with a burger.

Once the guy walked away to put their order in, Ash rubbed a hand down his face. His chest seemed lighter. That weight he'd been carrying around for the last year from the humiliation and guilt seemed to have evaporated. "Thanks, man. For coming. For setting me straight."

Never one for the touchy-feely, Luke nodded his response. Great with women in his bed, but shit with real feelings. "Enough about you," he said. "I want to talk about Samantha. Think she's a good idea given your track record?"

"You really wanna go there after the conversation we just had?" Ash sent him a lethal look. "Jesus, Luke. You know—"

"Hey, man." Luke raised his arms in defense. "Relax. No need to rehash old scars. I'm just saying. Watch yourself."

"Watch myself? What the hell do you think I've been doing over the last month? Shit. You think I wanted this to happen? You think I didn't try to stop it?" Ash closed his eyes and massaged his screaming temples. "She's..." A muscle tightened in his jaw. "She's hard to ignore."

Luke grinned. "I noticed. Slammed a door in your face—I

like her already."

Ash cracked an eye open, smiling. "Well, to be fair, I slammed one in hers first."

"Really?" Luke's eyes brightened. "I just met her, and I can imagine the shit-storm that brought on."

They both chuckled.

The waiter came back with a full tray of food. After asking if they needed anything else, he turned and left.

Luke picked up a wing and took a bite, and spoke between chews. "So why are you here talking about her instead of back at your place inside of her?"

Ash groaned. "It's complicated."

"With you, my friend, it usually is." Luke washed down his comment with a swig of beer, then said, "So what's the deal? She a bit hard to handle? Too wild for your type-A, anal tendencies? Give me two minutes with her, I'll show her—"

Ash's insides boiled, and his eyesight clouded.

Luke hid a smile behind the bottle. "Damn, you're a possessive bastard."

"It's crazy, man. I just…I can't explain it. Most of the time she makes me so nuts I want to bash my head into a wall. But then she does something that makes me want to"—Ash gave his friend a sidelong glance—"I'm sure you can figure out the rest."

"So why haven't you?" Luke asked, scooping a large helping of chili. "Figured out the rest, I mean."

Ash let out a loud exhale. "You know why."

"She's not worth it, you know. Lorena. This power you allow her to have over you. The sooner you get that shit out of your system, the sooner you can move on. Be happy. With Samantha, if you want."

"It's just…shit, Luke. I thought…you know, I thought I…*loved* her." The last part was muttered, but he knew Luke heard him.

"And now you can't trust your own judgment on the next one. That it?"

He leveled Luke with a glare. "I can't go around jumping into bed with every woman who gives me a hard-on."

"Why not? I do." Then Luke sobered. "I'll put a bullet in you myself if you don't listen to me the next time. And I'm not Lorena. I won't miss."

"What a relief," Ash added wryly.

Resting his spoon in the half-empty bowl, he placed it on the side of the table, moving his plate of fries in front of him. "So, you gonna go kiss and make up? Or are you gonna continue to give yourself blue balls?"

"They hurt less than a bullet."

"Yeah, but the recovery…" Luke closed his eyes, inhaling deeply through his nose.

"I can't get her to look at me, let alone talk to me."

"Does she know how you feel?"

He barked out a laugh. "Hell, *I* don't know how I feel."

Luke's eyebrows rose.

"I can't…I didn't…" Another sigh. "No, I didn't tell her."

Luke sat up straighter and grinned. "That might be your first step. Even I know that. Chicks respond to feelings. They want to hear flowery shit you spew from your heart."

Ash shook his head and laughed. "I'll keep that in mind." But he knew full well Sam wasn't the kind of woman who wanted anything spewed from his heart. She wanted honesty, so of course he'd tell her how he felt, but she wasn't a roses and wine kind of woman. She was a go-out-and-take-charge type. Make an impression. He just had to think of a way to do it. It'd be damn hard to impress a woman like Samantha Harper.

• • •

Ash and Luke returned to his house a few hours later. They'd settled on his worn sofa and watched a pair of commentators analyzing the baseball game that just ended. They both had slowed up on the beers at the bar, because Luke needed to be alert for recon later that night. Heinrich was apparently more active the last few days at the compound, which confirmed the team's assumption that he was getting ready for his shipment within the next week.

There'd been no other sightings of Davy Harper, or Jonah Michaels. The words cut right through him. He'd promised Sam if she gave the team more time, they'd tell her for sure if it was her father or not. That his team would make sure it was him before they took him down with Heinrich's other men. But it seemed he couldn't keep that promise. How was he going to tell her now they didn't know where the hell her father was? And how would she react to that information?

"We're doing what we can," Luke said. "But that's not our primary objective. We can't watch Heinrich, his men, *and* keep an eye out for Harper, all while prepping for the raid. The team's strapped as it is. You know that, man."

He did know that. And it was because of him. If he had followed directions in South America, he wouldn't be in this house. He'd be at the compound with his team, lending an extra hand.

But then you would have never met Sam.

Wow. A quick flood of heat coated his body. His heart thumped hard enough to vault out onto the floor. He shot to his feet, suddenly unable to sit still.

Luke jumped in reaction. "What the hell's the matter with you?"

"Nothing," he said, pacing in front of the TV.

He loved her. Jesus Christ. He loved Sam. And if he'd never gotten involved with Lorena, he would've never met her. What a twisted realization that was. But he didn't care.

He'd been excluded from his team and been an outcast for a year, trying to kiss up to Director Landry to get his job back. And this woman was in front of him, fulfilling him more than any job ever would.

He turned to Calder, knowing he must have had the most pathetic, lovesick grin on his face. But he didn't care about that either. He—

"Ashland!" a woman's voice shouted from outside. "Mr. Ashland!"

They both stiffened, their heads darting toward the door, hands instinctively going to their weapons.

No one called him by his given name. It was Ash or Cooper. Nothing else.

He dropped to the floor and crawled to the window. Luke took position on the left side of the room by the front door. Calder signaled that he'd be cover, when the voice shouted again. "Ashland! Please open up! It's about Sam!"

Ash was on his feet in an instant, ripping the door open. Before him stood the women from the neighborhood watch, minus Sam and her grandmother.

His gaze jumped from one wrinkled face to the next. "What happened? Where's Sam?"

Luke hung back, gazing down at the gaggle of older women with a puzzled expression.

"He took her," Maybel spoke. "Viktor Heinrich kidnapped Rose."

"And Sam went after him," a short one, looking like June Cleaver in pearls, said next.

His knees threatened to give out. And based on Luke's wide-eyed stare, Ash knew he'd turned noticeably white. Or maybe green.

The one wearing pearls held out something in her hand. "This note said he's going to keep Rose captive until the drop."

"That's next week!" Ash exclaimed.

The ladies passed terrified expressions to one another.

"Can't be," one looking like an older Daisy Duke said. "Why keep her that long?"

True. Why would Heinrich hold on to a hostage for a week? It would be more trouble than it was worth.

That could mean only one thing: he'd moved his shipment date up. Fuck.

He glanced at Calder, and his friend's expression said he thought the same thing. Luke reached into his pocket, yanked out his phone, and punched buttons on the keypad.

"She made me promise not to tell anyone," June Cleaver spoke again. "But—"

"I don't know why you listened to her." Maybel's words were clipped.

June's eyebrows sagged as red flamed in her cheeks. "She made me promise."

Maybel grunted, waving her arm in dismissal.

His heart stopped.

His stomach dropped to the floor, which was impossible since, at the same time, he thought he was going to puke. Shit. Sam. Going after Viktor Heinrich.

Goddamn it, why didn't she come to me? When she got that note, why didn't she ask me for help?

He hadn't been here. He'd hopped in the car with Luke, and they'd driven away. Even after seeing her terrified expression when that car with thumping music drove down the street, he still left her. He should've pressed her for information, should have made her tell him what she was so afraid of. But he didn't.

If only he'd been here. She could've come to him. He would've helped her. She had to know that, right? He wasn't sure. Not after the way they'd parted the last time she'd come over. He'd insulted her about not passing the police exam, which in turn insulted her confidence in their relationship. He'd seen her expression before she left. She didn't trust him. Hell, he didn't know if she ever had.

If anything happened to her… If Heinrich hurt her, or worse, *killed* her, he'd rip out Heinrich's throat with his bare hands. Fuck getting his team back. Fuck everything. Nothing else would matter.

"We're going to get them," Daisy Duke said, "and we need your help."

Ash took a step back from the force of her words. Luke's jaw dropped open. "*You* need *my* help?"

All the women looked at each other, and then turned to him, nodding.

"And hurry," Maybel said. "We don't have much time." She shot an unforgiving look to June, whose face flooded crimson as she looked away.

"Coop." Luke stepped forward, placing his hand on Ash's shoulder. "We gotta talk."

His nerves were already on edge, and Luke's solemn face sent him crashing to the ground.

"I didn't come to smooth things over." Calder hesitated, weighing his words. "Heinrich's club caught fire last week. Fire department said it was arson. After what happened the last time you went, Director Landry thinks you had something to do with it—"

"*What?*" His face went from cold to enflamed in an instant. "Why in the hell would he—"

Ash had a flash of Sam's withdrawn eyes as she avoided him over the last five days.

One week. Luke said Heinrich's club had caught fire a week ago. Right after she'd left Ash's house. After he'd crushed her dreams and said things he'd never meant.

Knowing her, and God knew he did, she would have gone after Heinrich trying to prove herself. Ash's words would have given her the stubborn-assed thrust she needed to confront Heinrich head-on.

Oh Christ. How could he have done this to her? If she was involved in that fire, Ash was to blame. This was his fight. He needed to protect her from it.

"Until word comes down on what happened at Club Hell," Luke's voice pulled him back from his thoughts, "you're definitely grounded, man. You can't go. The director'll have your ass for disobeying a direct order. Again."

Direct order, my ass. Ash's nostrils flared in protest.

The women stared at him, arms crossed, practically tapping their toes in impatience.

Was it really a decision? Sam's life or his career?

Hell no.

"Sorry, Luke," Ash said hoarsely, his emotions getting the better of him. *Please let her be okay. God please let her be alive.* "I get it if you aren't in. But I have to go."

Nodding, a slow grin crept over his friend's face. "The team never did know how to follow direction."

Startled, Ash stared at his friend.

"I told you," Luke said, "in as a team, out as a team. I already texted Tyke. He and Reese are on their way to the port now. Sawyer's team said Heinrich arrived about an hour ago. He had a woman with him. And it wasn't Lorena." He squeezed Ash's shoulder.

"Oh my God," the one with pearls said, her hand covering her mouth. "He has Sam too!"

Daisy Duke glared at her again. "Calm down, Celia. You're no good to us if you can't keep a level head." Then she turned her direct gaze to Ash. "Well," she said, hand on her hip. "Are you comin' or not?"

"I am," he said just as direct. "But, I'm sorry. I can't let you ladies come along. This is official law enforcement business—"

"But—"

"Now wait just a minute—"

"Who do you think you are—"

"If you think we're going to sit around and wait like a bunch of helpless old ladies—"

It was like a whole gaggle of Samanthas. "Enough!" Ash shouted, his nerves getting the better of him. The women's lips zipped shut, and they lurched back a step. "Time is of the essence, so unless you plan on arguing with me for another few hours, during which Sam and Rose could be seriously injured," he paused for effect, eyeing each woman in turn, "then I suggest you go back to your houses and wait for me to return."

When their mouths opened again, he cut them off by saying, "I love her." Then swallowed. The poufy heads of varying colors tilted as the women stared at him like he'd just said he was an alien and wanted to probe them. "I love her," he said again. "And I swear to you I will do everything in my power to bring them both home alive. Whatever it takes. Trust me."

The women remained quiet, and after a minute their jaws lifted back into place. He got a confident, stiff nod from each woman.

Whatever it takes.

Chapter Twenty-Six

How did she get here? Where was Grandma Rose?

Sam remembered driving to the docks, sneaking from shipping container to container, listening for signs of her grandmother. She'd approached the pier, coming up on a boat where she'd spotted Heinrich. Then a sharp pain drilled against her skull and everything went black.

Now she sat in a room, tied to a metal chair, with voices echoing around her. Gray evening light filtered through a nearby window. The floor was bare. The way her tennis shoes tapped against the ground told her it was covered in wood. Golden-toned sconces offered soft illumination on rich crimson-colored walls. The furniture around her was dark and masculine.

She sat in the middle of the room as if on display. Her stomach was unsettled. Off kilter. Queasy. The earth moved around her—swaying, sloshing from side to side.

A chill slid down Sam's spine, and her eyes stung with unshed tears. She was on the boat. She instinctively reached for her weapons only to feel the bite of the thick rope against her skin. Her weapons were gone.

Where's Grandma Rose?

No. She blinked the tears away. Nothing was going to happen to her. Sam would sacrifice herself long before she let harm come to those she loved. She had to figure out a way to loosen the tight restraints.

She wiggled in the steel chair, lifting her shoulders up and down. *If I could...just...slide it up...*

"Well, hello, sunshine." Heinrich's voice spoke through a satisfied grin. "How are we feeling?" His shadow approached from her front, coming into view within inches of her face. He leaned in, hands on his knees. A single strand of unruly bleached hair fell over his forehead. "Looking for these?" He pointed to a nearby table, which held the tranq gun, pepper spray, and air horn with earplugs she'd brought with her.

"I wasn't about to let you keep them." He lifted the air horn can and examined it. "I've seen what they can do."

"Where's my grandmother?" Sam asked, forcing determination in her tone. Never show weakness. No matter your position.

"She's fine for now." He placed the can back on the table, then reached his arm around his back. "You'll be together soon. But first, I want to talk to you."

"I have nothing to say to you, Heinrich." Sam twisted her head from his harsh features, focusing on a colorful painting on the opposite wall. Being this close to the man made her sick to her stomach even more than the sway of the boat.

He laughed with a dangerous glint in his eyes. "I find that hard to believe. You've been nothing but a thorn in my side lately. Looking for dear old dad, are you?" He lifted her dad's .38 service weapon she'd brought with her and turned it from side to side.

Her breath hitched.

"This was his, was it not?" He opened the cylinder and

peered inside. The six bullets she'd loaded earlier were still inside. Snapping it closed, he shut one eye and peered through the sight at her.

She strained against her restraints, the rope growing tighter with each twist. "You're going to pay, Heinrich. I'm personally going to see to it."

He lowered the gun and positioned his face close to hers again. His eyes were direct, and his stale breath blew against her lips when he whispered, "After what you did to my club, I should kill you right now. You don't know how much I had to pay the fucking cops and fire department to get off my ass." His lips pressed together as his gaze dropped to the bare skin of her upper thigh. "You know, I like you this way—all tied up." The barrel of the .38 grazed her kneecap and then slid up the inside of her leg. "Davy Harper's little girl."

She flinched but forced her body to relax, refusing to show fear. She hated herself for rushing out of the house in nothing more than a tank top and shorts. This was definitely not ass-kicking attire.

"I'm going to tear you to pieces," she said, baring her teeth. "You're going to be sorry you ever messed with my family."

"Testy, testy." He straightened and placed the gun on the table with a *thunk*.

"What do you want, Heinrich? Name it and it's yours. Just let my grandmother go." If her hands were untied, she would have snapped her fingers. It was that easy. Leave Rose out of it, and he could have anything he wanted.

He paced the area around her chair, his expensive alligator shoes tapping on the cherry floor with each step. "Such a simple question. 'What do you want?'" His body spun toward her, eyes black and expression monstrous. "I want the Harpers to stay the hell out of my business!" Then, heaving a deep breath, he flicked an invisible piece of lint from his shoulder and said, "But that doesn't seem possible. Every time I get rid of one of you, another pops up that I have to deal with." His gaze locked with hers. "No more. I'm going to be rid of you Harpers after tonight."

"Fine, Heinrich," Sam said, swallowing hard. "Do it. Kill me. But let my grandmother go. This is between you and me. She's got nothing to do with it."

"Ah, precious Samantha." He grinned, showcasing his perfect veneers. "That's where you're wrong. She's got *everything* to do with it." At Sam's confused look, Heinrich's grin widened. "I'm not going to kill you. What would be the fun in that? No, no. I'm going to make you watch as I turn your grandmother into a Vamp."

Bile rose in her throat, and the blood in her veins turned to lava. "You c-can't." She forced sharp intakes of air into her lungs to bolster her strength.

"I can." He leaned down and placed each hand on the arms of the metal chair, trapping her. "And I will. It's only a matter of time before she's an addict anyway." He cocked his head to the side to assess her. "Might as well be tonight under your watchful eye."

"What?" Her throat tightened, making it tough to get the word out.

He clasped his hands behind his back and strolled the room. "I forgot to tell you. By this time tomorrow, *everyone* in Baltimore will be a Vamp."

Her mouth dropped open and the lava in her veins turned to ice.

"Wonderful, isn't it? All your friends and neighbors flocking to me, begging for their next hit. Paying tens of thousands of dollars for one tiny piece of paper." He closed his eyes and shivered with what seemed like excitement. The disgusting monster looked back at Sam. "Baltimore is only the start. After this drop, we'll hit every port in America."

"Why?" What could possess a person to cause such devastation?

His expression said she should know the answer. "Money. Our friends in the Middle East are paying a pretty penny for this to happen."

He paced the room again, the tap of his expensive shoes pounding inside her head. "It's new-age terrorism. Infiltrate the country from the inside out. When I'm done, every American will be so hooked they won't want anything but their next hit. They won't eat. They won't sleep. They won't go to work. Everything will crumble. They'll kill each other. Destroy the entire country. It's fucking brilliant."

The picture he painted came quick and vivid. Grandma Rose, the ladies, her friends, coworkers all clawing at one another the way the Vamps at Club Hell had done, desperate enough to kill for more of the drug. She couldn't imagine loving or needing anything more than her family.

"How? How are you going to do it?"

"I haven't decided exactly how yet. It's between water or air. Which do you prefer? Would you rather drink or inhale your addiction?" He sucked in another deep breath, so proud of himself. "No matter. I have men ready for both, so I'll cover all bases. People can drink *and* inhale. It's untraceable, so no one would know they've ingested it. There'll be no stopping it. It'll grow until everyone everywhere is infected. We'd been using my club as the testing site, and I have to say, things worked out quite nicely." He rolled his eyes and gritted his teeth. "Before your interruption, of course."

"Like people won't notice what you're doing."

He flashed a smug grin. "So much to learn, Samantha. No one cares what we're doing. It's amazing how blind the police are when you throw enough money at them." He paused, examining his manicured fingers again, the arrogant bastard. "I have to admit, I agree with my new friends. It's about time

America the Superpower falls from grace. It's been destroying itself anyway; why not make a few billion dollars to help it along?"

"And where will you be during the destruction?"

He smiled. "On a beach, sipping Mai Tais while my personal masseuse pleasures me."

"Bastard!" Sam shouted.

"Yes, but a rich bastard." He shrugged again, showing no signs of guilt. "I've delayed long enough. Back to business." Heinrich snapped his fingers, and a large man appeared at his side. "Bring her."

Much like the brutes at Club Hell, this one was tall, built, and handled her with no problem. She shot a glance at her weapons on the far table, wishing like hell she could at least snag one on the way out. The man lifted Sam, still tied to the chair, and carried her through the doorway, down a long corridor, without breaking a sweat.

They strode into the warm night to a larger boat docked at a pier. The man hoisted her aboard, dropping the chair inside the cabin. This room was much less personal than the last. White walls and floor, knobs and buttons with a wheel, and an expanse of windows from which to see the harbor.

A scuffle sounded beside her, and she turned.

"Unhand me, you buffoon!" Rose shouted.

"She's a mouthy one, sir," the man holding Rose said to Heinrich.

"Seems to run in the family," Heinrich responded, looking at Sam. "Place her here." His finger pointed to a spot in front of Sam, just out of reach. Not that she could have reached her grandmother with her hands still tied. She wiggled her wrists and arms again.

Once Rose sat in front of her, also tied to a chair, Heinrich's lips curled. "Pay attention, Samantha, dear. You're not going to want to miss this."

"No!" she screamed. "Heinrich, you can't do this! Please! Take me!" Sam bucked against the restraints, lifting the chair from the hard ground. "Give me the Vamp! I'll take it!"

"Hold her still," he snapped at two others. It was eerie how many Hanses Heinrich had on staff.

They clamped on to Sam's shoulders, digging their fingers into her bare flesh.

Rose met her eyes. Her voice was calm and soothing, just like every other time Sam had been in trouble. "We're going to be fine, sweets."

Sam nodded, though she didn't believe it. How could they be? She'd made Celia promise not to tell the others where they were, she'd avoided Ash for the last week, and she wasn't due at work for another twelve hours. No one would come looking for them. Rose would be an incurable addict, and Sam would be dead long before anyone noticed they were missing.

She'd gotten her grandmother into this situation, and it was more than she could take. She'd provoked Heinrich when she set fire to his club. For all she knew she'd burned it to the ground. She'd driven him to kidnap her grandmother.

This was all her fault. She needed to get Rose out of this.

Heinrich's henchman brought a stack of white paper from somewhere on the boat. It didn't look much different than something a student would write on in class. But she knew it was.

This paper held the power to destroy people's lives. In a single day, it could annihilate an entire country built on morals and fortitude.

She had to stop this. She just didn't know how.

The German with the Vamp paper stepped toward Rose, while two of his buddies held her head and pried her mouth open.

"*NO!*" Sam fought against her restraints in a last ditch

effort to free herself, her muscles burning from being locked into place for so long.

The cabin door opened, warm air whisking in, and footsteps entered.

"Jesus Christ, Heinrich," a familiar voice said. "I'm here. What do you want?"

Sam's gaze jerked to the doorway.

"Sam?" The man's usually warm eyes opened wide, and his face drained of all color. The air in her lungs emptied in half a second.

Chapter Twenty-Seven

"So what's the plan?" Luke asked as he and Ash huddled behind a large shipping container, overlooking the port.

They positioned themselves about three hundred yards from a boat where intel said Heinrich held the women hostage.

The boat was docked at the pier, surrounded by a mass of other industrial-looking vessels. It was dark and quiet, the only activity coming from a shitload of Heinrich's men pacing with automatic rifles. Thick, white steam filtered into the night sky from nearby smoke stacks, creating an eerily unsettling aura for what they came to do.

They scoped out the area, waiting for Tyke and Reese to arrive. Ash with high-powered, thermal binoculars and Calder with a Laser Listening Device. It connected to a wireless earpiece, which Calder was currently using to keep tabs on Heinrich. They both had a secondary earpiece and mic to communicate to one another if they became separated. Once Tyke and Reese showed up, they'd be able to hook into the signal and communicate, too. Just like a team.

Where the hell were they? If they waited too long...

His eyes flashed to his sniper rifle lying at his feet. He could get two, maybe three shots off before compromising their location.

He raked a rough hand over his buzzed hair and surveyed the area again through his binoculars.

Twenty armed men surrounding the boat. Shit. Twenty. Twenty well-trained assassins with rifles to their two skilled agents, if Tyke and Reese didn't arrive soon. He slid a damp palm down his thigh. They couldn't wait much longer.

Correction—*he* couldn't wait much longer. Sam down there at Heinrich's mercy was a thought he didn't want to process. What Heinrich could be doing to her. The fact that Ash wasn't down there right now saving her from it was enough to give him an aneurysm.

"Got a plan yet?" Luke asked, the tone of his voice as thick as the air surrounding them. Obviously Ash's impatience was starting to choke Calder, too.

He turned the binoculars toward the entrance of the port. "First, we wait for the rest of the team." *Please let them get here in time.*

Luke held a finger against his earpiece. He turned, giving Ash a hesitant look. "Heinrich's threatening Sam."

"Goddamn it," Ash said louder than he meant. His brain jumped into hyper-speed. Scenarios zipped through his subconscious, calculating every possible ending to the situation. Each one got him or Sam killed.

"What's going on? Report. Now." Luckily Calder didn't comment about him barking orders like a team leader.

"Heinrich's talking," he said.

"Right. What's he saying?" Ash snapped back.

Calder held up a finger, signaling for a minute.

His nerves couldn't take it. "Give me that." He picked the earpiece out of Calder's ear and jammed it into his own.

Sam screamed. *NO! Please! Take me! Give me the Vamp!*

"Damn selfless woman," he grumbled.

In his mind, he couldn't see anything but Sam, offering herself up for Heinrich to do with as he pleased. Ash wasn't going to give her the chance.

Fuck the backup.

"I'm going down." He rooted inside his duffle bag for additional magazines. He slid them into his pocket, then hoisted his rifle onto this shoulder.

"Coop, you can't," Calder said.

"Like hell I can't."

"Stop and think about what you're doing. This is Lorena all over again."

Ash's head whipped to Luke and he snarled.

Luke's shoulders lifted. "It's the truth, man. Going down there without reinforcements—you're not gonna do anything but get yourself killed and maybe the women, too. You know that. Deep down, you do."

He did. But he'd slice his own throat before admitting it. "I have to do something, Luke. She's down there."

"Just a few more minutes, buddy. Give Tyke and Reese a few more minutes."

"Fine," he said. But he'd never forgive himself if something happened to Sam and her grandmother before he had a chance to do everything in his power to stop it.

"*NO!*" Sam's scream drilled through the earpiece, and his heart stopped. His hands started to shake, then his arm, before his whole body trembled with anticipation, rage, and irritation. "Get on the horn and call Tyke again. If his ass isn't here in five minutes, I'm going without him."

Pulling his service weapon from the back of his waistband, he gripped it, readying himself. All he could think about was getting to them in time. He had to reach them. Save them.

Soft footsteps sounded behind him, and a voice said, "Cool your ass, Cooper. We're here."

Ash whirled. "'Bout time. What the hell happened?"

Tyke shot him a nasty look but didn't comment.

As Ash gave Tyke and Reese the rundown of what had transpired so far, the two men prepared themselves. Tyke checked his weapons, his earpiece, and readjusted his bulletproof vest. Reese slid his earpiece in, adjusting the mic at his throat. Then he lay on his stomach with his long legs stretched out behind him, peering through the thermal binoculars Ash had put down earlier. His rifle was at the ready in front of him, pointed at the boat. Reese was the most serious of the group. Never had much to say, just did his job and did it well.

When Ash finished his explanation, Tyke asked, "Reese, what are you seeing?"

"Twenty outside with rifles. Five inside armed with rifles. Two strapped to chairs. And a handful of massive bodies pacing the area."

"Massive bodies?" Tyke asked through a smirk.

He shrugged and offered the binos to him.

Without taking the item, Tyke grinned wider. "Man, I love a challenge."

The largest of the team, Tyke stood at six-and-a-half feet and weighed damn near two-fifty. A big, gruff son of a bitch with an even bigger heart he tried like hell to cover up.

"All right, this is how it's gonna go," he said. "Sawyer and his team are around the perimeter. They'll run interference in case anyone else wants to join the party. Reese, you're the eyes and ears. Calder, Cooper and I are on the ground. We good?"

Ash pulled the second earpiece out of his ear and held it out to Reese. He would listen to what went on with Heinrich and Sam. "Anything crazy, I want to hear about it, you got me?"

Reese nodded.

"All right, fellas. Let's kick some ass."

• • •

The team remained in the shadows so they wouldn't be spotted by Heinrich's goons. Quietly they approached the first few men on guard, getting their arms around the thugs' throats and squeezing until the men went limp. Ash, Calder, and Tyke laid each guy on the ground, out of sight and advanced to the next target.

Ash pressed the mic button at his throat. "Talk to me, Reese. Where are they?"

Shhh. Static came through. "On your six," Reese's voice said into Ash's ear. *Shhh. Shhh.* "—three—" *Shhh.* "—one." *Shhh.*

Ash reached around the shipping container, gripped the man's head and twisted. The thug went limp and dropped to the ground. A second came around the same corner, and Tyke grabbed him, mimicking Ash's move.

"Goddamn mics are on the fritz, Reese," Ash whispered. "You hear me?"

"I—" *Shh. Shh.* "—of that. What did—" *Shh.* "—say?"

Ash tapped his finger against his ear. "Reese, can you hear me?"

"Loud and—" *Shhh.*

Great time for their equipment to stop working.

The three men gathered at the end of a shipping container, regrouping before moving onto the next obstacle.

In a low voice, Ash said to the men with him, "The damn mics aren't working. Hand signals from now on. Leave the COMs clear for Reese if the things come back up. You hear that, Reese?"

Shhh. Shhh. Shhhhhhhhh. Shh.

Shaking his head, Ash signaled to Calder to check the

area before they moved on.

Calder peered around the corner of the container, then gave an *all clear* signal with his hand.

Ash and Tyke nodded, following each other in a slow and uniform manner toward their target.

Hang on, Sam. I'm coming.

Chapter Twenty-Eight

The man had eyes the same shape as Sam and Grandma Rose—almond, but slightly upturned in the corners. His nose was a little crooked at the end from a scuffle he'd gotten into during his first year on the force. And his expression had been the exact same as the day she'd last seen him. The day he promised he'd come back to her. But those eyes, so much like hers, held one major difference.

They were black and red.

"No," she whispered. "It can't be."

"My dear, sweet Samantha," Heinrich said, smirking. "When are you going to learn that I always get what I want?"

"Daddy?" she asked, barely able to get the words past her dry throat.

Rose started and her gaze flickered to the form in the doorway. Her eyes widened, then sagged in disbelief. "Davy?"

His skin was dry and chalky, his lips peeling from being chapped for so long. Already a shorter man, his spine was curved and shoulders draped forward as if he was collapsing in on himself. His body trembled the tiniest bit.

How long had he been on the drug? The entire two and a half years he'd been missing?

She sagged in her chair. If she'd done something sooner. If she'd tried harder to find him. Maybe he wouldn't have ended up like this. Maybe she could have saved him.

Dad stood, frozen, his face the stark white his eyes should have been. "Sammie? Mom?" He jerked his gaze to Heinrich and said through clenched teeth, "What the hell are they doing here?"

Heinrich's shoulders lifted. "Just making sure you keep up your end of the deal."

"I've been keeping up my end, Viktor. Why did you need to include them?"

Heinrich directed an accusatory gaze at Sam. "Your daughter came after me. She set fire to my club. I'm simply returning the favor."

"Is that true, Sammie?" Dad asked.

She swallowed the emotions rocketing up her esophagus. "It was an accident, I swear. I was looking for you."

"And now you've found him," Heinrich said. "What a delightful family reunion."

"I want them released," Dad said. "Now. Otherwise our deal's off and I walk."

A smile played at the corners of Heinrich's lips. "We both know that's an idle threat, David. How far do you think you'd get? Ten? Twenty streets?"

Sam gasped. The Vamp. He needed it or else he'd die from withdrawal.

His red eyes softened as he looked back at her.

"Plus," Heinrich said, "if I let them go, they won't get to see all your hard work." He looked at Sam but gestured with a flick of his wrist to her father. "You'd be proud to learn that your father has made enormous strides in the field of drug testing."

So Ash was right. Dad had been forcing people to take Vamp. All that oxygen she'd wasted telling Ash he was wrong. That his teammates were wrong. And instead it was her.

"Why?" she asked her father. "Why would you do it?" Anger coursed through her though she wasn't sure at what. Was she mad because she'd been deceived? Or was she mad because Ash had been right? Or because Dad had a choice in all of this, and he chose to harm people?

Maybe all of it.

His gaze dropped to the floor like he couldn't bear to look at her. "It's not black and white, Sammie."

She waited to see if he'd say anything else, but he didn't. "That's it? That's all you have to say? 'It's not black and white?' What does that even mean?" He still wouldn't look at her. She released a choked laugh. "You willingly gave Vamp to people. People who probably have families who are worried about them. Did you think about that as you were shoving paper down their throats? Huh? Did you? And what about you? You're an incurable addict!"

"It's not that simple," he said, finally bringing his eyes up to meet hers. "I did what I had to."

"What you had to," she echoed. "You *had* to ruin other people's lives? Your life? That's who you are now? I guess Lou and all the others at the precinct were right. I didn't want to believe it, but the truth is staring me in the face right now."

He wrapped his arms around his stomach like someone had punched him. "You don't understand, I—"

"You're right, I don't understand. I don't even know you."

She snapped her head to the side, refusing to look into his guilty eyes for another second. Her gaze collided with Rose's. The blatant hurt and disappointment shadowing Grandma Rose's features almost crushed Sam's will. Heinrich stood to the side, arms folded and a satisfied grin on his face.

"What are you smiling at?" she asked. "So proud of

yourself for being able to corrupt one of Baltimore's finest?"

"Yes." Heinrich stepped forward, approaching her.

Dad lurched forward, too. "Viktor," he said in a low voice.

He held a finger in the air, and her dad stopped. "It's all about the right leverage, Samantha. You see, your father had you and your grandmother. So all it took was for me to threaten you both, and he agreed to do what I needed." He let out a dramatic sigh. "But then he got greedy and tried to escape so he could warn you. I couldn't let him do that. So I did the only thing I could to keep him under control." His devious gaze met hers.

"You drugged him," she said, barely getting the words out.

"I control the drugs up and down the eastern seaboard. He can't go anywhere to get a hit that I wouldn't know about. With a few calls, I could cut him off completely. He'd never get another taste of the drug."

And within hours, he'd be dead.

"So that's why you did it?" she asked her father. "That's why you turned those people into Vamps. Because you were trying to save us?"

"Yes," he said a bit too quickly. He skirted a glance at Heinrich, then back to Sam.

Shaking her head, she said, "So who cares about the rest of the people, is that it? As long as Grandma and I are okay."

"You two are the only thing that matters to me," he said. "I'd do it again if I had to."

Her father had damned those people to save Sam and Rose. Her stomach rolled, the motion in direct contradiction to the gentle sway of the boat. She was going to be sick right here all over the floor in front of everyone.

It wasn't that she didn't value her own life or her grandmother's. What she hated was the fact that other people had been affected. Their families torn apart. Because of her.

Why did she deserve to be safe when others didn't?

Dad wanted to protect her. She could understand that. She'd worked so hard to keep her grandmother and the ladies from the 19th Street Patrol safe in his absence. But that didn't mean hurting other people to accomplish the goal. If Heinrich had decided to come after them, she would have dealt with it. Maybe he would've succeeded, maybe not. But at least she could have a clear conscience that other people hadn't been sacrificed in order to keep her safe.

"As I said, Samantha," Heinrich said, still grinning, "one way or another, I always get what I want." He nodded to the goon standing beside her grandma.

The guy's meaty fingers dug into Rose's jaw, prying it open. Rose grunted as the German must have increased the pressure.

Heinrich approached the man holding the stack of Vamp paper and pulled a sheet off the top. "Now that the family is back together, let's get on with the show, shall we?" He glanced down at his gold watch, and said, "We still have a few minutes of fun left." He walked toward Grandma with paper in hand.

"What th-the hell do you think y-you're doing?" Dad's body shook with stronger tremors. "This wa-wasn't part of the deal. You promised to leave them out of it."

Heinrich gave him a look like he didn't care about their deal. "It's either tonight or tomorrow. Either way it's still going to happen."

"No." Sam rocked herself forward and back. The legs of the chair lifted and then clanged down on the hard ground. "Please don't do this. Please."

"Viktor, stop this, goddamn it." Dad sprang at Heinrich, but one of the goons grabbed him by the collar and yanked him back. The German wrapped his arms around her father and squeezed to hold him in place. "Wh-why, Viktor? Why are you doing this? She's an innocent woman f-for crying out l-loud."

Heinrich's eyes glazed over for a brief second. "We were all innocent at one time, David." He tore the paper in half, then in thirds.

A single tear broke free and rolled down Sam's cheek. "No," she whispered as her chin dropped to her chest. "No."

This was it. Her grandmother was going to become a Vamp, and there wasn't anything she could do to stop it.

She shifted her focus to Grandma. Sam would be strong. She wouldn't turn away.

Rose's eyes softened. Her expression was as clear as if she'd spoken the words: *Let me go.*

Tears streamed down Sam's face. This couldn't be happening. For everything good and right in the world, Rose was better. Her grandmother didn't deserve this. None of them did.

A thousand pound weight rested on her chest, making it harder to pull each breath.

The paper landed inside her grandmother's mouth and dissolved in seconds.

Sam's heart turned to stone. It could have stopped beating for all she cared. Her best-laid plans to keep her family safe had been demolished in those seconds.

It was done.

Rose Harper was a Vamp.

• • •

The men had taken out the twenty or so guards around the port and had been working their way toward Heinrich's boat when Reese's voice cut into their ears. *Shhh.* "Heads up. *Shhh.* "—another boat. It's—" *Shhh.* "—docks." *Shh. Shh. Shhhhhh.* "—east—" *Shh. Shh. Shh.*

They made their way east and settled behind wide pylons, giving them a clear view of the boat pulling in.

The port was industrial in look and use, catering to cruise liners and cargo vessels. But by the ostentatious look and size of this craft, it had to be the drop boat. This big ass thing belonged in a place like the Hamptons or Monte Carlo. Which was why it had to pull into another part of the port. No way that mammoth would fit where Heinrich had parked his boat. Only an overconfident drug smuggler wanting to flaunt his millions would travel in that kind of style. And when Ash caught sight of the name on the side of the vessel, it confirmed his suspicions. *Lorena.*

"It's her," he said.

Tyke and Calder nodded, acknowledging the message.

"We'll handle this," Tyke said. "You go after the women."

Ash hesitated. Being back with the team and it already felt unnatural to run off without them.

"Damn it, Cooper. We got this," Tyke said again. "If that bitch is on the boat, I don't want you here. Understand?"

When realization dawned that either Lorena or her father could be on that boat, he gave a stiff nod. It wasn't his fight anymore. His priority was Sam.

"As soon as we contain the threat," Tyke continued, "we'll be right behind you."

With a quick nod from Calder, Ash sprinted in the opposite direction, pressing his throat. "Keep an eye out, Reese. I don't want any surprises."

Shhhhhhhhhhhhh.

It was worth a try. He hoped like hell the COMs came back up before too long. Otherwise, he'd have no way to call for help if shit with Heinrich went haywire.

Chapter Twenty-Nine

"Grandma!" Sam needed to be free. Needed to touch her grandmother. Reassure her Sam was still there. Loving her. She'd see her through this. Somehow. Some way.

She bucked and twisted, the rope digging deeper, blood seeping down her arms. Maybe if the bindings dug farther into her skin, they'd eventually sever her arms. It couldn't possibly hurt half as much as her heart hurt right now. "Grandma, look at me." She whirled to face her father. "Look what you've done. All because you thought you were protecting us."

Her dad continued to shake in the German's arms, his gaze growing more distant. He looked at her, but it was as if he didn't see her. He drew long, harsh breaths through bared teeth.

Rose turned, tears in her eyes. She gave Sam a weak smile. Even after all she'd been through, she still attempted to ease Sam's fears.

Searching her grandmother's eyes, her breath hitched. They were still green. The same green they'd been her whole life.

Her body slumped in relief. Thank God. "How?"

"How what?" Heinrich asked, grinning. "How was I able to turn her so quickly?" He looked at Rose and his grin evaporated. "That can't be. I watched you take it." He grabbed Rose's face and forced her mouth open.

Rose whimpered and her eyes squeezed shut.

"I saw you. I saw you take it." Heinrich turned with his arm out to the German with the stack of Vamp paper. When a sheet didn't materialize in his hand immediately, he snapped his fingers. "Give me another."

Sam's body stiffened. Grandma Rose might have gotten a dud on the first dose. There was no way she'd survive a second. She wrestled with the rope, fighting like a caged animal to free herself.

But she was helpless. And her father stood to the side, panting and thrashing. The goon tightened his hold, muscles in his jaw working as he fought to keep her father from breaking away.

Heinrich shoved a second, much larger square of Vamp paper into Rose's mouth, then forced her jaw closed. Holding it, he glanced at his watch as if to time the transition.

The room was silent as everyone stared at Rose. She blinked back tears, likely from that scumbag's forceful grip on her jaw. Red welts appeared from where his nails dug into her skin.

Rage built inside of Sam. Instead of pushing it down, like she normally did when she thought about Heinrich and all he had taken from her, she let it bubble up. She let it rise to the point of almost exploding. Blood pounded in her ears, and her pulse raced. She was going to get him for this. Viktor Heinrich would pay, even if it killed her.

Heinrich paled. "But—I don't understand." He lifted the remaining paper and examined it.

Sam's head snapped toward Rose, scanning her

grandmother's face.

Wide, green eyes amplified by her bifocals stared back.

Sam's relief overshadowed any rage. It was more satisfying to have Rose alive and well.

Grandma was okay. Thank God, she was okay.

Sam didn't understand why the Vamp didn't work, and she didn't care.

Grunts and groans echoed from where her father stood, still held upright by the man behind him. Dad didn't seem to have a handle on himself, violent tremors shaking his body. His arms were crossed over his chest, immobile, but his hands bounced in place. His breathing increased to unhealthy levels, his chest heaving, as if he had to gather and conserve as much oxygen as he could.

"What's happening to him?" she asked.

"Withdrawal," Heinrich said. "He hasn't had a hit in a few hours."

This was worse than she'd ever seen. Far beyond any of the Vamps at Club Hell.

His eyes rolled back in his head, his black pupils disappeared so all that showed was red. The man holding him jostled in place, bouncing on his toes while trying to keep a steel arm locked tight.

"Do something!" she said.

Staring in fascination at her father, Heinrich said, "Why?"

"Because he's dying."

"Hmm. So he is."

"You don't care? What about all the help he gave you? All that crap you said about his drug testing?"

Heinrich shrugged. "I've never actually *seen* a person die from Vamp."

Her dad's face filled with color. Thick strands of spit trailed down his chin. He focused on the man holding the drug and tried to launch himself toward him.

"How long does he have?" she asked.

"Not long, I suppose," Heinrich said, still watching her father.

"What's it going to take for you to help him? Name it and it's yours." She couldn't bear to watch him die. It didn't matter what he'd done or what he'd turned into. He was still her father.

Heinrich swiveled to face her, excitement glittering in his eyes. "What are you offering, Samantha?"

"Anything. Anything you want. Just save my dad."

Bargaining with a drug dealer to give her dad more drugs was ridiculous. But if that's what would keep him alive until they could figure something else out, so be it. She'd rather have her father in her life as a drug addict than not in it at all.

"It's tempting," Heinrich said. "I could come up with so many useful things to do with you." His gaze fell between her legs and one corner of his lips hitched up.

A shiver ran through her at the thought. "Whatever you want. Just give him the Vamp. Please."

Her father's strained, high-pitched scream sounded as if it shredded his vocal cords.

"Please," Sam cried out. "Help him!"

"Fine," he said, glancing at his watch again. "My shipment is due any minute anyway. I don't feel like hearing that screeching while I'm conducting business." He reached for another slip of paper. He ripped it in half and balled up one side. He glanced back at her and said, "Anything I want?"

She swallowed her fear. "Yes."

Dad trembled, trying to rotate out of the larger man's embrace. Shadows played over his features, making sharp angles on his cheeks and chin. He definitely hadn't grown fangs, but as he snarled, his teeth seemed more pointed, hungry to sink into something.

He'd transformed before her eyes. The sweet, loving man

who'd raised her was gone. A feral addict stared back with sinister, uncaring eyes.

Her father was lost to her. Gone. Forever. Without a cure.

Would it have been better if she'd never looked for him? Assumed he was dead or corrupt? Would not knowing hurt less than seeing him this way?

She didn't know.

And what would happen if they couldn't find a cure? How would she protect Grandma Rose and herself from this monster?

But he's your dad. And family was meant to protect each other and care for one another, through the good and the bad.

She was going to see him through this.

The loud, slicing *bang* of a gunshot sounded.

Sam screamed and jerked her attention to the doorway.

Hans-Number-Forty-Five stiffened, then glanced down at his chest with a blank expression. A deep, scarlet stain expanded on his crisp, white shirt.

Chapter Thirty

Heinrich leapt back as his goon fell to the ground. Blood pooled from under the body, mixing with dirt and grime on the floor.

"Ash!" Sam's voice was an incredible sound. His first instinct was to go to her, his body leaning in her direction, but he had business to handle first. With the COMs out, he had no idea what was going on with Tyke and Calder. No idea who'd walk through that door behind him.

He spared a quick glance at the women, ensuring they were still in one piece. Spotting the dark streams of blood running down Sam's arms sent a tsunami of rage through him he didn't try to control. Goddamn it, Heinrich had hurt her. He stepped in that asshole's direction.

"No," Sam said. "Don't hurt him."

"Why the hell not?" he asked through tight lips.

An animalistic scream snapped his attention to the right. Her father. His eyes.

Heinrich, that motherfucker, was going to get it back tenfold.

"He needs the Vamp," she said, her chin gesturing in the direction of one of Heinrich's men.

The guy turned as if to shield the paper he was holding.

Ash pointed his gun in the larger man's face and signaled with a tilt of his head for him to move to the side with Heinrich.

The man holding Davy, who twisted and turned wildly in the larger man's arms, looked at Ash like, *Little help?*

"You will not let him go," Ash said. "Do you understand?"

He must have heard the finality in Ash's tone or realized the danger Davy could be to everyone in the room, because the guy nodded and squeezed his arms. Davy grunted and slanted forward as if reaching for his salvation just out of reach. With his service pistol trained on Heinrich, Ash reached in his pocket to retrieve a knife. With a flick of his wrist, he freed Sam and her grandmother from the ropes. Both stood, massaging their reddened wrists and arms.

He forced Heinrich and two remaining goons into the corner of the room, the door he'd entered through at his back, and positioned himself between the women and Heinrich.

Then silence.

"Daddy!"

Davy slumped over in the German's hold, head and arms dangling forward.

Sam dashed to her father, grabbing him around the biceps and shaking him.

His eyes were closed, and there was no indication whether he was breathing.

When Sam leaned her ear near his mouth, Ash said, "Wait."

She pulled back and looked at him.

"Let me," he said, approaching. He wasn't about to watch the man hurt Sam. Even if Davy couldn't help it.

He faced Heinrich as he placed his finger on the pulse at Davy's neck.

Nothing.

He pressed down on the man's vein, willing the goddamn thing to jump.

He dragged his gaze to Sam.

"No," she said. "Don't you dare say it."

His hand fell to his side and fisted. First she'd had to endure years of not knowing where her father was or if he was alive. Now, she had to witness his death. Had to see his demise with her own eyes.

Her face caved in, her features breaking apart. She shook her head back and forth. "No. I didn't come this far for you to be dead. I didn't go through all of this for you to give up now." She grabbed a handful of Davy's hair in her hand, and she yanked his head back up. "Do you hear me?" she shouted into his lifeless face. "You will not give up now!"

Ash put a hand on her back and stroked absently. He kept his attention on Heinrich, who wore a morose expression. Sam curled into Ash's arms, and he held her with one arm, while keeping the other with his gun at the ready.

"I'm sorry, Sam," he said.

Rose stared at her son with sagging eyes and shoulders.

"We were too late," Sam said, wetness soaking his arm. "He needed the drug sooner. We were seconds too late."

The Vamp.

Ash spun away from Sam and held his gun in the face of the German holding the stack of paper. Ash plucked a piece from the top and rushed back to Davy. Sam must have caught on to what he was doing because she clenched her father's jaw and strained to get it open. Ash tore a piece off, and once Davy's lips parted, he thrust the paper inside.

And they waited.

Moments ticked by as everyone kept their gaze on Davy.

Ash slid a glance to Sam. She had her arms around herself, her lips curled in as if in silent prayer.

The German holding Davy bent to look at the man in his arms. "Did it *verk*?"

Davy still hadn't moved.

Sam's eyes closed, and she released a ragged breath.

"Hmm, what a waste," Heinrich said.

Ash's gaze flicked to him, his finger itching to place itself on the trigger of his gun.

Then he caught movement. Davy's head slowly came up, and his eyes opened. He sucked in a sharp breath as if surfacing from a deep lake.

Sam gasped and threw her arms around her father. The German holding him smiled and let go. Davy swung a bony arm around her shoulders, and they hugged.

"It worked," she said. "I can't believe it. It worked."

"Wha-what happened?" her father asked. He rubbed his head like he might have a massive headache.

"We're not even going to mention it," Sam said.

Rose slipped under Davy's other arm, and the three of them hugged each other.

Ash breathed a sigh of relief. Thank Christ he'd survived. Vamp or not, he was still alive. There was still a chance to save him.

"I'm sorry, Sammie," Davy said, pulling out of the embrace. "I had to. I had to give those people Vamp."

"Shh. Tell me later." She reached for his hand, but he yanked it away.

"No. You need to know. I gave those people Vamp because I had to. I knew Heinrich was planning to release it to the public. I had to find a way to stop him. I'm not proud of what I did. But I had to do something. If I could find a cure. Something to help those people, then it would've been worth it." His chin dropped to his chest. "But I failed. There's no cure. I damned them for nothing. And now they'll die because of me."

He raised his head to look at his daughter. His expression softened into regret. *And so will I,* his expression said.

With his gaze on Heinrich, Ash spoke, "I think it's time you all make your exit." It was about to get fucking ugly, and he didn't need witnesses.

"No," Sam said.

She stepped forward, rubbing her shoulders. She wiped her palms against her shorts, leaving spatters of dark stains on the fabric. "I'm not leaving until I see for myself that he's hauled off in handcuffs."

She didn't glance at Ash for his opinion on the matter. And he knew better than to argue.

"Grandma, you need to go," Sam said. "Take Dad and—"

"But—"

"Please don't argue," Sam said, her hard gaze fixed on Heinrich. "I need to know you both are safe. Go home. I'll meet you there." She turned to her father. "You'll be okay, right? I mean, with, you know…"

His lips thinned and he nodded. "I'll keep it under control."

"Good." She shot her grandmother a steady look. "I'll be right behind you, I promise. Now go."

Her grandmother hesitated, rocking her weight from one foot to the other, but she must have seen the desperate look in Sam's eyes, because she nodded. She placed her hands on her granddaughter's cheeks and garnered her full attention. "Cuff him and then leave. This is over. Justice is served. You've gotten what you need. Now let it be done."

Sam gave one swift nod.

Rose turned to her son, glancing up into his red and black eyes. She kissed her right palm, then cupped his cheek with it. He leaned into the touch, offering a small smile. He bent to pick up the drugs, then tucked them under one arm. Holding his hand out to his mother, she took it and they exited.

Satisfaction was evident in Sam's voice when she approached Heinrich with cuffs in hand. "Orange is going to look great on you, Viktor." She pulled one arm behind his back, and then the other.

"You think you're so smart," Heinrich said, swishing his shoulders, making Sam struggle to keep his arms behind him. "But you don't know anything."

When Ash placed the barrel of his gun against Heinrich's forehead, he stopped moving.

"Go ahead," Ash said. "Give me a reason." Anything would do. Even a flinch. His fingers itched to end the lowlife with one pull of the trigger. But Sam deserved to see Heinrich brought to justice. Everything else on this mission hadn't been handled properly. This was going to be. He'd see to it for Sam's sake. Heinrich would be brought to justice through the legal system.

Heinrich might have stilled, but he continued to smirk. "This doesn't end with me. It'll never end. There'll be plenty of people to carry the torch. It's just too easy." Sam clasped one side of the metal cuffs with a snap, and then the other. Doubt clouded her eyes. She believed what he was saying—it wouldn't end with him. There would be others. Like her dad. And there wasn't anything she'd be able to do about it. She couldn't save everyone. Even if she wanted to. That's what he loved most about her—her giving heart. It was the size of the Empire State Building, and it seemed to grow more every day. Her heart got her into this situation, but it was also what was going to get her out. Ash was going to make sure of it.

"All you simple people, living your simple lives," Heinrich continued. "Americans are so arrogant. You're ignorant to the way the world really works. No one gives a shit about family. Or pride. Or decency. All they care about is money and greed." He gave Sam a snide look from the corner of his eye. The damn cloud wouldn't lift from her gaze. Ash's own body tensed. "You know I'm right. Just look at dear ol' dad. He didn't see things my way and look where that got him. He—"

Mother. Fucker. Ash should have pulled the trigger. Holy hell did he want to. Heinrich was the root of everything she'd had to endure. And for him to throw something like her father back in her face? He deserved to have *his* rearranged. Instead, Ash dropped the gun to his side and cold-cocked Heinrich in the eye. He put everything into that punch. All the rage and emotion he'd been feeling since meeting Sam; all the sorrow he'd wanted to take away for her after she'd lost so much.

Heinrich went limp, causing Sam to lose her hold on his wrists. He fell, slamming his cheek onto the ground. His eyes closed, and his breathing was steady. Ash's fist screamed in pain, and based on the intensity, it'd be awhile before that asshole woke up.

Sam's eyes, wide and misty, glanced from Ash to Heinrich. He noted a hint of gladness behind the sheen. She smiled, one of her big, special smiles, and his body pieced itself back together. He wanted to carry her home and show her exactly how happy he could make her.

What a turn of events. Trusting a woman again. Letting her heal him. He'd never thought it was possible for a man like him. But she did it. She showed him there was still a hell of a lot of good left in the world. And that good would always defeat evil, if you were brave enough to fight for it.

Samantha Harper made him braver than he'd ever been in his life. She made him want to fight again. For goodness. For justice. For her.

She leaped into his arms, nuzzling her cheek against his chest. He dropped the rifle from his shoulder, and it clattered to the ground. He squeezed her tight, locking her in the safety of his embrace, too caught up in the moment to care about appearances if anyone saw him.

"Thank God you came," she said, her voice muffled

against his thick bulletproof vest. "I didn't know how we were going to get out." She pulled back and looked at him, her smile dimming. "My dad's hooked, and I don't know what to do to help him."

Running a hand down the side of her face, he said, "We'll figure it out." He glanced at Heinrich's body on the floor. "By the time he wakes up, he'll be in custody, and we can use all sorts of fun methods to interrogate him. Before long, he'll be begging to tell us what he's been doing with the drug experiments. We'll find out what to do to help your father."

If there was anything they could do.

Her lips flattened, obviously thinking the same thing.

Once a Vamp addict, always a Vamp addict. Until death.

No. If it was the last thing he did, he'd get her answers. He'd find *something* to help her dad.

Shhhh. "Ash," Reese's voice rose through the static in his earpiece. *Shhhh.* "Ash. Are—" *Shhh.* "There?"

One arm tightened around Sam, and he lifted his other to place a finger at his throat, turning on his mic. "I'm here," he said. "What is it?"

Shhh. Shhh. "Lorena." *Shhh. Shhh.* "Way."

Shit! The shipment!

His grip tightened on his service weapon, and he started to spin toward the exit.

"Do not move, *mi amante*," a woman spoke, holding a handgun of her own.

Chapter Thirty-One

It was her. The beautiful woman from Club Hell. The one with the cat eyes who had squeezed Heinrich's junk.

"Lorena," Ash said, stepping in front of Sam.

Lorena? That's *Lorena*?

Sam leaned around Ash's body to get a better view of the woman who had once held Ash's heart.

Lorena's lips curved slow and deliberate. The white of her teeth gleamed brilliant against the deep crimson of her lips. Much like when Sam had seen her at Heinrich's club, the woman wore a tailored dress that accentuated her voluptuous curves. Her spiked heels reinforced her fierceness.

"Well, well," Lorena's voice, heavily accented in Spanish, spoke. "What have we here?" She focused her gun on Sam and Ash as her other hand gripped her full hip. "I did not think I would see you again, Ash. And with a woman. I am wounded. I thought we had something special."

Ash's body shifted, blocking Sam's view. "I'd say that was blown to pieces when you shot me and left me for dead, Lorena. Where are my men?"

She laughed and waved her hand nonchalantly through the air. "Yes, so imagine my surprise at seeing you now. Plus, I remember you shooting first."

"Answer my question, Lorena," he said in a tight voice. "Where's my team?" Fear rolled off his body in waves.

Lorena's eyes sparkled with unconcealed excitement, and Sam trembled in response. *Please let Ash's team be okay.*

"Stop toying with me," he said in a tight voice. "Where are they?"

Shrugging, she said, "Captured? Dead? Truthfully, I do not care. You are the one I wanted."

Sam slid a glance at Ash. His expression didn't crack, but horror flickered in his eyes. Her heart ached for him. Based on what she knew about Lorena, Sam could only assume the worst.

Lorena peered around Ash's large frame. "Who are you hiding, *mi amante*?"

Sam sidestepped from behind Ash, despite his arm reaching out to keep her in place. "Samantha Harper."

Lorena grinned, her expression telling Sam she remembered her from Club Hell as well. "Lorena Serrano."

Ash moved in front of Sam again.

Tempted to roll her eyes, she made a deliberate move around him. If he was going to face Lorena head-on, they were going to do it together. His evils were hers now, too.

Sam stood at his side and placed her hand in his, squeezing.

He slid her a look from the corner of his eye. His expression was so impassive, she couldn't tell if he was pleased or annoyed by the move. She didn't care. She was there for him. From here on out.

Lorena spread her legs a bit and balanced on the skinny heels, her gaze dropping to their joined hands. "You have moved on." One corner of her lips dipped as if she couldn't believe her statement.

Ash remained silent, neither confirming nor denying.

Sam's body thrummed with awareness. Lorena's weapon was fixed on Ash's chest. On his scar. The one she'd given him. Bulletproof vest or not, he wasn't invincible.

His gun hung in his hand at his side. He wouldn't be able to raise it before Lorena got her shot off. And the woman surely wouldn't miss. Only Sam's aim was that poor.

Sam squeezed his hand again. She needed to get the attention away from Ash. She hated that he was in the line of fire. Vulnerable.

Anger built inside of her. She couldn't stop it. Didn't want to. "You shot him," she said, spitting the words at the other woman.

Lorena's piercing gaze jerked to Sam. "As I said, he shot first."

Ash squeezed her hand almost to the point of being painful.

Sam stepped forward, ignoring his warning. "He didn't mean to get that little boy killed." Ash held her hand and pulled her back to his side. "It was an accident."

"Quiet, Sam," he said.

"Accident?" Lorena's grin disappeared. "*Accident?*" She sliced the gun through the air toward Sam. The barrel pointed at her heart. "It was no accident."

"Goddamn it," Ash said. "Lorena, stop this." He made a move to sidestep in front of Sam, but Lorena sent him a warning look.

"I would not do that, *mi amante*. Or I might *accidently* pull the trigger." The hand on her hip lifted to join the one grasping her 9mm.

He froze. "Lorena, don't do this. There's no justice in taking another life. It won't bring Armando back."

"Perhaps." She surveyed Sam, closing one eye as if gauging her aim. "But it would make me feel better to take someone from you. Someone you care about. I want you to feel my despair. I want you to wake up screaming in the middle of the night, remembering you will never see her again."

He dropped his hold on Sam's hand and lifted both hands in surrender. "Lorena, please." His tone was soft as he took a step toward her. "Think about what you're doing."

Sam couldn't let him do this. Lorena was unstable. Distraught with grief over losing her son. She wasn't thinking straight. He'd get himself killed trying to reason with her.

She had to do something.

"Do not take another step, Ash," Lorena said.

With Lorena's attention diverted, Sam jumped in front of Ash, stretching her arms open wide. "I won't let you hurt him again."

"Damn it, Sam," he said, reaching for her. She dodged him and stood an equal distance between him and Lorena.

Lorena's eyes widened, and her grin faltered. "That is not your decision. Ash and I have history." Her lips curled in disgust. "We are connected in a way you will never be."

Low blow, but Sam let it slide.

"Then you really don't want to do this. You can't hurt him. You'd regret it. And your son wouldn't want you to do that to yourself."

Lorena made a noise of disgust, and the gun trembled in her hands. "Do not speak of *mi hijo*!

"Sam," Ash warned. "Get back."

"No," she responded.

Lorena's features hardened as she shifted the barrel toward his chest. "Quiet!"

Sam softened her expression. "Think about it, Lorena. You said it yourself—you have history together. Why would you want to destroy that?"

"He took him," she said, her features still hard as a single tear glided down her cheek. "He took him from me, and I want to kill him for it." She aimed the gun at Ash's head. She inhaled a deep breath and then her grin reappeared. "But I think I will hurt him another way instead." She swung the gun toward Sam—

"No!" Ash leapt forward, crashing into Sam and tackling her to the floor.

The gun went off.

A searing pain invaded her skull and chest. She winced and bit back a scream.

Ash covered her body with his. She lay on her back, he on his stomach. His face buried in her shoulder.

He didn't move.

His breathing was slow and deep.

Sam scrambled to get up, but he was so heavy. He pinned her to the ground.

Lorena's heels clicked across the floor, circling their bodies. She locked eyes with Sam.

Lorena was coming back to finish the job.

Sam swallowed the enormous lump in her throat.

"Ash," she hissed into his ear. "Do you hear me? We need to move. Now!" She pushed against him, but he wouldn't budge.

Something warm touched her shoulder and spread across her chest.

Oh God. Blood.

The sound of his faint breathing filled her ears, the only indication he was still alive. But for how much longer? She had no way of knowing how serious his injury was.

"Ash," she said. "Ash, do you hear me?"

No movement.

Lorena raised her 9mm, the trajectory aimed between Sam's eyes. She was a goner for sure.

I'm not ready.

Lorena's lips curled into something resembling a gleeful

sneer.

As a last ditch effort, Sam bucked her hips with all her might. Ash shifted atop her, sliding slightly, his arm falling to the side. Something clunked onto the ground next to her hip, so she reached for it. The cool metal of his gun touched her fingertips.

"*Adios*, Samantha."

Sam gripped the handle and slipped her arm around Ash's body, hugging him between both arms and pointed the pistol at Lorena's chest.

As Ash's slowing heartbeat tapped against her, his shallow breaths blowing into her ear, she closed her eyes and pulled the trigger.

Chapter Thirty-Two

Beep. Beep. Beep.

Ash peeked one eye open, squinting at a bright light overhead. He blinked to clear his blurred vision. Voices echoed from a distance, a television talked on low volume, and a constant beeping sounded next to his ear.

He had trouble moving, his body feeling like he'd been whipped around in a blender. Everything hurt. Especially his left shoulder. He reached for it, but something held his right arm back. A cord connected to his wrist.

Ah, fuck. He was in a hospital. After being shot. Again.

How long had he been here?

Sam. Where was Sam?

He opened the other eye, trying to get his bearings, and attempted to lift his head.

"Take it easy, Coop." Calder lounged in a chair next to the bed, his feet propped up, and a soda can in his hand.

"What happened?" He hated being a goddamn invalid. Lying on his back, helpless. He searched for the button to incline the bed but winced when a pain sliced down his left side.

Calder's feet dropped to the ground, and he reached toward him. The bed inclined, almost folding Ash in two.

"Lorena used you for target practice again," Luke said, slouching back into the chair. "This time she clipped your shoulder. Same side though." He tilted his head all the way back and drank from the can. After swallowing, he said, "The hole Lorena's got is a hell of a lot worse."

Ash rubbed his forehead, trying to recall the events. He'd heard gunshots but that was all.

Luke placed the drink on the side table and laced his fingers behind his head. "You seem confused, so let's do a recap. Lorena went after Sam. You took the bullet instead. Passed out like a damn wimp. Then your girl shot Lorena. Hell of a shot. Tyke was pissed he didn't get to do it. It was all over by the time we got there."

"What happened to you guys? How the hell did Lorena get away from you?"

Luke made a sound that was half grunt, half snort. "Because she's a sneaky bitch. We were distracted by her men. She brought a whole damn fleet of them. Somehow while we were trying to contain them, she ran off. We tried to warn you, but all we got was static."

"Is Lorena dead?"

"Hell yeah, man. That bitch took a bullet in the face. No way was she walking away from that."

Lorena threatened Sam. Now she was dead. Jesus, Sam intentionally killed someone. Pointed the gun and pulled the trigger. The weight of that realization almost sent him into cardiac arrest. How was she coping? Was she racked with guilt? Knowing her, she was. Hurting another human being wasn't something she could take lightly. He knew exactly what kind of mind-fuck killing someone did to a person.

Where was she? Likely somewhere far away. She probably

couldn't bear to look at him for dragging her into his shit with Lorena.

Or... Oh Christ. What if... What if she'd been shot?

He cleared his throat. "Sam. Is she...?"

"She's fine. You were on top of her. Lorena couldn't get a clear shot."

"Where is she?" He had to see her. Wanted to see for himself that she was unharmed. He wanted to touch her. Hold her. *Tell* her.

"She went to grab a bite to eat with the guys." Luke stood and opened the blinds on the window, letting in a steady stream of bright light. "Better bring me something back."

Ash squinted and turned his head toward the hallway. Nurses and doctors buzzed past his room in a hurry. "Jesus, Luke."

When he turned back, his friend shrugged and sat in the chair again. He reached for his soda, tilted his head back, and then tossed the can into the nearby trashcan like a basketball. "Your girl won't leave. She's been here since they brought you in."

His body surged to life with that information. *She won't leave.* "How long?"

"Three days."

Three days. Sam had been here for three days, sitting by his side, waiting for him to wake up. She cared about him. She had to.

"What about Heinrich?"

"In custody," Luke said. "Sawyer helped clean up the mess with Heinrich while Tyke, Reese and I handled the drugs on Lorena's boat."

"So the COMs came back up long enough to dispatch Sawyer and his boys?" A freight train of a migraine pounded its way through his brain at everything he'd missed.

Luke shook his head. "Nope. Sawyer got nervous when

he didn't hear anything but nonstop static. He pulled his men back and headed to the port to offer extra hands. We had Lorena's men handled by the time they showed up, so Sawyer helped get the drugs into DEA hands."

Movement by the door caught his attention. Sam held a tray of plastic cartons piled high in her palm. Her smile was wide and exactly as he'd dreamt over the last three days. His gaze raked her trim body, a warmth spreading through him at the sight. She was safe. And she hadn't left him.

He smiled back, feeling absolutely no pain.

Tyke and Reese stood behind Sam, holding plastic containers of their own. They glanced at one another and shifted their weight from one foot to the other. "Guess we'll chow down in the cafeteria," Tyke grumbled.

Reese lifted his shoulders as if to say, *Cool with me.*

Luke glanced between Ash and Sam, a stupid grin on his face. "I'm gonna give you two some time to catch up." He stood and turned to the door, craning his neck back. "Good to see you among the living, Coop."

He stepped around Sam and reached for the plastic carton in Tyke's hand. Tyke growled and yanked it back. "Get your own grub, Calder."

"Aww, come on, man," he said. "I'm hungry."

The three stepped into the hallway and turned in the direction they'd just come from.

"You're always hungry," Tyke said as the group retreated.

Sam settled into the chair Luke vacated. She placed her cartons on the side table. "You're awake."

"I am."

"I went to get food with Bryan and Jason."

"I heard."

The air between them thickened, charged with everything that had gone unsaid. She stared at her flip-flops, wiggling her unpainted toes. She wore one of her slim-cut tank tops again.

He watched the rise and fall of her breasts as she breathed. She was nervous, though he had no idea why. "I'm glad you're okay."

"You too," he said, meaning it. If something had happened to her. If Lorena had hurt her... "Luke told me what you did."

Her gaze slowly lifted to his. Worry blanketed her expression.

His lips curled. "I'm proud of you."

A rush of air blew from her lips, and her blue eyes opened wide. "You are?"

He nodded. "I am."

"You're not mad? I mean, I killed your ex-lover. But I had to," she rushed to say. "She was going to kill me. She even told me good-bye. Well, she didn't say good-bye exactly. She said *adios*. But that's good-bye in Spanish. So I knew I didn't have much time. And you were passed out on top of me. I could barely breathe. You're so heavy. And your gun fell out of your hand. I grabbed it. And—"

He laughed at her rambling. "Sam."

She paused and looked at him.

"Come here." He opened his good arm, signaling for her to join him. He was so relieved she had saved them both, and she hadn't been hurt, he couldn't stand not touching her for another minute.

She paused, gazing at the monitors surrounding his body. "I don't want to hurt you."

"Right now, I don't give a shit if you cut off both my arms. I need you with me."

Her cautious expression changed, and the rigidness in her spine relaxed. She slid onto the bed, curling her body into his so perfectly.

He rested his chin on the top of her head. "You saved the day."

Wrapping her arm around his stomach, she squeezed.

"You saved my life. If you hadn't jumped in front of me and knocked me over, she would have killed me. I saw it in her eyes." She tilted her head up to look at him. "I can't believe you did that. You took a bullet for me." Her eyes were open and honest, making him feel ten feet tall. His goddamn ticker swelled in response.

"Of course I did. There was no other option. I wasn't going to let her take you from me." He leaned down and kissed her forehead. "You were right, you know."

When her eyebrows scrunched in question he said, "I do need you. I should have told you before. I thought keeping you away was the best way to keep you safe. But now I see I was stupid. I've never needed anything the way I need you. I can't imagine my life without you." He paused, preparing for the right execution. "Sam."

She peered at him, wearing the most beautiful smile.

He was finally whole again. Like a man who deserved her.

Tightening his hold on her, he looked into her eyes. "I love you."

Her smile transformed into a broad grin. "I love you, too. And I hope this means you're going to stick around for a while."

His hand caressed her back, and he chuckled. "Yeah, I think I can work something out."

They stayed in that position for a long while, holding tight to one another as if something terrible could separate them at any second.

"How's your dad?" He looked down at her face for an indication on his status.

She gave a half-hearted smile and shrugged. "Same as you last saw him. He's with your people right now. They're trying to figure out what to do. Especially since he was so bad off and yet Grandma didn't turn into a Vamp."

His back stiffened. "What?"

"Heinrich made Grandma swallow Vamp paper. He gave her two doses, but they didn't work."

"How?" He'd never heard of anyone ingesting the drug and not becoming addicted instantly. Especially after two hits of it.

She shrugged. "Weird, huh?"

Definitely more than weird. Hopeful was more like it. If he could figure out how Rose hadn't been turned, the Agency might be able to save others.

She leaned up and kissed him long and deep. When her tongue dipped out and touched his, he groaned.

"Have your fun now, woman," he said against her moist lips. "When I'm out of this damn hospital, I'm going to do more than just put my arm around you."

She grinned. "Is that a promise?"

His hand slid past her shorts to grip the smooth, bare skin of her thigh. "Think of it more as a threat. When I'm done with you, Samantha Harper, you'll be begging me for mercy."

Chapter Thirty-Three

"To Officer Harper!"

Sam sat on a barstool at Max's, surrounded by her family, friends, and coworkers, celebrating her achievement. She'd finally passed the Baltimore City police entrance exam. Just like the last six times she'd taken the test, she aced the written and physical parts. But this round, for the first time, she passed the shooting section, too.

Major Fowler sat beside her, grinning as he sipped his soda. He had to work the late shift, so he showed up to the bar in his uniform. He turned his attention from the O's game on a nearby TV and slapped her on the back. "You did good, Sam. Lieutenant Pool told me you ranked second highest among all the recruits." He beamed like a delighted poppa. "I'm proud of you."

Calmness suffused her body. She'd been through so much over the last few months. She'd witnessed the worst of humankind in Viktor Heinrich and Lorena Serrano. But she'd also witnessed the best in her grandmother, Ash, and the ladies of the 19th Street Patrol.

He placed his hand on her shoulder. "Your old man is proud, too, ya know."

Her smile dimmed, and she fought the onslaught of nerves and desolation. "How was he?"

Lou lifted one shoulder. "Same. Eyes are red and black. Still needs that paper to survive."

When her smile vanished, he said, "Don't lose hope, Sam. They're going to figure something out."

She nodded, even if she didn't agree. It had been months, and the DEA hadn't been any closer to learning how to help Dad. The DEA didn't have an explanation for why Grandma didn't turn, either. The hope was to find a breakthrough on one, which would shed light on the other. But it seemed hopeless.

Her arms wrapped around him in a big hug. "Thanks, Lou."

He checked his watch. "I gotta run, kid. See you at work on Monday?"

"Absolutely. I still have a few weeks until I have to report to the academy."

He placed a kiss on the top of her head. "Have fun."

As Fowler made his exit, Webb, Martinez, and Sinclair also waved good-bye.

"See you guys Monday," she shouted.

Ash snuggled against her back, kissing his—and now her—favorite spot on her neck. "Congratulations, Officer."

She smiled and craned her neck to place her lips on his. "Thanks. It wouldn't have happened without you."

"Bull," he said, spinning her stool so she faced him. He stepped into the open space between her legs and lowered his face to hers. "It happened because of you. Everything is because of you." He kissed her again, deeper, making her toes curl. He must have felt the same way because a sound of satisfaction rumbled from deep in his throat. "How long do you want to stay?"

"A little while longer. Why? You have something better in mind?"

His sly grin told her his answer.

She shook her head. "The doctors said you need to rest for three months with limited activity. You still have two weeks left."

It drove them both insane. The sexual tension was growing unbearable. But Sam refused to let him do anything that might jeopardize his recovery.

"True," he said, cupping her neck with his palm. He pulled her face forward to kiss her again. His tongue darted out and ran along the seam of her mouth. "But I seem to remember someone telling me to just lie back and let her do all the work."

She laughed out loud at the memory. Damn Estelle and her how-to-be sexy lessons. "That's when I needed something from you."

He pulled back, his eyebrows raised in question. "And you don't need anything from me now?"

She shook her head again, laughing.

In a flash, he gripped her hips, lifted her off the stool and threw her over his right shoulder.

She smacked his rear-end. "Your shoulder! Put me down before you hurt yourself!"

He grunted and slid her back onto her feet, rubbing his left shoulder. "Not the best idea."

"Are you okay?" She massaged his injury the way the physical therapist had shown her. Her fingertips tingled as she reached under the sleeve of his T-shirt to feel the bare skin.

He closed his eyes and sighed. "Jesus, Sam. When you touch me…"

Grinning, she said, "I think I'm ready to go home now."

His eyes opened and ignited into a deep, crystal blue.

"Just give me a minute to say good-bye to Grandma and the gang."

"One minute," he growled, slapping her butt.

She spun on her heels as a quiver tickled her belly. Her sandals practically bounced across the floor as she made her way to the end of the bar where her grandma sat with the ladies and Ash's team members.

"Hey, Sammie!" Estelle exclaimed, holding a shot glass with clear liquid. "Great party!"

Tyke and Calder sat to her left, gripping shots of their own. The three of them clinked glasses and then tipped their heads back and swallowed.

Reese positioned himself to the far left of his teammates, expressionless, sipping amber liquid. He turned when Calder flagged the bartender for another round. He smiled and then returned his attention to his drink. Nice guy once she got to know him, but *really* quiet. Ash said it was just the way Reese was. But Sam wondered if it was more than that. No one could remain silent for that long and not go insane. Or at least she couldn't.

Laughing at Estelle's antics, Grandma extended her arms for a hug. "We're so proud of you, sweets."

Sam grabbed her favorite girl tight and spoke into her ear, "I'm scooting out a bit early."

She pulled back, smiling. "Figured as much."

Maybel reached for a bowl of peanuts. She cracked one open and popped the nut in her mouth. "You kids have fun. Don't do anything I wouldn't do." She winked.

Estelle snorted. "Are they supposed to play Parcheesi all night?" She turned to Sam. "Do *everything* I would do." She swung around on her barstool to glance across the room at Ash, then turned back, smirking. "And then some."

Celia, seated far right, blushed and covered her mouth. "Oh, Estelle!"

Sam let out a huge belly laugh. "I love you girls."

"Right back at you, sweets," her grandmother said. "Now get out of here."

"Later, Bryan," Sam said. "See ya, Luke. Jason. Thanks for coming."

"Sure thing." Calder winked.

Reese lifted his glass.

"Wouldn't have missed it," Tyke said. He swallowed his shot, his Adam's apple jumping as the liquid went down. "We'll be back in a few weeks to check on you. Make sure you're not slipping up in the academy."

"Thanks, big guy. But I've worked too hard for this. There won't be any slipups." At least she hoped not.

She said her good-byes to the rest of the guys and gals from the precinct and a few neighbors. She turned and made her way to the front of the bar where Ash waited. He paced the hardwood floor, checking his watch every few seconds.

"Ready?" she asked.

His hooded expression was answer enough.

She placed her hand in his and pushed the door open.

They walked into the warm night, their steps in sync across the cobblestone street.

Could things get any more perfect?

"Tyke gave me a bit of news," Ash said, staring straight ahead.

"Really?"

He gave her a sidelong glance.

"Good news or bad news?" she asked, her heart pounding. "It's bad, isn't it?" When he didn't say anything, didn't change his stiff expression, she said, "Oh man, it is bad. I knew it. I knew things were going too well. I—"

His laughter cut her off.

"What?" She halted on the sidewalk outside a small café. She pulled back and placed her hand on her hip. "Why are you laughing?"

Streetlights cast dark shadows over his face, making him appear just as dangerous as the first day they'd met. But she knew better. Sure, he was dangerous to anyone who threatened those he cared about, but to her he was warm and sincere.

"You're cute when you're mad, you know that? You get a wrinkle right here." His finger touched a spot between her eyes.

She waited for him to tell her the news.

A second or two passed, and he didn't say anything.

"Out with it, Cooper!"

He laughed again. "Tyke told me he talked to the director. He stepped down from team leader."

Her muscles relaxed. So not bad news. "And that means you..."

He nodded, accompanied by a wide grin. "The job's mine if I want it."

"You're going to take it, right?" She searched his blue eyes for an indication of his thoughts. "I mean, I know it's not my decision, but if I were you, I'd take it. It's what you wanted. And your men love you. You're a natural leader. Anyone can see that."

He reached for her hand, glancing down when their fingers interlaced. "I told Director Landry I'd think about it."

"But—"

"I'll give the director my response in a few weeks." He lifted their linked hands to his lips, kissing the back of hers. "I want time with you."

"Oh," she said, her heart beating even faster. "Oh, well. Good. I want time with you, too."

His wide grin turned devilish. "We can start tonight."

Chapter Thirty-Four

"Holy shit, woman," Ash said from beneath her. His fingers dug into the skin at her waist, anchoring her in place above him.

Pleasure erupted inside her body, making her increase her speed. She rocked forward and then back, watching his expression darken with each stroke.

All the pent-up tension they'd fought with during his recovery had finally paid off. Being filled with Ash was more than euphoric. Stars exploded in her vision. She closed her eyes, relishing the sensation of his warm skin in hers.

"Goddamn, I love you," he said through a groan. "So fucking much."

"Me. Too," she said, with each pump.

A cell phone rang somewhere in the room.

Sliding a stray blond hair behind her ear, she slowed her pace, figuring he needed to answer.

"Ignore it," he growled, clamping harder on to her sides. He palmed the back of her neck and pulled her forward. His lips attacked hers, his tongue dipping into her mouth without reservation.

Against his lips, she asked, "But what if it's important?"

He groaned. "Sam, I don't give a shit if it's the President calling to tell me there's a new drug turning people into flesh-eating zombies. Nothing is going to stop me from having you right now."

She chuckled.

In one quick motion, he flipped her onto her back, pinning her to the mattress with his weight. "Are you laughing at me?" His pelvis drove forward, his length hitting her just where she needed him. Hot currents of energy ignited, and she sighed.

"No," she said through a ragged breath. "Never."

A wicked grin curved his lips.

"But what if—"

He thrust again, coaxing another sigh from her. Her eyes fluttered closed. "You're right, whoever it is can wait."

His hand traveled down between her thighs, and his fingers applied just enough delicious pressure to start her climb. Her breath increased, and her heart beat in a swift rhythm with his. He was close, too. His back went rigid beneath her fingers, his muscles taut from the strain. Blue eyes bored into hers. His expression was complete and utter awe.

Oh God. She pumped faster, reaching for what they both craved.

"Shit, Sam," he said, gritting his teeth. "Tell me you're close."

She was. So close. She squeezed her eyes closed and nodded.

"Look at me," he demanded. "I want to see you come apart."

Opening, she watched his expression change. His eyes widened and his back arched. A growl tore from deep in his chest.

Three more pumps and her vision darkened at the corners. She was right there. "Ash," she said. "Oh God. I'm—"

"Me too," he said through a tight jaw. "Now, Sam."

She let go. Her body erupted, giving in to the full force of the orgasm.

He dipped his lips to hers as his body shook with pleasure. His grip on her neck tightened, and he groaned her name.

• • •

His cell beeped from the nightstand, alerting him of a voicemail. Sam mumbled something in her sleep as he leaned over to grab the phone. Director Landry's voice came through the receiver.

Cradling the phone onto his ear, he rolled against Sam's naked form, his front to her back, and listened to the brief message. When Landry finished, Ash closed the phone and dropped it onto the carpet next to the bed.

Sam peered over her shoulder. "Everything okay?"

"Just the director," he said, touching his lips to her bare shoulder.

A murmur of pleasure drifted from her lips. She smiled as her eyes closed.

The sheet had been tossed onto the floor at some point, so she lay on his bed in nothing but her heart-stopping smile. The one that heated his blood and made him never want to leave his bedroom. "Was he calling to bug you for an answer on whether you're coming back?" she asked.

His tongue swept over the sweet skin of her shoulder. "No," he said. When she moaned, his groin stiffened, ready for round two.

He kissed the side of her neck, just below her ear. When his teeth grazed her earlobe, she asked, "It wasn't important, was it?"

His mouth hovered over her skin, wanting like hell to dive back in. "The test results came back on Rose."

Her body stiffened, and she flipped onto her back, damn

near pushing him off the bed. Her face whipped toward his with an eager glint in her blue eyes. "What did he say?"

Cocking his elbow, he placed his palm on his cheek and peered down at her. "Coumadin. She's on it. Apparently there's something in it that broke the drug down. It thinned her blood enough so the Vamp couldn't take over her organs. It just passed right through her system. There's no trace of it at all."

Sam's chest expanded, her bare breasts rising and falling with the motion, tempting him. "Thank God."

His finger traced lazy circles on her firm abdomen. "Landry said the agency's doing tests now to determine the amount needed to distribute to Vampers to counteract the drug."

Her eyebrows crunched. "You mean…?"

Nodding, he said, "He thinks we have a real shot at weaning addicts."

"Like my dad," she said, her voice was almost a gasp.

"That's the hope. Sounds like the tests are promising. They helped a new Vamper this afternoon. Her eyes turned back to brown within a day. Landry said she's doing well so far. There's still more testing to be done. We'll stop by to visit your dad this afternoon if you want." She gave him a smile that was less hesitant than it had been recently, making him smile in response.

"You're not going to let me give up, are you?"

"Never," he said.

Another wide, incredible smile spread across her face. "I love you."

His insides warmed, escalating to molten levels. "I love you, too," he said, nudging her onto her back. Positioning himself over her, he clasped her cheeks between his palms. Slowly, so he could look into her pale-blue eyes, he lowered his mouth to hers and savored the taste of what life was like with Samantha Harper in it. Forever.

Epilogue

One month later...

Sam bit her bottom lip, glancing out the passenger window at the gray stone building. It was more imposing than she'd expected. She'd seen it before, of course. But now that she'd be attending the academy as a student it took on new meaning.

A swarm of crazy butterflies circled her belly. This was it. What she'd been waiting for.

"You ready?" Ash's voice said beside her. He sat in the driver's side of her new Honda. She'd finally agreed that her old girl had been through enough for one lifetime. It was time for a fresh start.

When her leg started to bob, he lifted her hand and placed a soft kiss on her palm.

"I think so." She turned to him, squaring her shoulders and stilling her leg. "No. I *know* I am."

"That's my girl," her father said from the back seat. He leaned forward, resting a hand on her headrest and grinned. "I'm so proud of you, Sammie."

After they'd gotten the call from Director Landry about the blood thinners, the DEA had been able to cure almost all Vamps around the city. After weeks of trial and error, increasing and decreasing the dosage of Coumadin to her father, he had finally returned to normal. Or at least as normal as he could be. He was required to take the medication for the rest of his life and get a check up every six months as a precaution, but that was peanuts compared to what life had been like a month ago.

Ash stepped back in as Team Leader. According to the DEA's latest intel, Jose Serrano was still manufacturing drugs in his home country, so until he was stopped, the threat was very real. Like Heinrich said, there would be plenty of other people who would willingly pick up the torch and try to destroy America. Ash begged the director to allow the team to go to South America, because he was terrified once Jose Serrano found out what happened to his daughter, he'd want revenge.

Sam couldn't say she wasn't worried about Ash and his team, but she looked forward to the day when the threat of Viktor Heinrich, Jose Serrano, and whomever else wanted to do her family harm, was over.

For now she looked forward to each day spent with the people she loved. She had her father back. Rose had her son back. They were a family again. And there wasn't anything in the world that felt better than that.

Except maybe the man next to her, who had stood by her through thick and thin. Believed in her, though maybe not as she'd thought she wanted, but as she'd needed. Ash loved her for her. And accepted all of her. Even that stubborn Harper side.

"Do you have everything you need?" Ash asked.

Peering down at her lap, she surveyed the items she was told to bring on her first day—blue sweat pants, blue sweatshirt, and tennis shoes with white laces.

She was ready for this. More than ready.

But…

Her leg started to bounce in place again, the movement more erratic, causing the items on top to shift. She laid her hand over them to keep them from falling onto the floor.

"Sam," Ash said, all humor gone from his tone. "Sam, look at me."

She paused, nibbling on her bottom lip before turning.

He dropped his chin so their eyes were level, pinning her with his gaze. "You're going to do great. You were made for this." He leaned closer. "Remember, it's in your blood."

When she caught his meaning, her insides lit up. She looked back at her dad, whose blue eyes gleamed with delight. Damn straight. She was ready to follow in her father's and grandfather's footsteps and become a Baltimore City Police Officer. It was her turn to keep the long-standing tradition alive.

Gripping the handle with more determination, she shoved the door open and slid out.

Ash came around to her side, took the items from her arms, and placed them on the car's hood. Dad got out next and awkwardly backpeddled, looking down at the grass.

She turned to her father.

He slid a glance at Ash, so she followed his gaze.

Ash wasn't in her line of sight. Instead, he was low enough to stare at her bellybutton.

She zipped a look at her dad, then at Ash, then back at her dad. "What's going on?"

Dad winked. "Just go with it, Sammie."

"Sam," Ash said, his voice softer than she'd ever heard it. His Adam's apple bobbed twice before he went on. "I know it hasn't been that long. But I guess when you know, you know."

"Oh my God," she said. "Are you—?" Her gaze darted to

her father. "Is he doing what I think he's doing?"

"Not if you don't let me get it out," Ash grumbled.

Trying to contain an anxious smile, she squeezed her lips and nodded for him to continue. It seemed to take forever for him to start again. She bounced on her toes, waiting for the words to flow. *Just ask already!*

Ash tilted his head back and held her hand in his. He stared into her eyes. In that moment she knew. It didn't matter when the words came. Seconds, minutes, hours or days. Or not at all. They were bound. Whether he said it or not, they were linked more deeply than any words or a piece of paper could bind them. She loved this man, and he loved her. And that was all that mattered.

He did finally speak. She didn't catch most of it because she was too excited to listen. When he paused to take a breath, she shouted "Yes!" and leaped on him. They both tumbled to the ground, her on top of him, and she kissed him. Everywhere. His lips. His forehead. His left cheek. His right cheek. His lips again. Probably longer than she should have, given that her father stood a few feet away.

"I wasn't done yet," Ash said, laughing.

"Whatever you were going to say, it was still 'yes.' It'll always be 'yes.'"

When they finally got up, Ash pulled the diamond solitaire out of his pocket and slid it onto her finger. She gazed down at it, sparkling in the bright sunlight. The view started to blur a little, so she blinked to clear her vision.

Dad wrapped a strong arm around her and kissed the top of her head. "You're one of a kind, Sammie. I'm glad you found a guy who appreciates that." He stared at Ash as if to confirm his statement. Ash nodded, then shook her father's hand.

She glanced to her left, then to her right. Both men stood on each side. The flood of emotions was almost crippling. She had everything she wanted. Life wasn't going to get any better than this. Grandma and the ladies were safe. Her father had come back. And she and Ash were about to start their life together.

She clasped Ash's hand in hers, and she stepped toward her future.

Acknowledgments

There are so many people involved in writing a novel. It's amazing actually. All the people who had a hand in helping it come to life. The acknowledgements page is one of my favorite parts of a book. It gives the reader a wonderful glimpse into the author's life and support system. So if you're like me, here ya go. Below are my people. Without them, this story would have never seen the light of day.

First and foremost, BIG THANKS go to my family. From day one, my husband has been my biggest supporter. It doesn't matter what crazy idea I come up with, he supports me 100 percent. He never second-guesses me or tells me that I'm crazy, though I do enough second-guessing and calling myself crazy for the both of us. He helped me to get the technical points in this novel correct and was my biggest cheerleader during this entire process.

To my boys, Jameson and Bennett, for showing me what it's like to love so deep I can hardly breathe. Thank you for making me laugh and feel like superwoman, even on days when I just can't seem to get it together. You make it all worthwhile. I hope this book shows you that you can do anything you want to. Don't be afraid. Don't let others tell you that you can't. Don't worry about what others think. Be you and do what makes you happy. Even if it's writing romance novels.

To Mom and Dad for being hard on me when I needed it. You showed me what a strong work ethic looks like, and you taught me how to be humble through my struggles. Thank you for busting your tails in order to afford me a better life. This wouldn't have happened without your sacrifices. I do recognize and appreciate it.

To Jessie and Jim for supporting me and reading some of my early (and really sucky) work. Thanks for not acting too surprised when I said I landed an agent and also a book deal. And thanks for your poor attempts at helping me name this book. *A Bird In Her Hand And Two In Her Bush* isn't going to be published anytime soon. Don't hold your breath.

To Ninny, on whom every old lady I write about is based. You are the funniest, most grounded, most realistic, off-the-wall, supportive, encouraging, polite, hotheaded, quirky, smart-mouthed old broad I'll ever know. Thank you for teaching me to be ME no matter what.

To Misty, who is a far superior and more talented writer than I'll ever be. Your support means more than you know. I love that we "get" each other and that we can be there for one another outside of writing. Thank you for pushing me to be better and for laughing at my jokes.

To Mary, Patty, and the rest of the Maryland Romance Writers crew. Thank you for your endless support, encouragement, and tips to make my prose shine.

To Jillian, Tiffany, and Billy for dropping everything that weekend to read this book. Thank you for your time in finding my typos and inconsistencies. Your support is beyond measure. Truly, thank you.

To Chris Hemsworth by whom every hero I write is inspired (Yes, my husband knows). Thanks for starring in so many versatile roles and giving me an endless supply of inspiration to write about. Still kinda pissed you wore a wig in Thor though, not gonna lie. It ruined the fantasy for me. For the next one, please grow your own hair out.

To my agent, Margaret, for seeing something in me and giving me a chance. Thank you for your time in reading and re-reading this story to make it the best it could be. I appreciate your insight and your ability to push me to be a better writer.

To Alycia, my editor, who loves Sam and Ash as much as I do. Thank you for taking a chance on me, appreciating my kind of humor, and helping me share this story with others.

Thank you to Liz and everyone else at Entangled for their help and support in this journey. I very much appreciate your knowledge and expertise.

And last, but most definitely not least, thank you to YOU for picking up this story and giving it a read. I love to make other people laugh, so I hope this novel brightened your day.

About the Author

Christina believes that laughter really is the best medicine, which is why in her writing she adds a healthy dose of hilarious hijinks with gritty suspense. She lives near Baltimore with her husband and two sons, who give her an endless supply of humorous material to write about.

When she's not writing fun contemporary romance or quirky romantic suspense, Christina can be found devouring books in every genre, watching Chris Hemsworth on TV, playing board games with her family, working out, watching Chris Hemsworth on TV, napping, baking, watching Chris Hemsworth on TV, and shopping…for Chris Hemsworth's latest DVD.

She is a member of Romance Writers of America and Maryland Romance Writers. This is her first novel.

Discover more Entangled Select Suspense titles…

Lost in Tennessee
a novel by Anita DeVito

Heartache makes for good country music. It's what country superstar Butch McCormick keeps telling himself. How else could he reconcile another failed marriage, and more disappointment? Then Kate Riley appears out of nowhere with red hair and a peaches-and-cream complexion…and just so damned lost. But the longer Kate stays at Elderberry Farm, the stranger things get. For one, there's the crazy chemistry between her and Butch. For another, dead bodies are starting to turn up…and Kate might be the murderer's next victim.

Tattooed as Trouble
a *Vegas Vixens* novel by J.L. Hammer

Raegan Storm witnessed a double murder and enters the Witness Protection Program in exchange for her testimony. With her life on the line, the last thing she expects is to lose her heart to the mysterious, handsome Quinn Bronson, the U.S. Marshal protecting her. Driven by honor, Bronson rescues Rae from threats time and time again, but fighting off hit men is easier than ignoring his attraction for the one woman he should never desire: the witness. As danger presses in, neither knows who they can trust, and their forbidden love could be what destroys them.

Witness to Passion
a novel by Naima Simone

Fallon Wayland's having yet another lousy birthday. Fired from her job, dumped by her boyfriend, and oh yes, witnessing the murder of a high-ranking lieutenant in the local crime family? Yeah, birthdays suck. Up until now, soldier-turned-security specialist Shane Roarke has avoided his baby sister's reckless—

and gorgeous—best friend. Now he insists on protecting her. But as layers—and clothes—are peeled away, danger closes in. And Fallon and Shane might have a chance at love…if they can survive.

IMPOSSIBLE RANSOM
a novel by Kathleen Mix

Working as part of a yacht crew sounded like the perfect escape for senator's daughter Val Ferrell. But when the ship is hijacked, Val's fantasy turns into a nightmare. Her only hope is the ship's captain, her ex-lover. Covert operative Nick O'Shea is working with the tiny blonde who makes him crazy. But when her life is endangered, Nick must choose between fighting to retake the boat or risking their lives by escaping to an isolated Caribbean island. With the ransom deadline rapidly approaching, he's running out of time…

Made in the USA
Columbia, SC
17 January 2025

51955557R00198